The Heart of the Loch: A Mythic Highland Fantasy (Book 1 of the Riverborn Saga)

by Kevin Fraser

Table of Contents

Prologue: The Divided Waters

Chapter 1: The Restless King

Chapter 2: The Curious Daughter

Chapter 3: Forbidden Knowledge

Chapter 4: The Dance of Discovery

Chapter 5: Whispers in the Dark

Chapter 6: Mother and Daughter

Chapter 7: The Watcher in the Reeds

Chapter 8: Conspiracies and Councils

Chapter 9: The Journey Begins

Chapter 10: The Stone Arch

Chapter 11: Echoes of the Past

Chapter 13: The Quickening

Chapter 14: Shadows at the Door

Chapter 16: The Heart of the Loch

Chapter 17: The Tides of Sacrifice

Chapter 18: The Mourning Waters

Chapter 19: Hidden Among the Depths

Chapter 20: The First Stirring

Chapter 24: Breach of the Heart

Chapter 25: The Waters Awaken

Chapter 26: Whispers Beyond the Mist

Chapter 27: Envoys and Shadows

Chapter 28: Allies Awaken

Chapter 29: Gathering the Circle

Chapter 30: First Steps into the Wider World

Chapter 31: Shadows at the Crossroads

Chapter 33: Gathering Storms

Chapter 34: The Voice of the Heart

Chapter 35: Seeds of Rebellion

Chapter 36: Breaking of the Storm

Chapter 36 (Continued): Aftermath

Chapter 37: Rebuilding the Circle

Chapter 38: The Call to the Highlands

Chapter 39: The Day of Reckoning

Chapter 40: Murmurs from the Deep

Chapter 41: Seeking the Forgotten Powers

Chapter 42: Into the Wild Lands

Chapter 43: The Descent to the First Waters

Chapter 44: The Well and the Test

Chapter 45: Return from the Deep

Chapter 46: The Gathering Storm

Chapter 47: Clash at the Loch

Chapter 48: Heart Against Darkness

Chapter 49: A World Remade

Epilogue: The Watcher in the Mists

Published by Biscuits & Gravy Publishing

For Information and Requests on Reproducing Parts of this Book, Contact books@fraserlimited.com

Cave Creek, Arizona USA
First Edition, 2025

The Heart of the Loch: A Mythic Highland Fantasy
The Legend of the Kelpie King and the Selkie Maiden
A Novel Based on Scottish Folklore

Prologue: The Divided Waters

Long before men built stone castles upon Scotland's rugged shores, before crosses marked the sacred places, and before human songs tamed the wild winds, there existed two ancient peoples of the water—the Kelpies and the Selkies.

The Kelpies ruled the inland waters: the black lochs and rushing rivers, birthed from storm and sorrow. Shapeshifters with blood colder than the waters they haunted, they could become fierce black stallions, huge and wild, or transform into humans with eyes like winter skies. But no matter the form, their hearts beat with a merciless hunger that drove them to lure unwary travelers to watery graves.

The Selkies ruled the vast seas beyond, tender souls clothed in shimmering sealskin. Beings of gentle song and mourning eyes, they could shed their magical skins to walk as humans upon the shore. Yet their souls remained forever bound to the rhythm of the tides and the sorrows of the deep.

For centuries beyond counting, these two peoples never mingled. The waters of the loch stayed bitter and still. The sea remained wide and restless. An unspoken yet absolute law divided them—for should their blood ever mix, it was said the waters of Scotland would turn to blood and sorrow for a thousand years.

But fate, like the tide, cannot be commanded by ancient laws.

This is the tale of Brannach of the Thundering Hooves, King of the Kelpies, and Nerina of the Silver Eyes, daughter of the Selkie Queen. It is a story of forbidden love between river and sea, of ancient magic and bitter betrayal.

And perhaps, it is also a story of hope.

For even the oldest curses may sometimes be broken.

Chapter 1: The Restless King

The black waters of Loch Slochd churned as Brannach, King of the Kelpies, paced the depths of his great underwater hall. Carved from obsidian stone and adorned with twisted strands of silver kelp, the River Hall echoed with the frustrated steps of its master.

"My king," ventured Darran, his most trusted advisor, "the court awaits your presence. It has been three days since you've addressed them."

Brannach turned, his human form impressive even in the murky depths. Tall and powerfully built, with eyes the color of storm clouds and hair like midnight waves, he carried himself with the dangerous grace of a predator. His voice, when he spoke, was like stones tumbling in a riverbed.

"Let them wait."

"But sire—"

"What would you have me tell them, Darran?" Brannach growled. "That our hunting grounds grow barren? That the humans no longer wander our shores alone? That the old magic fades with each turning of the seasons?"

Darran, slim and pale like all river Kelpies, lowered his gaze. "The court needs your strength, my lord. They whisper of your... distraction."

Brannach's laugh was cold. "I am not distracted. I am awake." He moved to the hall's great window, carved from the living rock of the loch's deepest part. Beyond, the waters stretched dark and silent. "Do you not feel it, old friend? The hollow beneath our rage? The hunger that no mortal flesh can satisfy?"

"I feel only what I should feel," Darran replied carefully. "Pride in our strength. Joy in our hunts. Loyalty to our ways."

Brannach studied his advisor's face, noting what remained unsaid. "And fear," he added softly. "Fear that our time passes."

Darran stiffened. "We are the Kelpies. We have ruled these waters since before human memory. We will endure."

"Perhaps." Brannach turned away. "Inform the court I will address them tomorrow. Tonight, I ride."

"Where will you go, my king?"

Brannach didn't answer. He didn't need to. They both knew he would do as he had done increasingly these past moons—race across the highlands, following the river's course all the way to where fresh water met salt. Where river met sea.

When his advisor had gone, Brannach shifted his form. Bones cracked and realigned. Skin gave way to midnight hide. Arms and legs stretched into powerful limbs ending in iron-hard hooves. His face elongated, eyes growing wider, mane flowing like liquid shadow.

The Kelpie King, now in his truest form—a massive black stallion with eyes that held the promise of drowning—surged upward through the cold waters and broke the surface of Loch Slochd.

He galloped across the misty highlands, each thundering stride carrying him farther from his kingdom. The hunger that gnawed at him was not for flesh but for something unnamed, something forbidden.

Something that waited where the river emptied into the endless sea.

Chapter 2: The Curious Daughter

"Nerina! Nerina, return at once!"

The young Selkie ignored her mother's calls, diving deeper into the kelp forest that marked the boundary between the shallower waters and the true deep where the Selkie Court made its home. In her true form—a sleek, silver-gray seal with unusually bright eyes—she darted between the swaying fronds with practiced ease.

Only when she was certain she'd escaped her mother's watchful gaze did Nerina surface, her head breaking through gentle waves. The Scottish shore lay before her, misty and mysterious in the fading light. The tide was turning, and soon the narrow strip of sand would appear—her private stage for dancing under the stars.

With a graceful motion, Nerina swam to a hidden cove, familiar and safe. As the water grew shallow, she shifted, her sealskin peeling away as naturally as a cloak being removed. Beneath it emerged a young woman with skin pale as moonlight and hair that caught the fading sun like polished silver. She carefully placed her sealskin upon a high rock, knowing that without it, she could never return to the sea.

"Just a little while," she whispered to herself. "Just a little freedom."

For Nerina was the daughter of Queen Mhairi of the Silver Depths, ruler of the Western Selkies. And as such, her life was bound by tradition and caution. The Selkies had suffered much at human hands over the centuries—men stealing their sealskins, binding them to loveless marriages on land, or worse. Now they lived by strict rules, venturing to shore only during certain moon phases and always in protected groups.

But Nerina had been born with the second sight—rare even among her magical kin—and with it came an insatiable curiosity about the world beyond the waves. It was this gift that had drawn her repeatedly to this particular shore, this particular night.

For three moons now, she had dreamed of a great black horse, its mane flowing like night itself, its eyes filled with a loneliness that matched her own. The dream always ended the same way—the horse racing toward her across impossible waters, neither river nor sea, but something in between.

Tonight, free from watchful eyes, Nerina began to dance. She twirled upon the damp sand, her bare feet leaving delicate prints that the tide would soon erase. Her arms wove patterns in the air, and from her throat came a sound unlike any human music—a Selkie song, ancient and sorrowful.

She was so lost in her dance that she didn't notice the shadow that appeared at the edge of the strand. Didn't hear the soft intake of breath, or sense the eyes that watched her with wonder.

Not until the shadow moved, and a voice—deep as a river gorge—broke the spell of her solitude.

"You are not of the river."

Nerina froze, her silver eyes widening as she beheld the figure before her. No longer a horse but a man—tall and powerful, with storm-dark eyes and midnight hair that fell past his shoulders. His clothing seemed woven of shadows and river weeds, and around his throat hung a twisted cord of silver.

Fear flashed through her, but curiosity burned brighter. For she recognized those eyes. They were the same that had haunted her dreams.

"And you," she replied softly, "are not of the sea."

A smile touched the stranger's harsh mouth. "No. I am Brannach of the Thundering Hooves, King of the River Folk." He bowed with surprising grace. "And who are you, dancer of the tide's edge?"

Wisdom told her to flee, to grab her precious sealskin and return to the safety of the waves. But the second sight whispered otherwise. This meeting was meant to be.

"I am Nerina," she answered, choosing to withhold her lineage. "Why do you watch me, river king?"

Brannach studied her, his expression unreadable. "I do not know," he admitted, and the honesty in his voice surprised them both. "I have been drawn here night after night, pulled by... something I cannot name."

Nerina's heart quickened. "A hunger?"

"Yes." His eyes widened slightly. "How did you know?"

Instead of answering, she extended her hand, palm up—an invitation. "Dance with me, Brannach of the River Folk, and perhaps we shall both discover what we hunger for."

And to her astonishment, the fearsome Kelpie King stepped forward and took her hand. Neither noticed the small figure watching from the water, her seal eyes wide with horror, before diving deep to carry news to the Selkie Queen.

Chapter 3: Forbidden Knowledge

Queen Mhairi's private chambers reflected her position as ruler of the Western Selkies. Carved into a grotto beneath a remote Scottish island, the walls were inlaid with mother-of-pearl and luminescent sea glass. Soft light emanated from rare, cultivated anemones that glowed with gentle blue radiance. Upon shelves of polished stone rested treasures collected over centuries: a golden chalice from a Spanish galleon, jewels from a Russian princess's crown, and most precious of all—ancient scrolls preserved in special cases that kept the saltwater at bay.

It was to these scrolls that the Queen now turned, her elegant fingers trembling slightly as she carefully unwound a particularly ancient specimen. The writing upon it was neither human script nor the fluid symbols of Selkie record-keeping, but something older—a language from before the separation of land and sea.

"You are certain of what you saw, Calleen?" the Queen asked without looking up from her task.

The young Selkie messenger nodded, her large eyes still wide with shock. "Yes, my Queen. It was Princess Nerina. Dancing with a man upon the shore—only he was no man. Before he changed his form, I saw him clearly. A black stallion with eyes like whirlpools. A Kelpie, Your Majesty. And not just any Kelpie. From his size and the silver cord at his throat, it could only be their king."

Queen Mhairi closed her eyes briefly, pain etching her beautiful features. When she opened them again, they were filled with determination.

"You have done well to bring this to me directly," she said. "Speak of this to no one else. Not until I have consulted the ancient wisdom."

When the messenger had gone, Mhairi returned to the scroll, her silver-streaked hair falling forward as she bent over the cryptic symbols. For hours she worked, translating, interpreting, searching for guidance.

What she found made her blood run cold.

There, in faded ink and archaic symbols, lay the prophecy she had hoped never to encounter in her reign:

When river meets sea in forbidden embrace, Ancient boundaries shall be unmade. Blood of both, born of their passion, Will bring either doom or salvation. What was divided shall be rejoined, But only through sacrifice freely given.

Mhairi sank to her knees on the smooth stone floor, the scroll clutched to her chest. The Kelpies were violent, predatory creatures, anathema to the gentle Selkie way. For centuries, the two peoples had kept to their separate domains, divided by both geography and hatred.

If Nerina had indeed formed a connection with the Kelpie King, the consequences could be catastrophic. Yet the prophecy hinted at something more complex than simple disaster.

"Salvation," she whispered, the word feeling strange on her tongue. "Or doom."

A soft knock interrupted her thoughts. "Enter," she called, quickly returning the scroll to its case.

Her most trusted advisor, Finnol, slipped into the chamber. Ancient even by Selkie standards, with a beard like sea foam and eyes that had witnessed countless tides, he bowed low.

"Forgive the intrusion, My Queen, but I sensed your distress across the currents."

Mhairi gestured for him to sit. "Old friend, what do you know of the Kelpie King?"

Finnol's bushy eyebrows rose in surprise, but he answered promptly. "Brannach of the Thundering Hooves. He has ruled the River Folk for three centuries. Proud, powerful, merciless—as all Kelpies are. But..." He hesitated.

"But?" the Queen prompted.

"There have been whispers, carried by the river birds that sometimes visit our shores. They say he has grown... restless. Distracted. That he no longer takes the same pleasure in the hunt, in drowning unwary travelers. Some say he rides to the sea's edge night after night, staring into the waves as if seeking something."

Mhairi felt a chill that had nothing to do with the cool waters surrounding them. "And what of our own legends? The ancient prophecies concerning river and sea?"

Finnol's eyes widened. "Surely you don't think... The princess?"

"My daughter was seen dancing with him on the shore tonight," Mhairi confirmed grimly. "In human form, both of them."

The old advisor paled. "Then we must act quickly. The princess must be forbidden from returning to that shore. Perhaps sent to our cousins in the Northern Isles until this... fascination passes."

"And if it doesn't pass?" Mhairi asked softly. "If this is the beginning of what was foretold?"

Finnol shook his head firmly. "Those prophecies are from a time before memory, My Queen. Before the great division, when the waters of the world still spoke with one voice. They may have no meaning now."

"Or they may be more relevant than ever," Mhairi countered. She rose and began to pace, her flowing garments of woven kelp and pearls swirling around her. "If the prophecy speaks true, there may be more at stake than a foolish infatuation. 'Blood of both, born of their passion'—what could that mean except offspring? A child of river and sea."

"Such a union would be an abomination," Finnol protested.

"Or our salvation," the Queen replied. "The prophecy mentions both possibilities."

"What would you have us do, then?"

Mhairi stared into the glowing blue light of the sea anemones, her expression resolute. "For now, we watch. We learn. I will speak with Nerina, of course, but..." She turned back to her advisor. "I want to know more about this Kelpie King. Find our friends among the river birds, the otters, the creatures that move between our worlds. Learn everything you can about Brannach of the Thundering Hooves."

"And if what you learn convinces you that he is a threat to the princess?"

The Queen's eyes hardened to silver steel. "Then we will do what we must to protect our own. Even if it means breaking the ancient agreement not to interfere in river affairs."

After Finnol departed, Mhairi returned to the ancient scroll, running her fingers over a symbol she had not translated for her advisor—a symbol that appeared repeatedly in connection with the prophecy.

It represented a bridge. A connection between separate worlds.

And in the margin beside it, almost too faded to read, was scrawled a single word in the old tongue:

Rebirth.

Chapter 4: The Dance of Discovery

Brannach had never danced before.

The Kelpie people had their rituals, of course—wild, violent celebrations after successful hunts, or solemn ceremonies to mark the changing seasons. But nothing like this gentle swaying, this careful placement of feet, this awareness of another being moving in harmony with his own body.

Nerina's hand felt impossibly delicate in his much larger one. Her skin was cool and smooth, like polished stone worn by centuries of water. As she guided him through the steps of her dance, he felt awkward and powerful all at once—a creature of violence attempting grace.

"You're thinking too much," she said softly, a smile in her voice. "Feel the rhythm of the waves. Let your body follow mine."

"Kelpies don't follow," he growled, but there was no real anger in it. "We lead. We hunt. We take."

Nerina's silver eyes studied him with unsettling perception. "And does that bring you joy, King of Rivers? The hunting? The taking?"

The question struck him silent. Joy? When had he last felt such a thing? There was pleasure in the hunt, yes. Satisfaction in maintaining his kingdom's strength. Pride in his dominion over the waters. But joy?

"You ask strange questions, sea maiden," he finally said.

"And you give no answers, river king," she countered, spinning gracefully away from him before returning to his arms. "But your eyes speak what your lips will not."

"And what do they say?" he asked, suddenly curious.

"That you are lonely," she replied simply. "As am I."

The honesty of her response caught him off guard. Kelpies did not speak of such things. Vulnerability was weakness, and weakness was death in the river halls.

"How can a king be lonely?" he scoffed. "I rule the greatest of the river kingdoms. My subjects number in the hundreds. My territory stretches from the mountain springs to—"

"To here," she finished for him, gesturing to where the river mouth emptied into the sea. "To the edge of your world. But do any of your subjects see you, Brannach? Do they know the thoughts behind those storm-cloud eyes?"

Her use of his name—not his title—sent an unexpected warmth through him. "And do your people see you, Nerina of the Sea? Do they know why you dance alone on forbidden shores?"

A shadow passed over her face. "No," she admitted. "They see only the princess, the daughter who must be protected, the vessel of tradition."

"Princess?" he repeated, suddenly alert. "You are royalty among your kind?"

Nerina bit her lip, clearly regretting the slip. "I am Nerina of the Silver Eyes, daughter of Queen Mhairi of the Western Selkies," she said formally, lifting her chin with a dignity that impressed him despite himself.

"And does your royal mother know you dance with the king of her ancient enemies?" he asked, his voice low and dangerous.

To his surprise, Nerina didn't flinch. Instead, she stepped closer, her face upturned to his. "Do your subjects know that their fearsome king comes to the sea's edge not to hunt, but to search for something he cannot name?"

They had stopped dancing now, standing close enough that he could see the delicate silver flecks in her eyes, smell the salt and mystery of her skin.

"What are we doing, sea princess?" he asked, more softly than he had intended.

"I don't know," she whispered back. "But when I dream of you—"

"You've dreamed of me?" he interrupted, startled.

Her eyes widened. "You've haunted my sleep for three moons now. A great black horse with eyes like whirlpools, running across impossible waters."

Brannach felt something ancient shift within him. "And you have haunted mine. A maiden dancing on the shore, her hair full of starlight, her voice calling me from the depths."

Nerina's hand trembled slightly in his. "The second sight," she murmured. "A gift and a curse among my people. I see what may be, what must be."

"And what do you see now, sea princess?" Brannach asked, his voice rough with emotions he could not name.

She stood on tiptoe, her free hand coming to rest against his chest. "I see water that is neither river nor sea, but something new. Something that has never been before."

And then, with the courage that had always set her apart from her more cautious kin, Nerina pressed her lips to his.

The kiss lasted only a moment, but in that brief connection, Brannach felt something impossible—a vision of water flowing both ways, of boundaries dissolved, of a child with storm-cloud eyes and hair like seafoam, running across both land and wave.

When they broke apart, both were breathing heavily, staring at each other in wonder and fear.

"This is forbidden," he said, but made no move to release her hand.

"All important things begin as forbidden," she replied with surprising wisdom. "Before becoming necessary."

A distant call—haunting and mournful—drifted across the water, breaking the spell between them. Nerina's head snapped toward the sound, her expression suddenly alarmed.

"The dawn summons," she explained hurriedly. "I must return. My absence will be noticed."

She pulled away, moving swiftly toward the rock where her sealskin lay. With practiced grace, she wrapped it around her shoulders, the magical garment seeming to melt into her very being. Before his eyes, her human form shifted, limbs shortening, body elongating, until a sleek silver-gray seal regarded him with unmistakably intelligent eyes.

"Will you return?" Brannach found himself asking, hating the vulnerability in his voice.

The seal dipped its head once in clear affirmation, then slipped into the gentle waves and disappeared beneath the surface.

Brannach stood alone on the shore, the taste of salt still on his lips, a strange ache in his chest where her hand had rested. Above him, the stars were fading as dawn approached, and with them, his time of freedom.

He must return to his kingdom, to the dark halls and the cold politics of his court. To subjects who feared him but did not know him. To the endless cycle of hunting and killing that suddenly seemed hollow.

With a growl of frustration, he shifted back to his stallion form and galloped along the shoreline, his powerful hooves striking sparks from the stones. He ran until the sun crested the horizon, and only then did he turn inland, following the river's course back to the loch that was his home.

But as he ran, he knew with absolute certainty that he would return to the sea's edge the next night.

And the night after.

And every night until he understood what it was that pulled him toward the silver-eyed princess of a people he had been taught to hate.

Chapter 5: Whispers in the Dark

Darran waited in the shadows of the River Hall, watching as Brannach returned from his night's ride. The Kelpie King moved differently now, with a distracted air that set Darran's teeth on edge. Something had changed in his sovereign, and change was dangerous to their kind.

When Brannach had disappeared into his private chambers, Darran slipped away, moving through the underwater passages of their stronghold until he reached a seldom-used tunnel. Here, the black stone of the hall gave way to natural rock, and the passageway twisted upward toward the surface of Loch Slochd.

He emerged in a hidden cove, screened by ancient willows whose branches trailed in the water. The predawn light cast everything in shades of gray and silver, and mist rose from the loch's surface like spirits of the drowned.

"You're late," came a sibilant voice from among the reeds.

Darran didn't flinch, though the speaker had approached with supernatural silence. "I had to be certain the king had returned safely."

A figure emerged from the mist—neither fully human nor creature, but something in between. Female in form, with skin the pale green of river algae and hair like tangled waterweed. Her eyes were large and unblinking, the black pupils surrounded by rings of amber. A nixie—cousin to the Kelpies but smaller, weaker, bound to the shallow waters rather than the deep.

"And did he?" the nixie asked, her wide mouth curving in what might have been a smile. "Return safely?"

Darran considered his response carefully. His arrangement with the nixie, Lorelei, was both practical and dangerous. She provided information from the wider river network—things her kind learned from listening to human conversations, from the gossip of water sprites and the secrets carried downstream. In return, he protected her and her sisters from the more predatory of his kind and occasionally shared scraps from the Kelpie feasts.

"He returned," Darran said at last. "But something troubles him. He rides to the sea's edge night after night, and returns... changed."

Lorelei dipped her webbed fingers into the loch, creating ripples that spread outward in perfect circles. "Perhaps he has found a new hunting ground? A village near the coast where the humans are unwary?"

"No," Darran shook his head, his dark hair swirling in the water around his shoulders. "This is not about hunting. Something calls to him there, something that steals his attention from his duties, from his people."

The nixie tilted her head, her expression unreadable. "What would you have me do?"

"Find out what draws him," Darran instructed. "Your kind can travel the rivers swiftly, unseen by most eyes. Follow him tomorrow night, see where he goes, who he meets."

"And what will you give me for this service?" Lorelei asked, her voice taking on a hungry edge. "Information is one thing. Spying on the king is quite another."

Darran reached into a pouch at his belt and withdrew a gleaming object—a bracelet of intricate silver filigree set with small blue stones. "This was taken from a noble lady three moons ago. She drowned beautifully."

The nixie's eyes widened with desire. Such treasures were rare among her kind, who had not the strength to pull humans beneath the waters as Kelpies did. She reached for it, but Darran closed his fist around the prize.

"When you bring me useful information," he said coolly. "Not before."

Lorelei hissed but nodded her agreement. "Tomorrow night, then. I will follow the king and learn what secret he keeps."

"See that you do," Darran replied. "And Lorelei? Be certain he does not detect your presence. If you are discovered, I will deny any knowledge of our arrangement."

The nixie's laugh was like water trickling over stones. "Fear not, river lord. My kind invented stealth while yours were still learning to drown shepherds."

With that, she slipped beneath the surface, leaving only expanding rings to mark where she had been.

Darran remained a moment longer, staring across the loch toward the distant mountains. He had served the Kelpie court for three centuries, advising kings and princes, maintaining the delicate balance of power among the river folk. He had seen sovereigns rise and fall, had helped orchestrate the ascension of some and the downfall of others.

Brannach had been different from the beginning—fiercer, more independent, less willing to be guided. But he had also been a worthy king, expanding their territory, strengthening ancient alliances, ensuring their kind remained feared and respected in a world increasingly dominated by humans and their iron and their crosses.

If something threatened that strength now, Darran would find it. And if necessary, eliminate it.

For the good of all Kelpie-kind.

Chapter 6: Mother and Daughter

"You've been to the shore again."

Queen Mhairi's voice was carefully neutral as she brushed her daughter's silver hair. They sat in Nerina's private chamber, a smaller version of the Queen's own grotto, decorated with treasures the young princess had collected over the years—colored glass polished by the sea, unusual shells, and a small carved figurine of a horse that Mhairi eyed with new suspicion.

Nerina stiffened slightly but didn't deny it. "The tide was perfect for dancing."

"Alone?" Her mother's brush strokes never faltered.

A pause, just long enough to confirm what Mhairi already knew. "Does it matter? The shore is empty of humans this time of year. The village is too far inland, and—"

"Not all dangers come from humans," the Queen interrupted gently. She set down the brush and moved to face her daughter. "Nerina, look at me."

Reluctantly, the princess raised her eyes to meet her mother's identical silver gaze.

"You were seen," Mhairi said simply. "With the Kelpie King."

Nerina's face paled, but her chin lifted in that stubborn way that had both charmed and frustrated the Queen since her daughter's childhood. "His name is Brannach."

"I know what he is called," Mhairi replied, struggling to keep her voice level. "What I don't know is why my daughter, who has been taught the histories of our people, who knows the ancient divisions between river and sea, would place herself in such danger."

"He wouldn't hurt me," Nerina protested.

Mhairi's laugh held no humor. "Child, hurting is what his kind does. It is their nature, their purpose. The Kelpies are creatures of violence and deceit. They lure, they drown, they feed on fear and death."

"He's different," Nerina insisted. "Or at least... he wants to be. There's a hunger in him for something beyond what he's always known."

The Queen studied her daughter's face, noting the flush that had replaced her earlier pallor, the light in her eyes. With a sinking heart, she recognized the signs.

"You care for him," she said softly. Not a question.

Nerina looked away. "I hardly know him. We've only met once."

"And yet you dream of him," Mhairi guessed. When her daughter's eyes widened in surprise, she smiled sadly. "Did you think I wouldn't notice? The second sight runs strong in our bloodline. I had such dreams in my youth—visions of what might be, of paths that could be taken."

"Then you understand—"

"I understand that the second sight shows possibilities, not certainties," the Queen interrupted firmly. "And not all possibilities should be pursued, Nerina. Some doors are better left closed."

She rose and moved to a small chest carved from driftwood that sat on a shell-inlaid shelf. From it, she removed an object wrapped in shimmering fabric—a mirror of polished silver, its handle carved with intricate knots and symbols.

"This was given to our ancestress by the sea itself," Mhairi explained, handling the mirror reverently. "It shows not reflections, but connections. The ties that bind one soul to another, one fate to the next."

She held it out to her daughter. "Look, and see the truth of the Kelpie King."

Nerina hesitated, then took the mirror with trembling hands. For a long moment, she stared into its gleaming surface. Her expression shifted from curiosity to shock, then to something darker—a mixture of horror and fascination.

"He has blood on his hands," she whispered.

"All Kelpies do," her mother replied gently.

"So many lives... taken for sport, for hunger." Nerina's voice shook. "I see them all—men, women, even children. Lured by his beauty in human form, or driven mad with terror by his stallion shape. Dragged beneath the waters, their lungs filling as they struggle..."

"That is his nature," Mhairi said. "That is what he is."

Nerina continued to stare into the mirror, her expression now shifting to confusion. "But there's something else... a shadow over him. A sorrow. As if he's trapped in his own nature, unable to break free." She looked up at her mother, her eyes wide. "And I see myself, connected to him by a silver thread. Mother, what does it mean?"

The Queen gently took the mirror from her daughter's hands. "It means that fate has some design for you both—but fate is not destiny, Nerina. We make our own choices, even in the face of powerful visions."

"What should I do?" the princess asked, suddenly sounding very young.

Mhairi sat beside her daughter and took her hands. "For now, you will remain within our realm. No more visits to the shore, no more dances under the stars."

"But—"

"In three days' time," the Queen continued firmly, "you will journey to our cousins in the Northern Isles. The distance will help clear your mind of these... fascinations."

"You're sending me away?" Nerina pulled her hands free, her expression hurt and angry. "Like a child who's misbehaved?"

"I'm protecting you," Mhairi corrected. "Until we better understand what this connection means, what dangers it might hold."

"You fear the prophecy," Nerina said suddenly, her eyes narrowing. "The old tales about river and sea."

The Queen stiffened. "What do you know of such things?"

"Only whispers. Fragments of stories not meant for young ears." The princess rose and began to pace, her movements fluid and graceful even in agitation. "A joining of waters, a child of both worlds. The breaking of ancient boundaries."

"Those prophecies are ancient and obscure," Queen Mhairi said sharply. "Half-forgotten for good reason. They speak of cataclysm, of the natural order undone."

"Or of healing," Nerina countered. "The second sight shows me more than dreams, Mother. Sometimes when I touch the oldest stones beneath the waves, I hear whispers of a time before the division, when all water-folk lived as one people."

The Queen's expression darkened. "That time ended in blood and sorrow. The division exists because it must."

"But what if it doesn't have to?" Nerina's voice softened, grew pleading. "What if the prophecy speaks of reconciliation? Of something new and beautiful born from two worlds?"

"Enough!" Mhairi rarely raised her voice, and the sharpness of it now made Nerina fall silent. The Queen closed her eyes, composing herself before continuing more gently. "Forgive me, daughter. But you are young, and the young see only possibility, not danger."

She moved to the grotto's entrance, her shoulders straight with the weight of her crown. "You will remain within our territory until your journey north. I will set guards if I must." Her voice softened slightly. "It is for your protection, Nerina. One day you will understand."

When her mother had gone, Nerina sank onto her bed of soft sea moss, tears stinging her eyes. The mirror lay abandoned on the floor, its silver surface now showing only ordinary reflections. But she didn't need its magic to remember what she had seen—the blood on Brannach's hands, yes, but also the sorrow in his spirit. The loneliness that matched her own.

And that silver thread connecting them, pulsing with possibility.

"I'm sorry, Mother," she whispered to the empty room. "But some currents cannot be denied."

Chapter 7: The Watcher in the Reeds

Brannach arrived at the meeting place earlier than usual, the sun barely set beyond the western hills. The shore lay empty, the tide beginning its slow retreat to reveal the strip of sand where he had first seen Nerina dance.

He paced restlessly, still in his human form. Would she come tonight? Had she regretted their brief kiss, their shared confidences? Or worse—had she been discovered by her people, forbidden from returning?

The Kelpie King was unaccustomed to such uncertainties. In his world, he took what he wanted. He commanded, and others obeyed. This waiting, this hoping—it was new territory, uncomfortable yet somehow exhilarating.

As darkness deepened over the water, his keen senses detected movement—not from the sea, but from the river behind him. A subtle disturbance in the current, the faintest ripple where none should be.

He was being watched.

With practiced casualness, Brannach stretched and walked toward the river's edge as if to observe the flow. Then, with the explosive speed that made Kelpies such deadly predators, he plunged his arm into the water and seized the watcher.

He dragged the struggling creature onto the bank, his grip unbreakable around a slender green throat.

"Lorelei," he growled, recognizing the nixie. "Explain yourself before I squeeze the water from your worthless body."

The nixie's amber eyes were wide with terror. "M-mercy, my king! I meant no harm!"

"Spies seldom do," he replied coldly. "Who sent you? Answer truthfully, or I will ensure you never swim the currents again."

"D-Darran," she gasped. "He wanted to know where you go at night, who you meet."

Brannach's eyes narrowed. "And what have you seen?"

"Nothing yet, my lord," Lorelei insisted. "I've only just arrived. I swear by the dark waters!"

He studied her face, searching for deception. Nixies were known for their cunning, but not for their courage. The fear in her eyes seemed genuine.

"Listen carefully," he said, loosening his grip just enough for her to breathe. "You will return to Darran. You will tell him that I rode the highlands all night, hunting alone as is my right. You will say nothing of this place, nothing of my interest in the sea."

"Yes, my king," she whispered.

"And Lorelei?" He leaned closer, his voice dropping to a dangerous murmur. "If I ever find you or any other creature spying on me again, I will tear out your gills and leave you to dry on the shore. Is that understood?"

The nixie nodded frantically. When he released her, she scrambled backward into the water, disappearing with barely a ripple.

Brannach straightened, brushing sand from his hands. The encounter troubled him more than he cared to admit. Darran had been his trusted advisor for centuries. If he now set spies upon his king, it could only mean he sensed something amiss—something potentially threatening to the established order.

And he wasn't wrong.

A soft splash from the direction of the sea interrupted his troubled thoughts. He turned to see a sleek seal head emerge from the gentle waves, silver eyes unmistakable even at a distance.

His heart lightened instantly, worries temporarily forgotten as he moved to the water's edge. The seal swam closer, then disappeared beneath the surface. Moments later, Nerina rose from the shallow water, her sealskin draped around her shoulders like a cloak, her silver hair clinging to her like cascading moonlight.

"You came," he said, unable to keep the relief from his voice.

"I almost didn't," she replied, her expression troubled as she waded to shore. "My mother knows about us. I've been forbidden to leave our territory."

Brannach frowned. "Yet here you are."

A small, defiant smile curved her lips. "I've never been very good at following rules that make no sense." The smile faded. "But I haven't much time. The guards will soon notice my absence."

"Guards?" His voice hardened. "You're being watched too, then."

"For my protection, my mother says." Nerina sighed. "She fears what might come of our... friendship. She showed me things, Brannach. A mirror that reveals connections, truth."

She looked up at him, her silver eyes filled with a mixture of sorrow and determination. "I saw what you are. What you've done."

Brannach stiffened, taking a step back. Of course. How could he have forgotten, even briefly, the fundamental divide between them? He was a predator, a killer. She was a creature of grace and song.

"And yet you still came," he observed quietly.

"Because I saw more than blood on your hands," she said, stepping closer. "I saw your loneliness. Your hunger for something beyond violence. And I saw us, connected by a silver thread that neither time nor tide can break."

She reached for his hand, her cool fingers intertwining with his larger ones. "In three days, I am to be sent north, to our cousins in the distant isles. My mother hopes distance will cure me of... this." She squeezed his hand. "Of you."

"Will it?" he asked, surprising himself with the vulnerability in his question.

Nerina shook her head. "The second sight shows me many paths, Brannach, but all of them lead back to you. To us. To something neither Kelpie nor Selkie, but new."

"Your mother is right to fear, then," he said roughly. "For what could come of this except destruction? Our peoples have been divided since the world was young. There is no bridge between river and sea."

"Not yet," she whispered, her free hand coming to rest against his chest. "But there could be."

Her touch burned through him like fire, igniting something he had never known in his centuries of existence—hope. Dangerous, impossible hope.

"Nerina," he began, but fell silent as she stretched upward and pressed her lips to his once more.

This kiss was different from their first—deeper, more certain. And with it came another vision, stronger than before. A child standing between worlds, with storm-cloud eyes and hair like seafoam. Behind the child, something vast taking shape—not a bridge, but a meeting of waters, a place where river and sea flowed together in harmony.

When they broke apart, Brannach saw in her eyes that she had shared the vision.

"You see?" she whispered. "That is what could be."

"At what cost?" he asked, even as his arms tightened around her. "Your people would never accept it. Mine would see it as betrayal."

"Then we must find another way," she insisted. "Another place. Somewhere neither river nor sea, but both."

A sudden thought struck him. "The Loch of Whispers," he murmured.

"What?"

"An ancient place in my territory," he explained, excitement growing as the idea took shape. "A loch formed where a river was trapped by falling stones, creating a place apart from both flowing water and sea. Legend says it was once a meeting place between the water peoples, before the division."

Hope bloomed in Nerina's eyes. "Could we meet there?"

"Yes," he said, his mind racing ahead. "It's secluded, protected by cliffs on all sides. Few even among my own kind remember its existence." He gripped her shoulders gently. "But how would you get there? If you're being watched, being sent away..."

"The journey north will take us past the western coast," she said, her voice taking on a practical tone that surprised and impressed him. "I know the route well—my mother's guards will follow the deep channels, but there's a passage through the sea caves that I discovered as a child. I can slip away there."

"When?"

"Three nights from now, when the moon is dark," she said. "Can you meet me where the western cliffs meet the sea? There's a distinctive stone arch just offshore."

"I'll find it," he promised. "I'll be waiting."

A haunting call drifted across the water—the same sound Brannach had heard at their last meeting.

"The warning," Nerina said urgently. "My absence has been discovered." She clutched his hands tightly. "Three nights. The stone arch. Promise me you'll come alone."

"I swear it," he replied solemnly. "No one will know."

She kissed him once more, briefly but with fierce intensity, then pulled away and ran to the water's edge. With practiced grace, she wrapped her sealskin around her body, the transformation flowing over her like a wave. The seal that was Nerina looked back at him once, silver eyes gleaming, then disappeared beneath the dark waters.

Brannach remained on the shore long after she had gone, his mind churning with possibilities both wondrous and terrible. Something was taking shape between them—something that defied ancient boundaries and whispered of change to come.

And change, for beings as old as they, was both miracle and danger.

Chapter 8: Conspiracies and Councils

Deep within the River Hall, the Kelpie Council had gathered. Seven ancient beings sat at a table carved from the heartwood of an oak struck by lightning—the most powerful of Brannach's subjects, representatives of the major river systems within his territory.

Darran stood before them, his posture respectful but his eyes glittering with purpose.

"The king grows distracted," he said without preamble. "His rides become longer, his interest in the court's affairs diminishes. Something calls him away from his duties, from his people."

Morna of the Rapids, her hair a churning white like the waters she ruled, leaned forward. "What evidence do you bring, Darran? These are serious accusations against our sovereign."

"I sent a watcher," Darran admitted. "The nixie Lorelei."

"A risky choice," observed Kieran of the Deep Pools, a massive Kelpie with skin the blue-black of the deepest water. "Nixies are notoriously unreliable."

"She returned with strange news," Darran continued. "She claims the king spent the entire night riding the highlands, hunting alone." He paused significantly. "But when she returned, there was sand between her webbed toes—sea sand, not river sand."

Murmurs rippled around the table.

"You believe she lied," stated Ailsa of the Marshlands, her reedy voice as thin as her elongated form.

"I believe the king caught her spying and instructed her to lie," Darran corrected. "Which only confirms that he has something to hide."

"Even if this is true," rumbled Torquil of the Gorge, oldest of the council members, "the king's private affairs are his own. He has led us well for three centuries. Our territories are secure, our hunting grounds protected from human encroachment, our ancient ways preserved."

"But at what cost?" Darran moved to the center of the circle, his voice taking on an urgent edge. "Have you not felt it? The thinning of the old magic? The weakening of our connection to the waters we rule?"

Uncomfortable silence fell. They had all felt it—a subtle diminishing of their powers, a distancing of the water spirits that had once answered their every call.

"The world changes," Morna said at last. "The humans spread their iron and their faith ever wider. It is not our king's fault."

"Unless," Darran said softly, "he has betrayed our most sacred law."

Shocked gasps echoed through the chamber.

"You go too far," Torquil growled, rising to his impressive height. "To suggest the king would commune with the sea folk—"

"I suggest nothing," Darran interrupted smoothly. "I merely consider all possibilities. Something draws him to the coast night after night. Something he will not share with his oldest advisor, something he instructs others to lie about."

He looked around the table, meeting each council member's eyes. "If I am wrong, I will gladly accept punishment for my presumption. But if I am right, if our king indeed treats with the enemies of our kind, then the consequences could be catastrophic for all water folk."

Silence fell again, heavier this time, laden with ancient fears and hatreds.

Finally, Kieran spoke. "What would you have us do, Darran? Challenge the king directly? Muster our forces against him? Either path leads to civil war among our people."

"Nothing so dramatic," Darran assured him. "I propose only that we watch more carefully. That we learn the truth before acting. If he is innocent of wrongdoing, no harm is done. If not..." He let the implication hang in the air.

"And who will do this watching?" Ailsa asked suspiciously. "Not another unreliable nixie, I hope."

"No," Darran said. "This requires someone with greater skill, greater loyalty to our ways." He turned to the seventh council member, who had remained silent throughout the discussion. "Morvath of the Shadows, your talents are needed."

The figure stirred, hood shifting to reveal a face of disturbing beauty—neither male nor female, but something in between, with skin pale as moonlight on water and eyes black as a midnight pool. Morvath was unlike the other Kelpies, a creature of stealth rather than strength, of whispers rather than roars.

"You wish me to follow the king," Morvath stated in a voice like water sliding over smooth stones.

"I wish you to discover the truth," Darran corrected. "Wherever he goes next night from now, when the moon is dark. Whatever he does. Whoever he meets."

Morvath studied him with those unsettling eyes. "And what if the truth is as you fear? What then?"

Darran's expression hardened. "Then we act to protect our kind. As we have always done."

The council members exchanged uneasy glances, but none voiced opposition. Even Torquil, for all his initial defense of the king, could not dismiss the possibility that something was seriously amiss.

"Three nights," Morvath agreed at last. "I will bring you truth, Darran of the River Hall. But remember—truth is a double-edged blade. It may cut the hand that seeks it."

With that cryptic warning, the shadow Kelpie rose and glided from the chamber, leaving behind a chill that had nothing to do with the cold waters surrounding them.

Chapter 9: The Journey Begins

Nerina watched as her small traveling party made final preparations. Three of her mother's most trusted guards—veteran warriors who had protected the Selkie Court for centuries—checked their weapons and provisions. Though Selkies were peaceful by nature, the journey north would take them through territories frequented by humans, and occasionally by less friendly water folk. Silver daggers, coral spears, and nets of enchanted kelp were standard equipment for such expeditions.

The leader of the guards, Cailean, approached her with respectful deference. "We are ready, Princess. We should depart within the hour to catch the favorable currents."

Nerina nodded, her face carefully composed to hide her inner turmoil. "Thank you, Cailean. I'll just say my farewells to my mother."

The guard hesitated, clearly uncomfortable. "Your Highness, the Queen asked that I remind you... this journey is for your protection. Not punishment."

Nerina's smile didn't reach her eyes. "Of course. My mother means well. She always does."

Cailean bowed and returned to the others, leaving Nerina alone with her thoughts. The plan she had formed was dangerous, perhaps foolish. To slip away from royal guards during a sanctioned journey, to meet a Kelpie in secret—it violated every rule of her people, every warning she had been raised with.

And yet the visions persisted. Each night since she had last seen Brannach, the second sight had shown her the same images with increasing clarity: the child of two worlds, the meeting of waters, a new beginning for both their peoples. Sometimes, in the deepest watches of the night, she even glimpsed further—a time of reconciliation, of boundaries dissolved, of ancient hatreds finally laid to rest.

Could she ignore such visions? Turn her back on what might be the purpose for which she had been given the second sight in the first place?

"You're very quiet."

Nerina turned to find her mother standing behind her, regal in her formal attire of woven kelp and pearls. But there was softness in the Queen's eyes, a vulnerability rarely shown to others.

"I'm preparing myself for the journey," Nerina replied carefully.

Queen Mhairi stepped closer, reaching out to adjust her daughter's traveling cloak. "The Northern Isles are beautiful this time of year. Cousin Eilidh has prepared the pearl chambers for your stay."

"How long am I to remain in exile?" Nerina couldn't keep the edge from her voice.

"It is not exile," her mother corrected gently. "It is sanctuary, until we better understand what is happening." She hesitated, then added, "Finnol has been researching the ancient prophecies. There may be more to this connection than we first believed."

Nerina looked up sharply. "What do you mean?"

"Only that not all the old tales end in destruction," the Queen said carefully. "Some speak of... reconciliation. Of a time when the waters might once again speak with one voice."

Hope flared in Nerina's chest. "Then you understand? You see what might be possible?"

"I see danger," Mhairi replied, her voice firming. "Ancient forces stirring that might be beyond any of us to control. Which is precisely why you must be kept safe, away from the Kelpie's influence, until we know more."

The hope dimmed. Her mother still didn't trust her judgment, still saw her as a child to be protected rather than a seer with her own destiny.

"And if the visions continue?" Nerina asked. "If distance does nothing to break this connection?"

"Then we will face that challenge when it comes," the Queen said simply. "For now, go with Cailean and his warriors. Trust in the wisdom of those who have lived longer, seen more than you have."

Nerina embraced her mother, hiding her face against the Queen's shoulder so her expression wouldn't betray her. "I love you, Mother. I hope one day you'll understand that some currents cannot be denied, only navigated."

Queen Mhairi held her daughter tightly, as if sensing the farewell was more significant than it appeared. "Be safe, my silver-eyed one. Return to me when the moon has completed its cycle."

The journey began an hour later, with Nerina and her three guards slipping into the deep water channels that would carry them north. In their true forms—sleek, powerful seals—they moved with the graceful speed that was the envy of other sea creatures.

Nerina swam slightly behind the others, her mind racing ahead to the sea caves, to the stone arch where Brannach would be waiting. Three days of travel lay ahead—three days to strengthen her resolve, to prepare for whatever might come of this forbidden meeting.

Three days to say goodbye to the only life she had ever known.

Chapter 10: The Stone Arch

The western coast of Scotland rose harsh and magnificent against the darkening sky as Brannach made his way north. In his stallion form, he covered ground with supernatural speed, iron hooves striking sparks from the rocky terrain. He had left the River Hall at dusk, offering no explanation for his absence beyond a curt announcement that he would be patrolling the outer boundaries of their territory.

If Darran suspected anything, he had not shown it. But Brannach wasn't fooled. The failed attempt to spy on him had been only the beginning. His advisor was too clever, too experienced in the ways of court intrigue to abandon his suspicions so easily.

All the more reason to meet Nerina at the Loch of Whispers—a place so ancient and obscure that even most of his own kind had forgotten its existence. There, perhaps, they could find answers to the questions that plagued them both. What did the visions mean? What future was possible for a Kelpie and a Selkie? And what of the child they had both glimpsed—a being of two worlds?

As the moon rose, Brannach slowed his pace, scanning the coastline for the distinctive stone arch Nerina had described. The terrain here was wild and untamed, sheer cliffs dropping to the churning sea below, with only the occasional narrow beach where the rocks relented.

He found what he sought just as the tide reached its highest point—a massive arch of weather-worn stone standing just offshore, framing a view of the endless sea beyond. Ancient and powerful, it seemed a fitting gateway between worlds.

Shifting to his human form, Brannach picked his way down a treacherous path to a small, sheltered cove beneath the cliffs. Here, the sea's fury was gentled somewhat, creating a pocket of relative calm where a small boat might safely land—or a swimmer might come ashore.

He settled on a flat rock to wait, staring out at the dark waters. Would she come? Had her resolve weakened in the days since their last meeting? Or worse, had her escape plan failed?

The moon climbed higher, casting silver reflections across the restless surface of the sea. An hour passed, then another. Doubt began to gnaw at him. Perhaps this had all been folly—a momentary madness born of loneliness and the strange pull he felt toward the sea maiden.

A splash in the water jerked him from his thoughts. He rose, watching intently as a sleek dark head broke the surface some fifty yards from shore. Too large for an ordinary seal, moving with purpose rather than the random patterns of hunting.

Nerina.

Relief flooded through him, followed immediately by a warmth in his chest he was still unaccustomed to. He waded into the shallows, unmindful of the cold water soaking his garments, and waited as she swam closer.

When she reached the point where the water lapped at his waist, she disappeared beneath the surface. Moments later, she emerged in her human form, sealskin draped around her shoulders, her silver hair gleaming in the moonlight.

"You came," she said, her voice breathless with what might have been exertion or emotion.

"Did you doubt I would?" he asked, reaching for her hands.

"No," she admitted. "But the journey was more difficult than I anticipated. My guards are skilled and vigilant. Slipping away unnoticed required all my knowledge of the secret passages."

"They haven't followed you?" Brannach scanned the horizon, suddenly alert to potential threats.

"I don't believe so. I took a route few know—through caves that run deep beneath the cliffs. It would take powerful magic to track me there." She squeezed his hands. "But we shouldn't linger here. The Loch of Whispers—is it far?"

"A few miles inland," he said, helping her to shore. "Can you walk that distance? Or should I carry you?"

A smile lit her features, transforming her anxious expression into something luminous. "I'm not quite so delicate, river king. My legs are strong, though I prefer the freedom of swimming."

Together they climbed the narrow path up the cliff face, Brannach leading the way, occasionally turning to offer her a hand over the more difficult passages. At the top, they paused to catch their breath and survey the land ahead.

Rolling hills stretched before them, bathed in moonlight and shadow. In the distance, mountains rose like sleeping giants against the star-strewn sky.

"We'll follow the ancient river path," Brannach explained, pointing to a barely visible track that wound through the heather. "It's the swiftest route, though rarely used now except by deer and the occasional human wanderer."

They set off at a steady pace, Nerina adapting quickly to walking over rough terrain. For a time they traveled in comfortable silence, each lost in their own thoughts. Then, as the night deepened around them, Nerina spoke.

"Tell me about your people," she said. "Not the stories my kind tells of yours, but the truth. How do you live? What brings you joy? What troubles your sleep besides visions of sea maidens?" The last was said with a hint of teasing in her voice.

Brannach considered her questions carefully. No Selkie had ever asked such things of a Kelpie before—at least, not in all the long centuries of his memory.

"We are not so different from your kind in some ways," he began slowly. "We have our halls, our councils, our traditions. We celebrate the changing seasons, the waxing of our powers with the spring floods, the deep magic of winter when the waters lie still beneath ice."

"And the hunting?" she asked quietly. "The drowning of humans?"

He didn't flinch from her directness. "Yes. That too is part of our nature, our... sustenance. Not merely the flesh, though some of my kind do feed that way, but the fear, the life-force released in that moment between life and death." He glanced at her profile in the moonlight. "Does that disgust you?"

"It troubles me," she admitted. "Life is precious to my people. We sing to the dying, ease their passage. We don't hasten death's arrival."

"And yet, the greatest tragedies in human tales are not of Kelpies, but of Selkies," he pointed out. "Men who steal your sealskins, forcing you to remain on land as their wives. Children born of such unions, forever caught between worlds."

Nerina's expression grew sad. "Yes. Those tales are true enough. My mother's younger sister was taken that way—her skin hidden by a fisherman who loved her beauty but could not understand her nature. She withered like a sea plant left in the sun, growing weaker each year until she was nothing but sorrow and silence."

"What happened to her?" Brannach asked, genuinely curious.

"My mother found her after seven years of searching. Located the hidden skin and returned it to her sister. But by then..." Nerina's voice faltered. "By then, there were children. Two small ones with their mother's silver eyes and their father's human heart. She had to choose— remain in agony on land for their sake, or return to the sea and leave them behind."

"And she chose the sea," Brannach guessed.

"She chose life," Nerina corrected gently. "For to deny a Selkie the sea is a slow death. But she never stopped grieving for her children. She would swim close to shore, watching them grow from a distance, singing to them when the moon was full and the nights were calm."

"Did they hear her?"

"Yes. They grew up knowing their mother loved them, even if they couldn't understand why she left. When they were grown, they built their homes by the shore and learned the old songs. Their descendants live there still—humans with a touch of sea magic in their blood, who sometimes glimpse our kind in the twilight waters."

They walked in silence for a time after that, each contemplating the complexities of their separate worlds, the sorrows and joys unique to their kinds.

"Is that what you fear?" Brannach asked finally. "That any child of ours would be torn between worlds as those children were?"

The directness of the question startled her. "You've seen the vision too, then. The child with storm-cloud eyes and hair like seafoam."

"Standing between river and sea," he confirmed. "Neither one nor the other, but something new."

"I don't know what to fear anymore," Nerina confessed. "The second sight shows possibilities, not certainties. That child could bring great joy or terrible sorrow. Perhaps both."

"Perhaps it is not a child of flesh at all," Brannach suggested, "but a symbol. A new understanding between our peoples."

"Perhaps," she agreed, though her tone suggested she believed otherwise.

They crested a hill, and suddenly the landscape opened before them. Nestled in a valley surrounded by protective cliffs lay a small loch, its surface mirror-smooth in the moonlight. Unlike the dark, peaty waters of most Scottish lochs, this one gleamed with an inner light, as if the stars themselves had fallen into its depths.

"The Loch of Whispers," Brannach said reverently. "Sacred to all water folk before the division."

Nerina stared in wonder. "It's beautiful. I can feel the old magic even from here—pure and untainted by hatred or fear."

They made their way down the hillside, drawn by the loch's serene beauty. As they approached its shores, a strange sensation came over them both—a lightening of spirit, a sense of homecoming neither had expected.

"The waters here are neither river nor sea," Brannach explained as they reached the shore. "They are contained, yet connected to both through underground streams. That is why our ancestors considered it neutral territory, a place for councils and ceremonies."

"Why was it abandoned?" Nerina asked, kneeling to trail her fingers through the crystal water.

"The division," he said simply. "After the war between river and sea, such meeting places were deemed dangerous. Forbidden. Over time, most were destroyed or their locations deliberately forgotten." He gazed across the loch's still surface. "This one survived only because it is so remote, so well-hidden by the surrounding cliffs."

The moment Nerina's fingers touched the water, a soft glow spread outward in gentle ripples. She gasped, snatching her hand back in surprise.

"The loch responds to you," Brannach observed, fascination in his voice. "It recognizes the royal blood of the sea folk."

Tentatively, he knelt beside her and dipped his own hand into the water. The glow intensified, ripples meeting and merging with those still expanding from Nerina's touch. Where they intersected, sparks of silver and blue light danced upward like tiny spirits.

"And to you," she whispered. "The blood of the river kings."

As if responding to their combined presence, the entire loch began to glow, softly at first, then with increasing brilliance until the whole valley was illuminated with ethereal light.

"What's happening?" Nerina asked, wonder and a touch of fear in her voice.

"I don't know," Brannach admitted. "The old stories speak of signs and wonders at this place, but nothing specific. I think... I think the loch itself is welcoming us."

At the center of the waters, the light coalesced into a shimmering pillar that rose toward the night sky. Within it, shapes began to form—indistinct at first, then slowly resolving into recognizable images.

"Look," Nerina breathed, pointing. "It's showing us something."

They watched, transfixed, as the vision unfolded before them. A time long past, when the water folk were one people—neither Kelpie nor Selkie, but something that encompassed both natures. Beings of grace and power, harmony and strength, who moved freely between river and sea, who sang to the waters and danced with the tides.

Then came darkness—a great shadow falling across the vision. Conflict. Division. A terrible choice forced upon the water folk by some catastrophe the images couldn't clearly convey. The splitting of one people into two, each taking a different aspect of their original nature— the Kelpies embracing power and wildness, retreating to the rivers and lochs; the Selkies choosing grace and music, claiming the open sea as their domain.

The final image was of two figures standing exactly where Brannach and Nerina now stood, hands clasped above the waters of the loch. Male and female, neither fully Kelpie nor fully Selkie, but something that remembered the original unity.

Then the vision faded, the light receding until only the natural moonlight remained, casting silver reflections across the now-still surface of the loch.

"They were one people," Nerina said softly, awe in her voice. "Our ancestors. One kind, before the division."

"So it would seem," Brannach agreed, his mind racing to absorb the implications. "But what caused the separation? What catastrophe was so great that it split them into two distinct peoples?"

"And what does it mean for us?" Nerina turned to face him fully, her silver eyes searching his. "Are we meant to remember what was forgotten? To heal what was broken?"

Brannach took her hands in his, struck by how right it felt despite everything he had been taught about the sea folk. "I don't know. But I do know that since meeting you, the hunger that has haunted me for so long has quieted. As if something lost has been found, something long forbidden but now whispered as possible.

Chapter 11: Echoes of the Past

The Loch of Whispers lay before them, its surface mirror-smooth beneath the shivering moonlight. Neither river nor sea, it existed in the liminal space between worlds—a place of legend even among the magical folk of Scotland's waters. Ancient stones ringed its shores, their surfaces carved with symbols too old to be read by any living creature. The mountains surrounding it stood like silent guardians, their peaks lost in mist despite the clarity of the night sky.

Nerina and Brannach stood at the water's edge, their hands clasped, their hearts pounding with the gravity of what they were about to attempt. The visions that had plagued them both for months had led them here, to this sacred place that existed in the borderlands between their kingdoms.

Brannach's powerful frame was tense, his midnight hair stirring in the gentle breeze that seemed to whisper secrets across the loch's surface. In his human form, only his storm-gray eyes betrayed his true nature—fathomless and ancient, like the deepest parts of his river domain. Beside him, Nerina appeared almost ethereal, her silver hair falling in waves past her shoulders, her pale skin luminous in the moonlight. The sealskin that was her birthright was carefully folded and tucked into a pouch at her waist, a constant reminder of her true home beneath the waves.

"Three nights ago, I dreamed of this place," Nerina said softly, her eyes scanning the perfect stillness of the loch. "Though I had never seen it before."

"And I," Brannach admitted, his voice like stones tumbling in a deep riverbed. "Always the same vision. The loch at midnight, under a full moon. Us, standing together at the center."

Uncertainty gnawed at them both, despite the conviction that had driven them to defy their peoples, their traditions, the very laws of their existence. Could two beings, born of division and ancient hatred, truly forge a new bond that the world would not tear apart?

"My mother consulted the ancient scrolls," Nerina continued, her silver eyes reflecting the stars above. "She found a prophecy speaking of river and sea—of a union that could bring either salvation or doom."

Brannach's jaw tightened. "Darran spoke of similar legends. That is why he betrayed me—why the Kelpie court now hunts for my return."

A shadow crossed Nerina's face as she remembered her own narrow escape from the Selkie guards sent to escort her to the Northern Isles. Had her mother intended protection or imprisonment? The question still haunted her.

"We have sacrificed much to be here," she whispered, the weight of their choices heavy in her voice.

Brannach turned to face her fully, his storm-gray eyes dark with a fierce tenderness that would have shocked his subjects, who knew him only as a merciless hunter and an unyielding king.

"Are you certain?" he asked, his large hands enfolding hers. "Once we begin, there is no turning back. Your people may never accept you again. Mine would sooner drown me than bow to a king who has broken the ancient divisions."

Nerina raised her chin with the quiet dignity that had first captured his attention on that fateful shore where they had danced. "The second sight has never led me astray, though often its messages are shrouded in mystery. The currents of fate have brought us here. We must trust them."

Something in her certainty steadied him, as it always did. For centuries he had ruled through fear and strength, never once seeking counsel from another soul. Yet this slender creature of the sea had somehow breached the walls around his heart, bringing with her a wisdom that balanced his power as perfectly as the tide balances the shore.

"Then we begin," he said, voice deep with resolve.

Together, they stepped into the loch. The water, cool and clear, rose around them, embracing them in a silence older than any spoken language. As they moved deeper, the ancient magic of the place stirred, responding to their presence. The moonlight fractured across the surface, creating patterns like secret writing all around them.

Nerina felt the change immediately—this water was neither fresh nor salt, but something in between. It cradled her body differently than the sea, yet did not reject her as a river would. Beside her, Brannach moved with his natural predator's grace, though she sensed his heightened alertness to the unfamiliar sensations.

The water rose to their waists, then their chests. Still they waded deeper, drawn to the center where the loch's magic felt strongest. Small lights began to appear beneath the surface—not the phosphorescence of deep sea creatures that Nerina knew well, nor the glimmering river sprites that Brannach commanded in his kingdom. These were older beings, watchers perhaps, awakened by the unprecedented presence of Kelpie and Selkie together in this sacred place.

At the center of the loch, where the reflected stars seemed to burn brightest, they halted. The water now reached their shoulders, the gentle pressure surrounding them like an embrace. Brannach released Nerina's hand only to place his palm over her heart, feeling the steady, courageous beat beneath.

"By the waters that bore us," he murmured, voice low and reverent, beginning the ancient bonding ritual that neither of their kinds had performed in countless generations.

"By the winds that sing our songs," she answered, her own hand rising to rest over his heart, feeling its powerful rhythm match her own.

The loch's surface rippled outward from where they stood, a luminous ring of light expanding toward the shore. Above them, the stars seemed to wheel faster, a great vortex of destiny spinning into being. The small lights beneath the surface grew brighter, rising to surround them in a nimbus of ancient magic.

"By the depths that hold our secrets," Brannach continued, his voice deepening as the ritual power built around them.

"By the tides that mark our days," Nerina responded, her silver eyes now glowing with an inner light that matched the surrounding radiance.

A wind rose suddenly, circling the loch, stirring the perfect surface into concentric rings that spread from the center where they stood. The carved stones around the shore began to emit a soft, pulsing glow, their ancient symbols briefly legible once more—telling a story of division and potential reunion that had waited centuries to unfold.

"I, Brannach of the Thundering Hooves, King of the River Folk, bind my fate to yours," he declared, his voice carrying across the water with supernatural clarity. "No longer shall I be only of the river. Your waters shall be my waters, your path shall be my path."

"I, Nerina of the Silver Eyes, daughter of the Western Selkies, bind my fate to yours," she answered, her voice harmonizing with his in a way that made the very air vibrate around them. "No longer shall I be only of the sea. Your currents shall be my currents, your journey shall be my journey."

Their lips met in a kiss that was both a promise and a prayer. Around them, the loch erupted in a column of light that shot toward the heavens, momentarily turning night to day. The waters rose around them, wrapping them in a cocoon of shimmering silver and deepest blue. They felt their souls stretch toward each other, intertwining, merging, forging a bond that was not river or sea, but something new.

Within that sacred unity, images flashed between them—shared visions of a future taking shape. A child with Brannach's storm-gray eyes and Nerina's silver hair, running along shores where river and sea met in harmony rather than division. A new age where the waters spoke again with one voice, where ancient hatreds dissolved like morning mist beneath the sun.

And in that moment, beneath the ancient stars and the murmuring waters, their child was conceived—a being of two worlds, destined to walk where none had walked before. The very first blending of Kelpie and Selkie blood since the great division, carrying within its forming essence the potential for both the doom and salvation the prophecy had foretold.

As the light began to fade and the waters settled once more, Brannach and Nerina remained embraced at the center of the loch, forever changed by what they had experienced. The ritual was complete, the bond forged. Whether it would bring harmony or chaos to their divided worlds remained to be seen.

Chapter 12: Currents of Betrayal

Far from the loch, hidden in the shadows of the heathered hills, Morvath of the Shadows watched.

The spy had followed the lovers, slipping unseen through land and water alike. Now, witnessing the forbidden union at the Loch of Whispers, Morvath's black eyes glittered with a cold satisfaction.

It was worse than Darran had feared. Not merely affection, not even lust — but true merging, a binding of magics that could unravel the ancient divisions and doom the Kelpie people to dilution and weakness.

Morvath turned and slipped away into the night, carrying the news back to Darran.

Within hours, the Kelpie Council had been roused from slumber. Heated arguments echoed through the River Hall. Some argued for caution, others for swift and brutal action.

In the end, fear won.

Darran assembled a war party: swift, deadly warriors who had hunted humans and rivals with ruthless efficiency for centuries. Their orders were clear — find the lovers, capture or kill them, and ensure that whatever had begun at the Loch of Whispers was ended before it could take root.

Meanwhile, across the sea, Queen Mhairi received disturbing whispers from her own spies. With a heart heavy with dread, she summoned her fastest couriers.

"Find Nerina," she commanded. "Bring her back. Alive, if possible."

The tide of betrayal rose swiftly, and neither Brannach nor Nerina knew how soon the darkness would fall upon them. And as the full moon continued its arc across the night sky, the Loch of Whispers kept its own counsel, having witnessed the beginning of a new chapter in a story as old as Scotland itself.

Chapter 13: The Quickening

Inside their refuge, Nerina awoke to the sound of Brannach gathering kindling. She watched him through half-lidded eyes, studying the way his movements betrayed his dual nature—fluid like water one moment, powerful as a wild stallion the next. Even after weeks of sanctuary, she still marveled at their unlikely bond.

"You're staring again," he said without turning, a hint of amusement warming his usually guarded voice.

"The day I stop watching you will be the day my eyes no longer see," she replied, rising to her feet. The sealskin cloak slid from her shoulders, revealing her simple linen shift beneath.

Something had changed in her dreams the previous night—a shift as subtle as the turning tide but no less significant. She had dreamed of laughter—not her own, nor Brannach's, but the bright, bubbling sound of a child's joy. A child with storm-gray eyes and hair like Highland mist.

Throughout the day, the vision lingered. As they fished together at the loch's edge, as they repaired the shelter's roof, as they gathered heather for their bedding—the child's laughter echoed in Nerina's mind like a prophecy.

Later, as twilight painted the loch in shades of amber and cobalt, Nerina sat beside Brannach on their favorite outcropping of rock. Their hands entwined naturally, her slender fingers threading through his calloused ones.

"The waters speak differently to me now," she said softly, breaking their comfortable silence.

Brannach turned to her, dark brows furrowing. "How so?"

"They sing of beginnings when they once sang only of endings." She placed her free hand lightly on her abdomen. "Brannach... I carry our child."

The stillness that followed was absolute. Even the loch seemed to hold its breath. Brannach's expression shifted through disbelief, wonder, and finally, a deep, primal fear that darkened his eyes to the color of stormy depths.

"Are you certain?" he whispered, his voice rough as shale.

Nerina nodded. "My body changes. The dreams come clearer each night. And there's a new magic in my blood—two heartbeats where once there was one."

Brannach released her hand only to press his palm against her still-flat belly. He closed his eyes, and Nerina watched as emotions warred across his features. When he opened them again, they shone with unshed tears.

"A child of both worlds," he said, his voice breaking. "Half-selkie, half-kelpie. The first of its kind."

"A bridge between enemies," Nerina added softly.

"A target," Brannach countered, suddenly fierce. He pressed his forehead against her hands, his shoulders trembling. "Nerina, do you understand what this means? Neither side will accept this child. They will hunt us more relentlessly than before."

She threaded her fingers through his dark hair. "I understand the danger. I've always understood it."

He raised his head, eyes burning with a determination that caught her breath. "Then we must be stronger than fate itself."

"We will protect our child," Nerina said, the fierceness in her voice matching his own. "Whatever the cost may be."

"Whatever the cost," Brannach echoed, a vow as binding as blood.

That night, as moonlight dappled their shelter, they spoke of possibilities—of distant shores where ancient magic still held sway, of allies who might shelter them, of spells and enchantments that could hide their presence.

"The old ones might help us," Brannach suggested, sketching plans in the earth with a charred stick. "The river guardians remember debts older than either of our kinds."

Nerina shook her head. "They're too bound by tradition. And my people would never ally with river folk, even the oldest among them."

"Then we make our own path," Brannach said resolutely. "We carve it through the impossible."

As they spoke, the waters of the Loch of Whispers lapped gently against the shore, the sound like whispered promises. The ancient magic of the place seemed to listen, to weigh their words and their worth.

"Tomorrow," Nerina said as they finally settled into their shared bed of heather and moss, "we begin to weave protections. I know spells from my grandmother—secrets of the deep currents."

Brannach pulled her close, his breath warm against her neck. "And I know the ways of the river's rage. Together, we might just forge something new."

"Something powerful enough to save our child," Nerina whispered, her hand resting protectively over her belly.

Outside their shelter, the loch waters shimmered under starlight, silent witnesses to vows that would soon reshape the destiny of all water folk.

Chapter 14: Shadows at the Door

The warning came with the first hint of false dawn—that fragile, gray moment when night begins its reluctant surrender to day. Brannach's eyes snapped open, his body tense before his mind fully registered what had disturbed him.

He lay motionless, every sense straining. There—beneath the familiar chorus of the loch's gentle lapping and the soft breathing of Nerina beside him—a dissonant note. River birds crying out in panicked patterns, their wings striking water in chaotic flight.

"Sentinels," he muttered, the word like ash in his mouth.

Nerina stirred beside him, instantly alert in the way of those who have lived with danger as a constant companion. "What do you hear?" she whispered, her voice barely a breath.

"The river birds flee from something in the west," he replied, already moving to gather their essential possessions. "And the loch water carries strange vibrations from the east."

Nerina rose swiftly, her sleep-warmed skin prickling in the predawn chill. She placed one hand instinctively over her abdomen, now showing the first subtle curve of their growing child.

"From both directions," she said, her voice steady despite the fear that threatened to close her throat. "The river and the sea—they come together."

Brannach paused in his movements, the reality of their situation settling over him like a shroud. "Darran leads the river folk. Who comes from the sea?"

"My father would never dirty his hands with pursuit," Nerina said bitterly, wrapping her sealskin cloak around her shoulders. "But my cousin Mairenn has always envied my place as heir. She would see this as her opportunity to prove herself worthy of leadership."

"Two hunting parties, then." Brannach's expression hardened. "How much time do we have?"

"The mist is still thick," Nerina said, peering through a gap in their shelter's walls. "That will slow them, but not for long. An hour, perhaps less."

They moved with practiced efficiency, gathering only what couldn't be abandoned: a pouch of dried seaweed and berries, medicinal herbs wrapped in oiled cloth, the carved bone charm given to them by an ancient otter spirit for protection, and a blade forged from river-stone and coral—a weapon that could harm both river and sea folk alike.

"The eastern path is too exposed," Brannach said, securing the blade at his hip. "And the western route would lead us straight into Darran's forces."

Nerina's eyes gleamed with sudden certainty. "The Heart of the Loch," she whispered. "The sacred center—where the oldest magic still dwells."

Brannach hesitated. "No one has walked those grounds in generations. The protections there are unpredictable."

"Precisely why it might shelter us," Nerina countered. "The ancient powers recognize no loyalty to either river or sea. They existed before our kinds drew their arbitrary boundaries."

Outside, the first howl rose—distant but unmistakable. The baying of a kelpie war-hound, a beast born of river currents and moonlight, trained to track prey across any terrain.

"That decides it," Brannach said grimly. "We go to the Heart."

They slipped from their shelter like shadows, moving swiftly through the thinning mist. The terrain grew increasingly treacherous— slick stones and sudden dropoffs demanding their full attention. When the path narrowed dangerously along a steep incline, Brannach swept Nerina into his arms despite her protests.

"I can manage," she hissed, though her face had grown pale with exertion.

"I know you can," he replied, navigating the treacherous slope with sure footing. "But you carry more than yourself now. Let me be your strength when you need it, as you have been mine."

The simple honesty in his words silenced her objections. She relaxed against his chest, allowing herself this moment of vulnerability.

Behind them, the baying drew closer. A second howl joined the first, then a third—the hunting pack finding their scent.

"Brannach," Nerina whispered urgently. "They're closing in."

He quickened his pace, muscles burning with the effort. "Just beyond that ridge," he said between labored breaths. "The Heart lies in the basin below."

They crested the ridge as the first rays of true dawn pierced the mist. Below them, nestled in an ancient crater of stone and shadow, lay a perfectly still pool surrounded by standing stones. Trees with silver-barked trunks leaned inward, their branches forming a natural canopy above the water. Even from a distance, the air around the place seemed to shimmer with power.

"The Heart," Nerina breathed, awe momentarily overshadowing her fear.

Brannach set her down carefully. "Can you make the descent?"

She nodded, determination hardening her delicate features. "Together."

They started down the path, steep but navigable. Halfway to the basin floor, Nerina gasped, clutching Brannach's arm. He followed her gaze and felt his blood turn to ice.

Dark figures moved through the mist behind them—some on two legs, others on four, all pursuing with relentless purpose. At their head strode a tall figure with copper-bright hair: Darran, River Lord and once-brother to Brannach in all but blood.

"Run," Brannach urged, drawing his blade. "Get to the Heart. I'll hold them."

Nerina's fingers dug into his arm. "No. We face this together or not at all."

Their eyes met in a moment of perfect understanding—equals in this as in all things.

"Then we run together," Brannach conceded. "But promise me—if they break through, if I fall, you will save yourself and our child."

Pain flashed across Nerina's face, but she nodded. "I promise. Now, run!"

They descended in controlled haste, hearts pounding in desperate rhythm. The ground leveled beneath their feet as they reached the basin floor. Just yards ahead, the first standing stone waited—a sentinel of ancient days, covered in spiraling runes that pulsed faintly as they approached.

Behind them, the hunting party gained ground. The baying of the hounds grew frenzied, the sound of pursuit like thunder in their ears.

"Almost there," Brannach gasped, pulling Nerina forward.

As they crossed the threshold marked by the first standing stone, a curious sensation washed over them—like passing through a veil of water that left them dry. The sounds of pursuit dimmed slightly, though they did not cease entirely.

"The boundary recognizes us," Nerina said wonderingly. "It grants us passage."

Brannach glanced back, his expression grim. "But it won't stop them for long. Hurry!"

They wove between the standing stones, moving deeper into the Heart's sanctuary. Each step brought them closer to the central pool—a perfect circle of water so still it mirrored the sky above without ripple.

A howl rent the air—closer now, much closer. The boundary had slowed their pursuers but not halted them.

"Here," Brannach said, leading Nerina behind a massive leaning stone near the pool's edge. "Stay hidden."

"What are you planning?" Fear edged Nerina's voice.

Brannach met her gaze steadily. "To buy you time. The Pool of Voices—it lies just beyond that silver-barked tree. If I fall, go there. The old ones say it's a doorway to places beyond mortal sight."

"I won't leave you," Nerina insisted, gripping his tunic with white-knuckled hands.

He covered her hands with his own. "You promised, Nerina. For our child. Our hope."

Tears welled in her eyes, but she nodded, the movement almost imperceptible.

Brannach pressed his lips to hers—brief, fierce, full of unspoken words. Then he stepped away, drawing his blade as he moved into the open space between the standing stones.

CHAPTER 15: Pursuit

The hunting party emerged from the mist like nightmares given form—Kelpie warriors with bodies that flowed between human and equine aspects, their eyes burning with cold fire. Among them ran the war-hounds, creatures of current and shadow with too many teeth and too little mercy.

Darran stood at their center, his copper hair gleaming like blood in the strengthening sunlight. His own blade—forged from the heart of a mountain stream—gleamed with deadly purpose.

"Brannach," he called, his voice carrying across the sacred ground. "You dishonor yourself with this chase. Stand down. Return to your people."

Brannach widened his stance, blade at the ready. "I stand with my people," he replied evenly. "She is my people now. The child she carries is my future."

Shock rippled through the hunting party. Darran's face contorted with disgust. "Abomination," he spat. "You would pollute our bloodline with seal-spawn?"

"I would create a new beginning," Brannach countered. "An end to ancient hatred."

"Then you will die a traitor's death." Darran raised his blade. "Take him!"

The warriors surged forward. Brannach met them with controlled fury, his blade singing as it cut through air and occasionally flesh. He fought not with wild abandon but with calculated precision—every move designed to keep the attackers from discovering Nerina's hiding place.

From her concealment, Nerina watched with heart-stopping fear as Brannach held off three, four, five attackers at once. His movements were beautiful and terrible—the dance of a river in storm. But even his considerable skill could not prevail indefinitely against such odds.

She pressed her hands against the ancient stone that sheltered her, feeling its pulse of dormant power. The Heart of the Loch had slumbered for generations, its magic undisturbed by the petty conflicts of water folk.

"Awaken," she whispered, drawing on memories of spells taught by her grandmother in secret caves beneath the western isles. "Béithe uisce, éist le mo ghlao."

The stone warmed beneath her palms.

Out in the open, Brannach took a wound to his shoulder but continued fighting, driving back a snarling war-hound with a vicious kick. Blood darkened his tunic, but his stance remained strong, his blade unwavering.

"Éirigh anois, seanmhaighistir na doimhneachtaí," Nerina continued, her voice rising slightly as the ancient words of power took shape on her tongue. "Cosain do leanaí."

The pool's surface trembled. The air thickened.

Darran pressed forward, engaging Brannach directly. Their blades met with a sound like thunder, the force of the impact sending ripples of power across the sacred ground.

"You cannot win this, brother," Darran growled, pressing his advantage.

"I already have," Brannach replied through gritted teeth, blood trickling from a cut above his eye. "She lives. Our child lives. That is victory enough."

Nerina felt power surging through the stone beneath her hands, building like pressure beneath ice. The Heart of the Loch was stirring, ancient consciousness rising from ages-long slumber.

The waters trembled. The stones shivered.

And fate, so long fixed in patterns of hatred and division, began to shift its course.

Chapter 16: The Heart of the Loch

Metal sang against metal, the discordant music of battle echoing through the ancient hollow. Brannach moved like a tempest unleashed, his river-forged blade carving silver arcs through the clinging mist. What he lacked in numbers, he made up for in desperate fury—each strike calculated, each defense born of a lifetime spent honing his craft.

"Fall back!" he shouted to Nerina, though he dared not turn to see if she obeyed. "To the pool!"

Three hunters came at him simultaneously, their forms fluid and terrible as they shifted between mortal and equine aspects. Brannach recognized them all—Sorvan with his distinctive scar, Lirren whose blade work had once earned his praise, young Adran who had looked to him as mentor. Now their eyes burned with the cold fire of duty, their features twisted by an ancient hatred he had once shared.

"You dishonor your kind," Sorvan growled, his blade whistling dangerously close to Brannach's throat.

Brannach parried the strike and countered with one of his own, opening a shallow gash across Sorvan's chest. "I honor something greater," he replied, voice steady despite the exertion. "Something you've forgotten."

Behind him, he could hear Nerina's voice rising in cadence—words ancient and powerful flowing from her lips as naturally as breath. The old tongue of the sea folk, melodic and haunting, seemed to resonate with the very stones beneath their feet.

A blade slipped past his guard, carving a line of fire across his shoulder. Another scored his thigh. Brannach gritted his teeth against the pain, forcing himself to maintain position. Each moment he held them back was another moment for Nerina to complete her work.

"Brannach!" Darran's voice cut through the chaos, commanding as always. The River Lord pushed through his warriors, copper hair gleaming like blood in the strange light. "End this madness! Yield now, and you may yet be spared."

"And her?" Brannach demanded, not slowing his defense. "And our child?"

Darran's expression hardened. "Some lines should never be crossed. Some magics never mingled. You know this."

"I know nothing of the kind," Brannach spat, knocking aside a thrust meant for his heart. "I know only that love is not meant to be bound by ancient hatreds."

Another hunter lunged from the left. Brannach twisted, but too slowly—the blade bit deep into his side, drawing a grunt of pain. He staggered but did not fall, driving his attacker back with renewed ferocity.

The ground beneath them trembled. The air grew thick, charged with energies long dormant. Behind him, Nerina's chanting reached a crescendo, her normally melodic voice taking on harmonics that seemed impossible from a single throat.

"Éisteacht liom, a sheanchroí na locha," she sang, the words rippling through the air like visible currents. "Múscail ó do chodladh domhain."

The sacred pool responded, its still surface beginning to churn. Luminous ripples spread outward, washing over the moss-covered ground. The standing stones surrounding the hollow pulsed with answering light, ancient runes flaring to life.

One of the hunters—Adran, eyes wide with fear—broke from the main group, darting toward Nerina with blade drawn.

"No!" Brannach roared, hurling himself between them.

His blade met Adran's with a clash that sent sparks flying. The force of his counter-drive the younger warrior back several paces, but the exertion cost him. Blood flowed freely from his wounds now, each breath becoming a struggle.

"You will not touch her," Brannach snarled, voice guttural with pain and determination.

Adran faltered, something like recognition flickering in his eyes. "Captain," he whispered, using Brannach's old title. "Please. This isn't worth dying for."

"On the contrary," Brannach replied, straightening despite the agony it caused him. "This is the only thing worth dying for."

Darran pressed forward, his expression grim. "Brannach, stop this madness! It is not too late. Yield, and your life may be spared."

Brannach bared his teeth in a snarl. "Spare my life, and take hers? Never."

Then came a sound that chilled Nerina's blood—the hunting call of her own people. From the opposite side of the clearing emerged new figures: sleek and silver-eyed, with sealskins draped around their shoulders. The Selkie hunting party had arrived.

At their head walked Mairenn, Nerina's cousin—beautiful and terrible in her cold perfection.

"Well met, river-filth," she called to Darran, though her contemptuous gaze swept over the entire Kelpie hunting party. "It seems we hunt the same prey."

Darran's expression twisted with disgust, but pragmatism won out over ancient enmity. "The traitors hide within the Heart. The male defends them both."

"Both?" Mairenn's silver eyes narrowed. "Explain."

"Your cousin carries his spawn," Darran spat. "An abomination against nature itself."

Shock rippled through the Selkie party. Mairenn's beautiful face contorted with horror, then settled into lines of cold determination.

"Then our purpose aligns, however distasteful the association." She gestured to her hunters. "Surround the clearing. None escape."

Brannach, seeing himself trapped between two deadly forces, fell back to the stone where Nerina hid. His breathing was labored, his skin ashen beneath the blood and grime.

"Nerina," he whispered, eyes never leaving the approaching hunters. "I cannot hold them all."

Nerina's chanting reached a crescendo. Her body shook with the strain of channeling the old magic, the energy coursing through her threatening to tear her apart.

The mist thickened abruptly, swirling with unnatural speed. From the sacred pool came a sound unlike any Brannach had heard before—a resonance that vibrated in bone and blood rather than air. The loch itself was responding, ancient beyond reckoning, terrifying in its power.

"Brannach!" Nerina's voice carried to him, strained yet triumphant. "The Heart answers!"

He risked a glance back and his breath caught. Nerina knelt at the pool's edge, her silver eyes blazing with inner light. The waters before her had risen into a twisting column of luminescence and mist, and within that column, shapes moved—figures neither wholly mortal nor entirely spirit. Guardians of the ancient waters, awakened from centuries of slumber.

The Kelpie hunters faltered, some stepping back involuntarily. Even Darran's confident posture weakened, his blade lowering slightly.

Brannach seized the moment to stagger to Nerina's side. He dropped to one knee beside her, his hand finding hers amidst the storm of power that surrounded them. Her skin burned feverishly against his calloused palm.

"What have you awakened?" he gasped, blood dripping from his wounds to mingle with the sacred waters.

Nerina turned to face him, and in her eyes he saw both joy and a terrible sorrow. Tears streamed down her face, glowing with the same light that emanated from the pool.

"Not what," she said softly, though he heard her clearly despite the rising tempest around them. "Who. The First Ones—those who were here before Selkie and Kelpie drew their boundaries. They offer us a way."

"A way?" he repeated, hope surging despite the dire circumstances.

"To save our child," she explained, squeezing his hand with painful intensity. "But Brannach... the cost..."

He searched her face, understanding dawning like a cold sunrise. "We must bind ourselves to the Heart," he whispered. "Become part of it."

She nodded, fresh tears spilling. "Our lives for our child's future. Only by giving ourselves fully to the waters can we create a protection strong enough to weather the storm that comes."

Brannach looked back at the Kelpie hunters—at Darran, whose face now showed confusion and the first flickers of doubt. Beyond them, at the edge of the hollow, new figures had appeared: Selkies with their distinctive silver eyes and fluid grace, led by a woman whose bearing marked her as nobility among their kind.

They were surrounded, with no hope of escape by conventional means.

Brannach turned back to Nerina, lifting a hand to brush away her tears despite the blood that stained his fingers. "Then let it be so," he said, his voice steady with resolve. "I would rather become part of these waters with you than rule all rivers without you."

Together they stood, facing the sacred pool and the ancient guardians that swirled within its waters. Their voices joined as one, speaking words that seemed to flow into their minds directly from the Heart itself—a language older than the divisions between their peoples.

"By current and tide, by storm and stillness, we offer ourselves to the waters eternal," they intoned, the words resonating with power. "Take our flesh, take our spirits, forge from our sacrifice a sanctuary for our child, born of river and sea."

The light from the pool surged upward, engulfing them in a blinding torrent. Pain lanced through Brannach's body as the ancient magic took hold, beginning the transformation that would bind them forever to this place. Yet alongside the agony came a sense of rightness, of completion long sought but never found—until now.

Through the veil of light, he saw the Kelpie hunters thrown backward by the force of the magic's awakening. Even Darran, powerful as he was, could not stand against this tide.

"Remember," Brannach called out, his voice amplified by the energies flowing through him. "Remember that love broke these ancient chains!"

Nerina's hand tightened in his as the binding deepened. Their bodies began to shimmer at the edges, flesh becoming light, bone becoming water. The process would not be quick, nor would it be painless. But they would endure it together, as they had endured everything since the moment their paths crossed.

As the magic of the Heart of the Loch rose around them like a cresting wave, Brannach felt a strange peace settle over him. Whatever came next—whatever form their sacrifice would take—they had chosen it freely, and for the highest purpose.

For love. For their child. For a future where the bitter divisions between river and sea might finally be healed.

The waters of the loch responded to their offering, ancient and renewed. And in that moment, fate itself seemed to hold its breath.

The waters of the pool erupted upward in a great column of light and mist, casting the entire hollow in an otherworldly glow. Figures formed within the light—shadowy shapes of ancient guardians, beings of river and sea who had once ruled these waters in peace.

The Kelpie hunters faltered, fear etched on their faces. Even Darran took an unconscious step back.

Brannach, bleeding and bruised, staggered to Nerina's side. He dropped to one knee beside her, his hand finding hers.

"What must we do?" he rasped.

Nerina turned to him, tears streaming down her face—tears of sorrow, of love, of terrible understanding.

"We must bind our souls to the Heart," she said. "Only by giving ourselves fully can we protect our child."

Brannach searched her eyes, finding no fear there—only fierce, unwavering love.

"Then let it be so," he whispered.

Together, they stood, facing the sacred pool. Together, they spoke the binding words, their voices merging into one.

The light engulfed them, and the Heart of the Loch roared to life, sending a shockwave through the mists that threw the Kelpie hunters to the ground.

In that blinding moment, two souls became one with the ancient waters.

And the fate of the river and sea was forever changed.

Chapter 17: The Tides of Sacrifice

For a moment, silence reigned.

The mist recoiled from the Heart of the Loch, revealing the stones now blazing with ancient light. The Kelpie hunters, thrown to the ground by the magic's awakening, scrambled to their feet, dazed and fearful.

Brannach and Nerina stood at the center of it all, hands entwined, faces lifted to the torrent of light. Their bodies shimmered at the edges, already becoming part of something greater than flesh and bone.

Nerina looked at Brannach, her heart full to breaking. "There is still time," she whispered. "You could go. You could survive."

Brannach only smiled, a tender, broken thing. "Without you, I am already dead."

The guardians within the light—vast shapes of seal and stallion, river serpent and sea bird—circled around them. They sang in voices older than stars, weaving the binding spell that would protect the unborn child.

The ground trembled as Darran stepped forward, blade still in hand. His face twisted with despair and rage.

"Brannach! Nerina!" he shouted, his voice cracking. "You do not have to do this! Surrender—we can still find a way!"

Nerina's hand tightened around Brannach's. "It is too late for that."

Brannach took a step toward Darran, his body outlined in silver fire. "You were my brother once, Darran. Remember that, when the tide turns and the old ways crumble."

Darran faltered, lowering his blade slightly. But the other hunters behind him murmured and shifted, fearful of the unknown forces gathering.

A rumble rose from the depths of the loch, a sound like the voice of the world itself waking from sleep. The waters surged upward, tendrils of pure energy spiraling around Nerina and Brannach.

Pain lanced through them as the binding deepened, knitting their souls into the very fabric of the Heart. They gasped, but neither cried out. They bore the agony together, as they had borne everything else.

Nerina's voice trembled as she began the final invocation.

"By river and sea, by blood and bone, we bind our souls to the waters' heart."

Brannach echoed her, their voices overlapping, entwining, becoming one.

The light surged, blinding. The Kelpie hunters shielded their eyes, some falling to their knees. Even Darran stumbled back, overwhelmed by the sheer force of it.

Within the storm of magic, Brannach leaned close, pressing his forehead to Nerina's.

"I love you," he said, his voice raw.

"And I you," she breathed.

The stars shimmered overhead, reflected in the water as if the heavens themselves had bent low to watch.

"Will he remember us?" Brannach asked his voice barely more than a whisper.

Nerina pressed her lips to the boy's forehead. "Not in ways he will understand. But he will carry us. In his blood. In the currents of his soul."

A shudder went through her, the strength of her grief pressing down like the deepest tides. Still, she did not cry. She would not let their son see her weep—not tonight.

From around Brannach's neck, he drew a leather cord, threaded with a single stone—smooth, worn, carved long ago with a spiral of river and sea entwined. The same symbol the boy would one day come to wear with pride.

"A promise," Brannach said. "That he will find his way. That the rivers and seas will remember him even when we are dust."

Love, Brannach thought, was sometimes the fiercest sacrifice of all.

Their forms blurred, melted, merged into the very waters of the loch.

When the blinding light receded, silence descended upon the hollow. The Kelpie hunters who had been thrown to the ground by the magic's awakening rose unsteadily, their expressions a mixture of awe and terror. The Selkie warriors at the periphery remained frozen in place, their silver eyes wide with disbelief.

At the center of it all stood Brannach and Nerina, transformed. Their bodies still maintained their mortal forms, but their substance had changed—skin now bore the translucent quality of water caught in sunlight, hair moved as if stirred by unfelt currents. They hovered slightly above the sacred pool, their feet no longer quite touching its surface.

Around them, the guardians of the loch circled—vast, ancient beings now fully visible to all. Some bore the aspects of seals with eyes like polished jet, others the flowing manes and powerful limbs of river horses. Still others took forms beyond mortal understanding—creatures of mist and memory, of current and tide.

The guardians sang in voices that resonated through bone and spirit, weaving the complex enchantment that would bind these two souls to the Heart forever.

Nerina turned to Brannach, her eyes luminous with unshed tears. The pain of the transformation showed in the tightness around her mouth, but her gaze remained clear and certain.

"The binding is not yet complete," she whispered, her voice carrying a new resonance, like water flowing over stones. "There is still time for you to turn back. You could return to your life."

Brannach's laugh was gentle, though it cost him. "What life remains for me without you?" He reached for her hand, their fingers intertwining—still solid enough to touch, though their substance had begun to change. "I made my choice the moment I first saw you on the shore. I will not unmake it now."

The ground trembled as Darran stepped forward, his blade hanging loose at his side. The River Lord's face was no longer twisted with rage but slack with shock and a dawning grief.

"Brannach," he called, his voice uncharacteristically hesitant. "What have you done? What are you becoming?"

"Something new," Brannach replied, meeting his former friend's gaze steadily. "Something necessary."

Nerina's grip tightened on his hand as a fresh wave of transformation energy rippled through them. "It grows more difficult to maintain form," she murmured.

Brannach nodded, feeling the truth of her words in his own increasingly fluid body. The bindings that once held spirit to flesh were loosening, their essence beginning to merge with the ancient powers of the loch.

"Darran," he said, his voice strong despite the pain, "you were my brother once—in all ways that truly matter. I ask one final thing of you."

The River Lord took another step forward, his eyes suspiciously bright. "Name it."

"When the time comes, remember today not as a tragedy but as a beginning. Watch for our child. Protect what we have sacrificed everything to create."

Darran's expression contorted with fresh conflict. "You ask too much."

"I ask only what you would have done before fear and hatred poisoned your heart," Brannach replied.

From the other side of the hollow, the Selkie noblewoman approached, her movements cautious but her bearing proud. Snowdrops, woven into her silver-blonde hair, marked her as royalty among her kind.

"Cousin," she addressed Nerina, her voice cool yet not entirely without feeling, "is this truly your choice? To dissolve your very self for this... union?"

Nerina lifted her chin. "It is, Mairenn. Not for the union alone, but for what grows from it." She placed her free hand over her abdomen, where the subtle curve spoke of new life.

Mairenn's eyes widened. "A child? That is why you fled?"

"A child of river and sea," Nerina confirmed. "The first of its kind—and, if the hatred between our peoples continues, perhaps the last. We bind ourselves to the loch to ensure our child survives. To give hope a chance to take root."

A rumble rose from the depths of the waters, a sound like the voice of the world itself waking from endless sleep. The guardians circling Brannach and Nerina began to move faster, their forms blurring as they tightened the spiral of magic.

Pain lanced through the pair as the binding deepened, knitting their souls into the very fabric of the Heart. Brannach gasped as he felt his ribs dissolving into currents, his blood becoming one with the sacred waters. Beside him, Nerina trembled, her outline blurring further.

"It is time," she whispered, her voice already sounding distant, as if coming from the depths of the loch rather than her throat.

Together, they began the final invocation, their voices overlapping, entwining, becoming a single harmonious current.

"By river and sea, by blood and bone, we bind our souls to the waters' heart. Take what we freely give. Protect what we most cherish. Let our love become the bedrock upon which a new world may be built."

The light surrounding them intensified, becoming almost unbearable to witness. The Kelpie hunters shielded their eyes; some fell to their knees, overwhelmed by the raw power emanating from the ancient pool.

Even the Selkie warriors, accustomed to strange magics, stepped back in reverent fear.

Within the storm of transformative magic, Brannach leaned close to Nerina, pressing his forehead against hers—a final touch while they still possessed forms capable of touch.

"I love you," he said, his voice raw with emotion and pain. "Beyond death. Beyond dissolution. Beyond time itself."

"And I you," she breathed, her tears now flowing upward rather than down, defying mortal laws as her body surrendered them. "Always."

Their forms blurred further, edges dissolving into the very waters of the loch. Flesh became current; bone became stone; blood became the sacred waters themselves. The guardians closed in, their ancient voices rising in a paean to sacrifice freely given.

With a final surge of light that momentarily turned night to day, the transformation completed itself. Where two figures had stood, now only the gently rippling surface of the pool remained—yet somehow more alive, more aware than before.

The Heart of the Loch had changed forever, bound now by the willing sacrifice of two souls who had dared to love beyond the ancient laws.

The light gradually diminished to a soft glow emanating from the pool's depths. As it faded, something new appeared at the water's edge—a small bundle wrapped in woven strands of mist and kelp, luminous as moonlight on water.

For several heartbeats, no one moved. Then Darran approached slowly, his face ashen with shock and sorrow. He knelt beside the bundle, one trembling hand reaching out to fold back the delicate coverings.

Inside lay an infant, perfectly formed and peacefully sleeping—a child with Brannach's dark curls and Nerina's delicate features. Around its tiny neck gleamed a river stone inscribed with interwoven spirals, symbolizing the union of river and sea.

A great, terrible grief washed over Darran's face. "What have we done?" he whispered, his voice breaking. "Forgive us, brother. We understood too late."

From the mist beyond the pool stepped a figure unlike any they had seen before—neither Selkie nor Kelpie, but something more ancient than either. Tall and slender, with skin like polished silver and eyes reflecting depths beyond mortal comprehension, the guardian approached with silent grace.

"The child must be protected," the guardian said, its voice like water flowing over stones. "Such was the price paid. Such was the promise made."

Darran looked up, conflicting emotions warring across his features. "Where will you take it?"

"To safety," the guardian replied simply. "Beyond the reach of those who would harm it for the blood that flows in its veins."

"And when will it return?" This from Mairenn, who had drawn closer, her silver eyes fixed on the child with an intensity that blended wonder and apprehension.

The guardian's smile was mysterious as the depths of the loch itself. "When the time is right. When the waters call it home. When both river and sea are ready to hear what it has to teach."

With infinite tenderness, the guardian lifted the sleeping child. The infant stirred but did not wake, small hands curling against the guardian's silvery chest.

"Remember this day," the guardian said, its gaze sweeping over all assembled. "Remember what was lost. Remember what was gained. And when the child of two worlds returns, ask yourselves if the price of hatred has been worth its cost."

Then the guardian turned and walked into the mist, the child cradled securely in its arms. Within moments, both had vanished from mortal sight.

One by one, the Kelpie hunters turned away, many weeping openly. Even the proud Selkie warriors bowed their heads, moved despite themselves by what they had witnessed.

Darran remained kneeling by the pool's edge, his blade forgotten on the ground beside him. Across the water, Mairenn stood equally still, her proud posture softened by the weight of what had transpired.

Their eyes met over the gently rippling surface—river lord and sea princess—and in that moment, something passed between them. Not friendship, not yet. Perhaps not even understanding. But acknowledgment, at least, of a shared witness to something profound.

Something that might, in time, change everything.

Beneath the now-calm surface of the Heart of the Loch, currents moved with new purpose. The waters, ancient and renewed, held within them the essence of two who had loved beyond all boundaries.

And deep within those sacred depths, a gentle heartbeat pulsed—a rhythm that would continue until the day when the child of river and sea returned to claim its birthright.

A promise flowing through water. A love stronger than death itself.

That one day, the child of river and sea would rise.

And the world would change again.

Chapter 18: The Mourning Waters

The Heart of the Loch grew still once more, though the echoes of the great sacrifice lingered in every ripple and breeze.

Darran remained kneeling by the pool's edge, staring into the mist that had swallowed the child. His blade lay forgotten at his side. Around him, the Kelpie hunters shifted uneasily, some murmuring prayers, others gazing at their hands as though only now seeing the blood upon them.

"What have we done?" one whispered, the words trembling with guilt.

Darran rose slowly, as if the very weight of his guilt pressed down upon his broad shoulders. His eyes, once sharp and sure, were now clouded with grief. He turned to face his warriors.

"We must leave this place," he said, his voice hoarse. "We have witnessed something greater than ourselves. Greater than our laws."

No one argued. Silently, one by one, the Kelpie hunters faded into the mist, their steps heavy, their spirits broken.

Darran lingered a moment longer, gazing once more into the Heart. Somewhere within, the blood of Brannach and Nerina had mingled with the ancient waters. Somewhere within, a new future was stirring.

He bowed his head, touching his forehead to the sacred stones. A silent vow passed his lips, a vow to remember, to protect the memory of those who had fallen for a dream of peace.

The journey back to the River Hall was slow and somber. The currents seemed to resist their passage, and the very waters whispered of betrayal and loss. Word of Brannach and Nerina's fate traveled swiftly, carried on the tides to every corner of the river and sea.

In the Selkie Court, Queen Mhairi received the news in silence.

She stood alone at the highest cliff, gazing out over the restless sea. Her silver hair whipped about her in the wind, and her heart, so often shielded behind duty and pride, ached with an unfamiliar sorrow.

"Fools," she murmured to the waves. "We were all fools."

When her attendants came seeking counsel, she dismissed them with a wave of her hand. There were no decrees she could give to heal what had been broken. No punishment she could mete out that would undo the sacrifice that had been made.

Instead, she sent her most trusted envoy, a Selkie wise-woman named Maelis, into the heart of the loch.

"Find the child," Mhairi commanded. "Guard it with your life. For within that child lies the hope of river and sea alike."

Maelis bowed and disappeared into the surf, her sealskin gleaming like polished pearl.

As the days turned to weeks, the Heart of the Loch grew ever more guarded. Few dared to venture near its sacred waters. Strange lights were seen beneath the surface, and the songs of ancient spirits echoed across the shores.

But the child remained hidden, nurtured in the deep places of the loch, cradled by magic and guarded by forces unseen.

In time, the memory of Brannach and Nerina faded from common tongue, becoming a whispered legend passed from parent to child around hearthfires and tidal pools.

Yet the old ones remembered.

And in the depths of the loch, a heartbeat continued—steady, strong, and patient.

Waiting for the day when the child of river and sea would rise to fulfill the promise sealed by love and sacrifice.

Waiting for the tides of fate to turn once more.

Beneath the still waters of the Heart of the Loch, where the currents whispered secrets no mortal could hear, the child of Brannach and Nerina lay nestled in a cradle woven of living kelp and shimmering mist.

The guardian who had taken the infant was not a creature known to river or sea. She was of the oldest magic—a being birthed in the dawn of the world when water and air had first touched. Her form shifted between that of a great silver fish and a woman clothed in flowing riverweed. She bore the child deeper into the loch, into places where no light pierced, and where only the oldest spirits remembered the songs of the first waters.

There, in a cavern adorned with crystals that pulsed with the heartbeat of the loch itself, she made her home.

The child grew swiftly, nourished by the ancient magic. Though still an infant, there was an awareness behind the child's eyes that startled even the guardian. He would reach toward the patterns of light that danced on the cavern walls, giggling with a joy that warmed the cold stones.

Maelis, the Selkie wise-woman sent by Queen Mhairi, found the guardian after many days of searching. She approached the cavern with reverence, bearing offerings of woven sea-grass and starfish shells, gifts of peace.

The guardian regarded Maelis with eyes that were older than mountains. There was no need for words; in that sacred place, thoughts flowed like water between them.

He must remain hidden, the guardian said, her voice like the rushing of underground streams.

Maelis bowed her head. "I will watch. I will protect."

The time is not yet right. The world is not ready for him.

And so it was agreed. Maelis took up residence at the edge of the loch, building a humble dwelling of driftwood and stone, blending into the landscape so well that even the most curious of travelers would overlook it.

Each day, she would visit the cavern, singing songs of the sea and the river, weaving tales of courage and unity into the fabric of the child's dreams. The guardian would listen, ever watchful, her presence a shield against any who might seek the child with ill intent.

Years began to pass.

The child, known to none yet by name, grew into a curious boy with hair the color of storm clouds and eyes that mirrored the loch's shifting depths. He spoke little, but his laughter was like the chiming of bells across the water, and his gaze held an ancient knowing.

He learned to swim before he could walk, gliding through the loch's waters as naturally as breathing. The fish and birds and even the ancient trees seemed to recognize him, bending closer as he passed, whispering their secrets to him.

But always, Maelis warned him: "You must not stray beyond the Heart. Not yet."

And the boy, though restless and filled with questions he could not yet voice, obeyed.

For deep within him, a memory stirred—a memory not his own, of a woman with hair like silver mist and a man with eyes like thunderclouds, standing hand in hand at the center of a great light.

In his dreams, he heard their voices calling him.

Be patient, little one, they seemed to say. Your time will come.

And so the child waited, growing stronger, wiser, and more restless with each passing season.

Waiting for the tides of fate to summon him forth.

Chapter 20: The First Stirring

"You're staring at nothing again," Maelis said, her weathered hands continuing their work with the silverweed, nimble fingers weaving protection charms with practiced ease.

The boy turned, a half-smile touching his lips. "Not nothing. The patterns. They speak, if you listen long enough."

Maelis studied him, this child who was not truly a child—who had never truly been one. Seven seasons had passed since she'd found him in the guardian's care, seven seasons of watching him grow with unnatural swiftness, of teaching him the old ways, of waiting for the inevitable.

"What do they say today, then?" she asked, setting aside her work.

The boy's eyes—eyes that mirrored the loch's ever-changing depths—grew distant. "They speak of change. Of things stirring beyond the mist." He frowned. "Maelis, why must I remain hidden here?"

She had expected this question for years, had rehearsed her answer countless times. Yet now, faced with his direct gaze, the carefully crafted words dissolved like morning mist.

"Because there are those who would fear what you are," she said finally, truthfully. "Some would seek to use you. Others... would destroy you."

"And what am I, exactly?" The question hung between them, sharp as a blade.

Maelis sighed, setting aside her weaving. "You are the impossible made flesh. The union of river and sea, of ancient enemies brought together in love." She moved closer, kneeling before him. "But more than that, you are hope. A hope that must be protected until it is strong enough to flourish in the harsh world beyond."

The boy's fingers traced patterns in the damp sand at the cavern's edge. "I dream, Maelis. Almost every night now."

Her shoulders tensed. "Tell me."

"I see a river choked with darkness—not natural darkness, but something... wrong." His voice dropped to a whisper. "I hear weeping— so many voices. And then there's a light, breaking through, calling to me." He looked up suddenly. "The dreams are getting stronger. As if they're trying to pull me somewhere."

"The time draws near," Maelis murmured, almost to herself.

The boy caught her wrist, his grip surprisingly strong. "What time? You always speak in riddles about my future, but never plainly. Tell me what awaits me, Maelis. I deserve to know."

The selkie wise-woman held his gaze, seeing in him the echoes of Brannach's determination and Nerina's fierce compassion.

"Very well," she said at last. "When you were born—when your parents gave their lives to create the Heart—a prophecy was whispered across the waters. It spoke of a child who would either unite the divided peoples of river and sea, or become the instrument of their final destruction."

"And that child is me." It wasn't a question.

"Yes."

The boy released her wrist, turning back to the dancing lights. "How will I know which path to choose? How can I be certain I won't destroy everything my parents died to protect?"

Maelis reached out, brushing a stray lock of hair from his brow—a gesture so human, so maternal, that for a moment he looked like any other young boy seeking guidance.

"The choice itself reveals the path," she said softly. "It is not destiny that determines your future, but the small decisions you make each day. The compassion you show, the courage you find, the truth you choose to face."

The guardian, silent until now, moved closer to the surface of the pool that connected her realm to theirs. Her form wavered between woman and fish, her ancient eyes fixed on the boy.

"He grows restless," she said, her voice like water flowing over stone. "The Heart can feel it."

Maelis nodded. "He dreams of what lies beyond."

"As all prisoners do," the boy said quietly.

The guardian's expression shifted—something like sorrow, if such ancient beings could feel as mortals did. "Not a prison, child. A sanctuary. But sanctuaries, too, have their season."

Later that night, as Maelis sat by the shore singing softly to the stars—an old selkie lament for those lost to the depths—the boy slipped silently to the edge of the cavern. Beyond the protective mists, he could just make out the distant shores of Loch Ness, where tiny fires flickered like fallen stars.

He pressed his palm against the iridescent barrier that separated him from the world beyond.

"Soon," he whispered to himself. "Soon."

In the waters behind him, the guardian watched, her ancient heart heavy with the weight of what was to come. For she had seen the darkness gathering beyond the mist, had felt the poison spreading through the rivers that fed the loch.

The boy would step beyond the Heart's protection. It was inevitable now.

And when he did, the tides of fate, once loosed, would never be dammed again.

Seasons turned upon themselves, weaving the endless cycle of mist and tide across the Heart of the Loch. The boy grew, no longer a babe in swaddling kelp, but a lithe figure whose every movement was poetry, whose very breath seemed to sing in harmony with the waters.

Maelis watched him with a gaze at once proud and sorrowful. She saw the change that was coming, the slow unfurling of destiny in the way the boy stood longer at the edge of the sanctuary, staring into the swirling mists as if searching for something just beyond his reach.

He was no ordinary child. His blood—the mingling of river and sea—gave him senses far keener than mortal folk. He could feel the moods of the waters, taste the shifting currents of magic in the air. Dreams came to him often now, vivid and troubling: dreams of cities in ruin, of rivers running red, of creatures—neither Selkie nor Kelpie—rising from darkened depths.

Maelis, who knew the prophecies as well as any, grew anxious. She began to weave stronger protections around the Heart—spells of misdirection, enchantments to lull the curious into forgetting their very purpose should they wander too near.

Yet even she could not halt what stirred within the boy himself.

That night, as the boy slept beneath the glimmering crystals of the sacred cavern, Maelis sat by the shore, singing low and sad to the stars.

For she knew that soon—too soon—the mist would thin, the protections would waver, and the boy would step beyond the Heart.

It happened subtly at first. The silver veils thinned on certain mornings, revealing distant glimpses of the hills and forests beyond. Strange scents drifted in on the wind—the tang of iron, the acrid sting of distant fires.

The boy—now nearing manhood, his frame lean and strong—felt the pull in his bones. It was a summons he could no longer ignore, a call older than language, older even than the magic that had birthed him.

Maelis watched him with growing unease. She had known this day would come, had prepared for it as best she could. Yet knowing and accepting were two different things.

One morning, as the sun struggled to pierce the heavy clouds, she found him standing at the very edge of the Heart's protection, the mist swirling about his ankles.

"You feel it too," he said without turning.

Maelis wrapped her sealskin cloak tighter around herself. "Yes."

"Something is wrong beyond the mist," he said. "I can hear it. I can feel it—like a wound in the water."

"There is conflict," Maelis said carefully. "The rivers are poisoned. The seas grow restless. Old hatreds have risen again."

He turned to her then, his storm-gray eyes alight with a fire she had never seen before. "Then I must go."

"You are not ready," Maelis said quickly, stepping closer. "There are those who would see you undone the moment you reveal yourself."

"And if I do nothing?" he asked. "How many will suffer while I hide behind these stones?"

Maelis's heart broke at the certainty in his voice. He was so young—and yet he carried the weight of a thousand lifetimes.

"At least wait," she pleaded. "Wait until the signs are clearer. Until the waters themselves call you forth."

The boy hesitated, conflict raging within him. Duty pulled him in one direction, destiny in another. He looked back at the mist, where the faint outlines of the wider world beckoned.

"One more night," he said finally. "I will wait one more night."

Maelis nodded, relief warring with dread.

That night, as the boy slept restlessly beneath the ancient crystals, Maelis walked alone to the water's edge. She whispered prayers to the old gods, begging them to hold back the tide a little longer.

But deep within the loch, forces already stirred. The bonds woven by Brannach and Nerina's sacrifice strained against the tide of destiny.

And far beyond the mist, unseen but inevitable, something dark and ancient turned its gaze toward the Heart of the Loch—and the child who would soon step into legend.

CHAPTER 21: Evil Emerges

No more than a long day's travel from Loch Ness, the ruins of the old river fort had long since been forgotten by the proud clans of the Highlands. Moss covered the crumbled stones, and the river that once ran swift beneath its archways now whispered sluggishly through the reeds. It was a place of abandonment, a place where broken things gathered.

Malcontents of every order, man and monster, land and sea, had gathered at the call. Duncan MacAuley stood beneath the shattered remnants of the great hall, his cloak snapping in the chill wind. His hands, once steady and strong as a healer's, now trembled with a different kind of power. A bitter one.

One by one, figures emerged from the mists — men and women drawn by anger, fear, and the promise of something the old ways could no longer provide. Cousin Malcolm MacAuley led them, his scarred face half-hidden beneath a battered hood. Riverfolk, outcast Highlanders, even a few dark-eyed Kelpies whose allegiance shifted like the river's own currents.

They formed a rough circle around Duncan, their faces grim and expectant.

"You summoned us," Malcolm said, his voice low, grating like stone on stone.

Duncan surveyed them — the desperate, the forgotten, the dangerous. His voice rang clear in the ruined hall.

"Our world is slipping away," he said. "Brannach of the Kelpies turned his back on tradition. The Selkies whisper peace when war is needed. And now they rally behind a child — a child who will bind us all with soft words and weaker laws."

He let the words hang in the mist.

"They offer you unity," Duncan spat, "but unity for the rivers means death for the strong. It means rule by those who have never tasted blood in their mouths, never earned what they claimed."

A murmur ran through the gathering. Duncan could see it — the flaring anger, the tightening fists.

An older riverwoman, wrapped in a tattered gray cloak, stepped forward. Her eyes, milky with age, saw more than most. "And what would you do, MacAuley? Declare yourself king of bones?"

A ripple of uneasy laughter passed around the circle. Duncan smiled, a grim curl of his lips.

"I would do what must be done. I would stop the child before his power roots too deep. I would break the false alliances before they choke the rivers dry."

He stepped forward, lowering his voice.

"We strike at their heart. Quietly, swiftly. We turn their dreams into ash before they can awaken."

Malcolm MacAuley crossed his arms. "You ask much. Blood will spill — and not just theirs."

Duncan nodded. "Yes. Some among us may fall. Some will curse my name. But in the end, they will thank me — when the rivers run strong and free again, not shackled to the whims of Selkies and song-weavers."

Another figure spoke — a lean Kelpie with silver threading his black hair. "And what of the clans that resist? The loyal ones?"

Duncan's eyes hardened. "They will drown with the rest."

Silence fell, heavy and final.

Above them, clouds rolled across the night sky, smothering the stars. The river lapped hungrily at the broken stones, as if tasting the promises made here.

Slowly, Malcolm MacAuley extended his hand. Others followed — rough hands, webbed hands, hands scarred by years of hardship and hatred.

Duncan clasped each one, sealing the pact.

"We are the storm," he whispered. "And the tide will turn at our choosing."

The wind rose, howling through the shattered fort like a ghost called to witness.

And in the gathering dark, the first seeds of rebellion took root. And like weeds will do, grew with frightening speed.

CHAPTER 22: Alasdair Fraser

The encampment on the shores of Loch Ness hummed with purposeful activity. Gone were the scattered fires of uncertain allies; in their place stood orderly rows of tents, organized training grounds, and the steady rhythm of a people united in common cause.

Alasdair Fraser, his weathered face creased with concentration, studied the map spread before him. Beside him, Caelan—a kelpie warrior with skin that shimmered faintly green in certain lights—traced potential attack routes with a finger still damp from the loch.

Clan Fraser controlled the lands surrounding Loch Ness, and had for centuries. Their oath to protect not just the land, but the waters and its dwellers, were the strength of the clan. Their motto, Je Suis Prest stood them proud and always ready to defend.

"They'll come from the North," Caelan said, his voice carrying the burbling undertone of his river origins. "Duncan's forces have been gathering in the shadow of Ben Nevis for three days now."

Alasdair grunted, pushing a hand through his graying hair. "And what of the eastern passes? My scouts report movement there as well."

"A diversion," said a voice from the tent's entrance.

Both men looked up to see the boy—no, not a boy any longer, but a young man who carried himself with quiet certainty. His simple clothes were unadorned save for the spiral of riverstone clasped at his throat, yet something in his bearing drew the eye.

"How can you be so sure?" Alasdair asked, not unkindly.

The young man stepped forward, studying the map. "Duncan knows these lands too well to commit his forces to the eastern valley. It's too exposed, too easily defended." He touched the map where the loch narrowed. "He'll send enough men east to draw our attention, but his main force will strike here, where the water is shallowest."

Caelan's eyes narrowed. "Where the boundary between water and land blurs. Clever. It would allow his men to attack while keeping our water-folk at disadvantage."

"Exactly." The young man straightened. "We need to strengthen that position immediately."

Alasdair studied him with a mixture of respect and lingering uncertainty. Since emerging from the mists of the Heart three weeks ago, this child of prophecy had transformed their ragtag assembly into something approaching an army. Riverfolk who had never taken up arms now drilled alongside Highland warriors; selkies shared ancient water-magic with clan children; even several normally solitary kelpies had joined their cause.

Yet doubts remained—whispers in corners, uneasy glances when the young leader walked by.

"I'll see to the defenses myself," Alasdair said, rolling up the map. "Caelan, gather your river-scouts. I want to know the moment Duncan's forces move."

As they prepared to leave, the young man caught Alasdair's arm. "There's something else. Something... wrong."

Alasdair paused, recognizing the tone. In the short weeks of their alliance, he'd learned to trust the young leader's instincts. "What do you sense?"

"Not all eyes in our camp look outward for enemies." The young man's voice dropped lower. "Some look inward, watching us. Waiting."

"Spies," Caelan hissed, his hand dropping to the bone-handled knife at his belt.

"Worse," the young man said. "Saboteurs. I found two water-magic wards disabled this morning. And the maps—"

"What about the maps?" Alasdair demanded.

"The eastern pass is marked incorrectly. The trail doesn't fork until much later than shown."

The three exchanged grim looks. Someone was deliberately misguiding their defensive plans—someone with access to their war council.

"We need to identify them," Alasdair said, "but quietly. If we start hurling accusations—"

"The alliance fractures," the young man finished. "Exactly what Duncan wants."

"I'll speak with Maelis," Caelan offered. "She may have ways to reveal deception without alerting the deceivers."

After Caelan departed, Alasdair turned to the young leader. "You've given these people hope," he said gruffly. "Something many haven't felt in a long time."

The young man looked across the camp where riverfolk and Highlanders worked side by side. "They gave themselves hope. I merely reminded them it was possible."

Alasdair smiled faintly. "You sound like your father."

The young man's head snapped up. "You knew my father? Truly?"

Something like regret crossed Alasdair's face. "Saw him, heard him. During his final battle I was just cresting the valley walls when he was taken up by the water spirits. I watched him fight, I watched him sacrifice for you. I saw him well enough to see him in you—in the way you speak, the way you stand your ground." He reached beneath his plaid, pulling out a worn stone strung on faded leather. "This was his. I found on the shore that next morning, and have kept it safe, so many years ago."

The young man stared at the simple stone, emotions warring on his face. "I have... nothing of them. Nothing but stories and dreams."

"Then take this," Alasdair said, pressing it into his palm. "A piece of the river that carried your ancestors. It's yours now."

That evening, as dusk painted the loch in shades of amber and gold, Maelis moved silently among the gathered warriors and riverfolk. The feast—hastily assembled but welcome after days of preparation—had drawn everyone together around the central fires.

The selkie wise-woman's fingers traced invisible patterns in the air, her lips moving in ancient prayers as she wove magic through the gathering. Beside her, Eira—a young selkie with unusual silver-streaked hair—did the same, though her eyes never left the crowd.

"There," Eira whispered suddenly. "The trader with the red sash. His aura flickers wrong when the Heart is mentioned."

Maelis nodded subtly. "And the woman near the western fire. Watch how she never drinks when others toast."

The young leader moved casually through the crowd, sharing bread, exchanging words of encouragement. Each time he passed near a suspected spy, the Heart of the Loch pulsed faintly against his chest—confirming Maelis's suspicions.

Three infiltrators. Three potential breaking points in their fragile alliance.

He caught Alasdair's eye across the gathering and gave an almost imperceptible nod.

What followed happened with such swift efficiency that many in the camp barely registered it until it was over. Alasdair and Caelan closed in from opposite sides, their movements casual until the last moment. Six warriors—three Highland, three riverborn—followed their lead.

There was no clash of weapons, no shouted accusations. The spies were simply surrounded, disarmed, and restrained before they could react.

A hush fell over the camp as the infiltrators were brought before the central fire. The light revealed them clearly now: a river-trader with a red sash, a woman claiming kinship with a minor Highland house, and a thin man who had presented himself as a fisherman.

"What is the meaning of this?" demanded the woman, struggling against her bonds. "I am Fraser kin! You have no right—"

"Silence," Alasdair said, his voice cutting like a blade. "No Fraser blood flows in your veins. Your accent betrays you—northern, not Highland. And no Fraser would misspell our clan motto as you did in your pledge."

The young leader stepped forward, addressing not the spies but the watching crowd. "We will not be undone from within," he said, voice clear in the stillness. "Our strength lies not just in our swords or our magic, but in our trust. That trust is sacred—and those who would poison it will find no mercy here."

The river-trader spat at his feet. "Pretty words from a half-breed abomination. Duncan knows what you are! He knows the prophecy is false—a selkie trick to subjugate the true folk of the Highlands!"

Murmurs rippled through the gathering. Uncertainty. Fear. The first cracks in their unity.

The young leader felt the weight of every gaze, the fragility of the bonds he'd worked so hard to forge. He stepped closer to the trader, close enough to speak for his ears alone.

"I know what you are," he said softly. "I can see the magic that binds you—old magic, blood magic. You are as much a prisoner as those you seek to betray."

Something flickered in the trader's eyes—confusion, then a moment of terrible clarity, quickly extinguished.

"Take them away," the young leader commanded, stepping back. "They will be judged according to the laws of both river and clan."

Later, as the fires burned low and most had retired to their tents, the young leader sat alone by the dark waters of the loch. The Heart pulsed gently against his chest, a reassuring presence.

"You handled that well," said Maelis, appearing silently beside him.

"Did I?" He looked up at her. "I saw their faces, Maelis. The doubt. The fear."

"Such is the burden of leadership." She settled beside him on the rocky shore. "Your parents faced the same challenges. Trust is not given freely in times of conflict—it must be earned, again and again."

"The river-trader," he said after a moment. "Something was wrong about him. Beyond the deception."

Maelis nodded grimly. "Blood-binding. Duncan's work, without doubt. He has grown powerful in dark magics—magic that twists the will of others to his purpose."

The young leader stared out across the dark water. "Then what we face is worse than I feared."

"Yes," Maelis said simply. "But not beyond hope. Never beyond hope."

They sat in silence as the mist crept in from the loch, wrapping around them like a living thing. Somewhere beyond that silver veil, Duncan MacAuley waited, gathering his forces, weaving his dark magic.

The true battle had yet to begin.

CHAPTER 23: The Camp at Loch Ness

The encampment on the shores of Loch Ness had transformed overnight.

Where once there were scattered fires and uneasy strangers, now there rose the sound of hammers striking iron, of warriors sparring in tight, disciplined circles, of riverfolk weaving magic into nets and shields. The mist still clung to the earth, but within it, purpose burned bright.

At the heart of it all stood the boy. Ready now, emerged finally from the waters that had raised and protected him.

He wore no crown, no robe of office — only a simple cloak clasped at the throat with a spiral of riverstone. Yet as he stepped onto the rise overlooking the camp, conversations stilled. Heads turned. Even the Selkies lounging by the water's edge paused their songs.

The boy lifted his voice, steady and sure.

"We stand on the edge of a tide that will either carry us into a new world or drown us in the old."

Murmurs stirred the air. Some looked away; others clenched fists tight around spear shafts and sword hilts.

"They come for us," the boy continued. "Not as open warriors, but as cowards hiding in the dark. They would cut the heart from our alliance before it can beat."

Beside him, Alasdair Fraser stepped forward, his hand resting on the hilt of his blade.

"Let them come," Alasdair said, his voice carrying easily across the assembled. "They will find Highland steel and river magic waiting for them."

A rough cheer rose from the warriors nearest the front. But farther back, there was unease — the shuffling of feet, the tightening of jaws.

One of the elder riverfolk, his face lined like the bark of an ancient tree, spoke up.

"And if we lose? If the dark tides rise and we are swept away?"

The boy met his gaze without flinching.

"Then we fall standing together," he said. "Not scattered and broken as they would have us. Together, we are stronger than any tide."

Eira stepped forward then, her sealskin cloak glistening faintly with morning dew.

"We do not fight for conquest," she said, her voice a song woven with sorrow and hope. "We fight for the right to choose our own future. For the rivers to sing free, for the seas to carry our children's dreams."

Caelan said nothing. He simply drew his blade — a simple thing, unadorned — and planted it in the earth at the boy's feet, a silent vow.

One by one, others followed.

Swords, daggers, spears — placed point-down in the earth, a growing circle around the boy. A symbol of allegiance. A promise.

Not all stepped forward. Some lingered on the edges of the mist, faces shadowed, doubts unresolved.

But enough came.

The boy looked out across the gathered circle and felt the Heart of the Loch pulsing faintly against his chest — not commanding, not demanding, but offering strength drawn from the waters and the stones and the living will of those who chose to stand.

"Go now," he said. "Sharpen your blades. Whisper your prayers. Bind your hopes to the tide."

He lifted his hand, and the circle broke, warriors returning to their tasks with renewed urgency.

Messengers slipped away into the mist, carrying word to distant clans and hidden strongholds.

Weapons were honed, spells were woven, oaths were spoken beneath the darkening sky.

And as the sun dipped low over Loch Ness, casting long shadows across the water, the boy stood alone for a moment longer.

Watching.

Waiting.

The storm would break soon.

And they would be ready.

In the days that followed the boy's call to the Highlands, the encampment around the Heart of the Loch grew not just in numbers, but in spirit. The old barriers of suspicion and fear between riverfolk and Highlanders began to crack, slowly giving way to tentative trust.

Every morning, drills began at the break of day. Alasdair Fraser would stride among the lines of warriors, barking orders that rang across the misty fields. "Stand as one! Blade and breath as steady as stone!"

Laughter sometimes bubbled up amid the discipline—a Fraser boy slipping in the damp grass, a riverborn woman conjuring a spray of mist to startle a boastful young Kelpie. The boy watched it all unfold with quiet satisfaction, knowing that these small moments of joy would one day forge bonds stronger than fear.

In the evenings, the fires burned bright. Warriors shared tales—of battles fought, of rivers crossed, of loved ones waiting at home. Riverfolk sang songs of deep waters and lost isles, and Highlanders answered with ballads of mountains and wind.

One twilight, as the mist curled low and the stars began to prick the sky, the boy sat by a small fire, carefully carving a charm from a piece of riverstone. Alasdair approached, lowering himself onto the ground beside him.

"A charm?" Alasdair asked, his voice gruff but warm.

The boy nodded. "For the youngest among us. Something to hold when the darkness presses in."

He turned the stone in his fingers—a simple spiral carved deep into its surface, echoing the ancient symbol of the waters.

Alasdair watched him for a long moment, then pulled something from beneath his cloak—an old, worn stone of his own, strung on a faded leather cord.

"My father gave me this before my first battle," he said, voice thick with memory. "Said it was a piece of the river that carried our ancestors to this land."

He placed the stone in the boy's hand alongside the new charm.

"Yours now."

The boy blinked back sudden emotion, feeling the weight of generations pass into his palm.

"Thank you," he said simply.

All around them, the camp breathed with life—the low hum of conversation, the crackle of flames, the soft lapping of the loch against its banks.

The boy looked out across the gathering and saw not strangers, not divided peoples, but the shape of something new—a family forged by choice, not by blood.

And in his heart, the Heart of the Loch pulsed once, slow and strong, as if in approval.

Later, as the fires died down and the mist reclaimed the night, the boy sat alone by the dark waters of the Loch.

The Heart of the Loch throbbed gently, like the distant beat of war drums.

They had won a small victory, capturing the spies. But the true battle still loomed ahead.

And somewhere beyond the mists, Duncan MacAuley smiled, knowing full well that the boy's trials had only just begun.

Chapter 24: Breach of the Heart

The mist that had sheltered the Heart of the Loch for so long began to change.

"It's thinner again today," Eira observed, her seal-dark eyes narrowed as she gazed across the water. "I can see the far shore clearly now."

The young leader nodded, feeling the shift in his very bones. For weeks, the protective veil had been retreating, pulling back like a tide before a storm. With each passing day, more of the world beyond became visible—and more of the world could see them in return.

"It's not just changing," he said quietly. "It's dying."

Eira looked at him sharply. "The magic fades? But how? The sacrifice that created the Heart—"

"Was meant to last until I fulfilled my purpose." He touched the spiral stone at his throat. "The magic knows its time grows short. It calls me forward now, not back."

Around them, the encampment had transformed into a formidable stronghold. Defenses ringed the shore—some built of Highland stone and timber, others woven from riverborn magic. Warriors drilled in tight formation under Alasdair's watchful eye, while Maelis and her circle of selkie mages reinforced the protective wards.

Unity had come at a cost. The capture of the spies had proven their vulnerability, forcing closer cooperation even among those who still harbored suspicions. Necessity, if not trust, bound them together.

"Caelan's scouts returned," Eira said, changing the subject. "Duncan's forces move tonight."

The young leader's expression hardened. "Then so do we. Gather the Circle."

Within the hour, the war council assembled in the largest tent. Maps covered the central table, weighted down with stones and weapons. The air hung heavy with tension and the tang of magic.

"His main force approaches from the north, as we predicted," Caelan reported, indicating positions on the map. "But there's something else—something the scouts couldn't identify. A darkness that follows them, something that taints the very water it touches."

"Blood magic," Maelis said grimly. "Duncan has embraced powers no mortal should wield."

Alasdair Fraser planted his hands on the table, his scarred knuckles whitening. "Magic or no, his men will bleed like any other. We hold the high ground and the water's edge. We can—"

"He's not coming for the camp," the young leader interrupted, his gaze fixed on the map. "That's not what this is about."

The tent fell silent.

"He's coming for the Heart itself," he continued. "Everything else—the attacks, the spies, even the blood magic—it's all to clear a path to the Heart of the Loch."

"But why?" asked a young Highland warrior, confusion plain on his face. "What could he want with—"

"Power," Maelis answered. "The Heart contains magic older than Scotland itself. In the right hands, it protects and nurtures. In the wrong hands..."

She didn't need to finish. Everyone present understood the stakes.

"Then we must protect it at all costs," Alasdair declared. "We'll position our strongest fighters in a ring around the Heart's access point."

The young leader shook his head. "No. We must move it."

Gasps and protests erupted around the table.

"Impossible!" "The Heart cannot be moved!" "Its roots go deep into the loch itself!"

"Listen!" His voice cut through the chaos, not through volume but through a resonance that vibrated in the very air. "The Heart is not just a place—it's a manifestation of will. Of sacrifice. It can be relocated, but only by one who carries its essence."

All eyes turned to the spiral stone at his throat, the physical anchor of the Heart's power.

"Even if that's possible," Caelan said carefully, "where would you take it? Nowhere in these lands would be safe from Duncan for long."

The young leader took a deep breath. "To its source. Where river meets sea."

Maelis stepped forward, alarm evident in her weathered features. "That journey would take you through the heart of Duncan's territory. It would be suicide."

"Not if his attention is elsewhere." He looked to Alasdair. "Your warriors can provide that distraction. Make Duncan believe we're preparing for a last stand here."

Silence fell as they considered his words. It was Eira who broke it, her voice soft but determined.

"I'll go with you."

"As will I," Caelan added immediately.

One by one, others stepped forward—a small band of the most trusted among them, river and Highland alike.

Alasdair studied the young leader's face. "You've been planning this. How long?"

"Since the first spy was discovered." He met the older man's gaze steadily. "I've seen what's coming, Alasdair. In dreams, in the patterns of the water. This is the only way."

That night, as final preparations were made in hushed tones and hurried movements, the young leader stood alone at the edge of the loch. The Heart pulsed against his chest, stronger than before, as if sensing the proximity of its fate.

Soft footsteps approached behind him.

"I remember the day we found you," Maelis said, her voice thick with memory. "So small, yet your eyes held such knowing. I wondered then what you would become."

He turned to her, this woman who had been mother, teacher, and guardian all at once. "And now?"

"Now I see the son of Brannach and Nerina," she said, reaching up to touch his cheek. "A bridge between worlds. Neither river nor sea, but something new entirely."

"I'm afraid, Maelis," he admitted quietly. "Not of Duncan, not of the journey. I'm afraid of failing them—all of them. Those who have followed me, those who sacrificed for me."

"Fear is wisdom in the face of danger," she replied. "It is not the absence of fear that makes a leader, but the courage to act despite it."

A horn sounded in the distance—three long blasts. The signal.

"They come," he said, straightening his shoulders.

Maelis pressed something into his hand—a small pouch of woven rivergrass. "Waters from the sacred springs. When all seems lost, remember that even the smallest drop can change the course of a mighty river."

He tucked it carefully into his belt, then embraced her fiercely.

"Go now," she whispered. "The tide waits for no one, not even the child of prophecy."

As he pulled away, his gaze swept over the encampment—these people who had become his family, his purpose. Highland warriors checking their weapons one last time. Riverfolk weaving last-minute protections into cloaks and shields. Selkies slipping into the water to take up positions as scouts.

United, despite centuries of mistrust. Fighting not just for survival, but for a future where their children might know peace.

In that moment, seeing them through the thinning mist, he knew with bone-deep certainty that this—this fragile, hard-won unity—was what his parents had died to protect. What they had believed possible.

The Heart of the Loch pulsed once more against his chest, strong and sure.

It was time.

With Eira, Caelan, and a small band of the most trusted at his side, he slipped away from the camp. Behind them, the forces of river and Highland prepared for battle, a shield to cover their true purpose.

Ahead lay a journey through shadow and peril, to the ancient place where river met sea—where the Heart of the Loch might find its final sanctuary.

And somewhere in the darkness, Duncan MacAuley waited, weaving spells of blood and hate, well aware that the very prize he sought was attempting to slip beyond his grasp.

Chapter 25: The Waters Awaken

But this battle was not to be avoided, not left to others. This was a chilling, deep conflict that could only be met by the boy himself. And so it came to pass, his effort to divert from the main camp foiled.

The mist parted like a theater curtain, revealing the boy standing alone before the gathered darkness. The weight of the pendant pressed against his chest, its gentle warmth a stark contrast to the cold fear that threatened to freeze his limbs.

Ahead, the black-armored riders sat atop their twisted mounts, creatures that had once been horses before corruption had seeped into their flesh and bone. Behind them writhed things made of mud and shadow, their forms constantly shifting as if unable to decide what manner of nightmare they wished to become.

For a heartbeat that stretched into eternity, neither side moved.

The boy could feel eyes upon him—not just the hollow stares of Duncan's forces, but the desperate gazes of those who had placed their trust in him. Somewhere behind, Maelis whispered ancient prayers. Caelan and his river-warriors stood ready at the water's edge. Alasdair Fraser and his clansmen gripped their blades, the steel catching what little light remained in this twilight confrontation.

"So," came a voice from among the darkness, "this is the great savior of the waters? A half-grown boy with a trinket?"

A figure urged his mount forward—taller than the others, his armor forged from some black metal that seemed to devour light rather than reflect it. His face remained hidden behind a helmet crowned with antlers of iron.

Duncan MacAuley. The boy knew him instinctively, as prey knows predator.

"I am what I am," the boy replied, his voice clear despite the pounding of his heart. "And you are what you've chosen to become, Duncan MacAuley."

The figure stiffened. "You speak my name as if you know me, child."

"I know enough." The boy's fingers brushed the pendant. "I know you were once sworn to protect these lands, not poison them. I know you once pledged fealty to the covenant between river and sea."

A harsh laugh echoed from within the black helmet. "Ancient history. Fairy tales for children who still believe in honor." Duncan raised a gauntleted hand. "The waters bow to strength alone. Allow me to demonstrate."

The boy closed his eyes, drawing in a deep breath that seemed to pull not just air but essence into his lungs. He felt the waters of the loch moving within him—not just the cool depths he had swum in as a child, but the rivers that crisscrossed the land, the deep currents of the sea, the mist-laden breath of the hills. All of it was part of him, and he of it.

He stepped forward, opening his eyes to meet Duncan's invisible gaze.

The first rider—not Duncan, but one of his lieutenants—spurred his corrupted mount. The beast surged forward with unnatural speed, its hooves striking sparks from stone. The rider lowered his lance, its tip aimed unerringly at the boy's heart.

Behind him, Alasdair bellowed a warning. Caelan shouted a curse.

But the boy stood unmoved. At the last possible instant, the pendant flared with blinding light, and the waters answered his unspoken call.

A wall of liquid rose from the ground itself, gleaming with magic older than Scotland. The black lance struck it and shattered like glass, fragments scattering in all directions. The corrupted horse screamed in terror, rearing and throwing its rider before bolting into the mist.

The boy lowered his hand slowly, feeling the magic pulse through his veins. There was no need for thought now; instinct guided him, the old power responding to his will as naturally as breathing.

The mud-creatures surged forward, their forms coalescing into things with too many limbs and gaping maws. More riders charged, weapons raised, voices raised in harsh battle cries.

The loch answered each threat. Great tendrils of mist coiled around riders, plucking them from saddles with deceptive gentleness before flinging them away. The ground beneath the mud-creatures liquefied, swallowing them whole. Waves rose like walls, crashing down with the force of ancient storms.

Yet with each defense, each attack repelled, the boy felt the cost. The pendant grew heavier, its light burning into his chest. Each manifestation of power threaded his essence deeper into the Heart of the Loch, binding him to its fate as surely as his parents had been bound.

"Stop this!" Maelis cried, seeing the strain etched upon his face. "You'll burn yourself out!"

But retreat was impossible now. From among the chaos, a new figure emerged—not mounted, not armored, but somehow more terrifying for its lack of protection.

A wraith of poisoned waters, its form constantly shifting between liquid and vapor, its voice a gurgling hiss that spoke of stagnant pools and drowned hopes.

"Child of broken laws," it rasped, gliding closer. "You are an abomination. A thing that should never have been."

The boy straightened, though each movement sent pain lancing through his overtaxed body. He met the creature's empty gaze without flinching.

"I am the future," he said, voice steady despite his exhaustion. "You are the rot of the past."

The wraith's form trembled with rage. "Insolent whelp! I am the voice of the old ways—the true guardian of the waters!"

"No," the boy said simply. "You're just a shadow. A memory of hatred that should have been washed away long ago."

With a shriek that drove several warriors to their knees, the wraith lunged forward, its form elongating into a spear of corrupted water.

The boy braced himself, feeling the last reserves of strength gathering within him. He would not fall. He could not. Too many depended on him now.

"Remember who you are!" Maelis shouted, her voice cutting through the chaos. "Remember your parents' sacrifice!"

The words struck deeper than any physical blow could have. In his mind's eye, the boy saw them again—not as abstractions or stories, but as real people who had loved and lost and given everything for a hope they would never see fulfilled.

Something ancient and powerful stirred in response to his need. From the depths of the loch, the guardians—creatures of legend that had slumbered since the days when the first stories were told—awakened.

Silver serpents with scales like starlight. Birds of living flame that trailed sparks as they soared. Great beasts born of river and sea, their forms too vast to fully comprehend. Their voices rose in harmony, a song of power and protection that shook the very stones of the Heart.

The boy felt their strength flowing into him, freely given. He grasped the pendant with both hands and lifted it high.

"Enough," he said, and the word carried the weight of mountains, the persistence of rivers, the inevitability of tides.

Light exploded outward—not the harsh brilliance of lightning, but the gentle, inexorable illumination of dawn breaking over water. It washed over the battlefield, piercing the wraith's form. Where the light touched, corruption burned away like mist before the sun.

With a scream that echoed across the waters, the creature unraveled, its darkness dispersed by the mingled magic of river and sea.

In the silence that followed, Duncan MacAuley's voice rose above the battlefield. "This isn't over, child! The waters will know their true master!"

But even as he spoke, his forces were retreating, broken and leaderless, disappearing into the mist like nightmares at daybreak.

The boy stood a moment longer, the pendant's light gradually fading. Then his knees buckled, and he collapsed to the earth, utterly spent.

Maelis was the first to reach him, gathering his limp form into her arms. Her weathered face showed equal parts awe and terror.

"It has begun," she whispered, brushing damp hair from his forehead.

Alasdair Fraser knelt beside them, his scarred face solemn. "Is he—?"

"He lives," Maelis said. "But the power nearly consumed him. He is bound to the Heart now, more deeply than before."

Caelan joined them, water dripping from his greenish skin. "The enemy has retreated beyond the eastern ridge. Our scouts are tracking them, but they move as if in disarray."

"We've won a reprieve," Alasdair said, "not a victory."

Maelis nodded, her eyes never leaving the boy's face. "Help me get him to the sacred pool. The waters there will help restore him."

As they carried him away, something stirred in the depths of the loch—a ripple that traveled outward, bearing whispers that would soon reach distant shores. The whispers carried a word—a name. The true name of the child born of sacrifice and hope.

But that name would remain hidden a little longer, cradled in the heart of the waters, until the world was ready to hear it.

Chapter 26: Whispers Beyond the Mist

The loch lay silent once more, its surface a mirror reflecting clouds that scudded across the sky like thoughts too swift to capture. Yet the stillness was a lie—beneath the placid surface, currents raced with urgent purpose, carrying whispers far beyond the Heart.

In a small stone dwelling built into the shoreline, the boy lay in healing sleep, his breathing steady now but shallow. Three days had passed since his stand against Duncan's forces, three days of anxious watching and whispered consultations.

"His fever breaks," Eira said, removing a damp cloth from his forehead. Her selkie heritage showed in the subtle sheen of her skin, the slightly too-large eyes that missed nothing. "But he remains distant. As if part of him lingers elsewhere."

Maelis, who had barely left his side, nodded grimly. "Part of him does. The Heart claimed more of his essence than I feared it would. Each time he calls upon its power, the connection deepens."

Alasdair Fraser paced the small room, his massive frame making the space seem even smaller. "Will he recover?" The Highland chieftain's voice was gruff, but genuine concern underlay the brusqueness.

"His body, yes," Maelis said. "As for his spirit..." She trailed off, unwilling to voice the dread that had settled in her chest.

Caelan, who had been silently watching from the doorway, spoke up. "The word spreads. The rivers carry news of his stand against Duncan. The tales grow with each telling—some say he called down lightning, others that he commanded an army of water spirits."

"Tales are useful," Alasdair grunted. "Fear may keep Duncan's forces at bay longer than our swords."

Maelis shook her head. "It's not just fear these stories will inspire. Hope, yes. But also envy. Ambition. Others will come—not just to witness, but to claim."

As if confirming her words, a messenger arrived that evening, breathless with news of strangers approaching the Heart from all directions. Some bore banners of peace, others traveled in shadow.

Far beyond the mist-shrouded shores of Loch Ness, the ripples of the boy's stand against darkness spread through the hidden waterways of Scotland.

In the scattered courts of the Selkies, hidden in sea caves and forgotten isles, ancient songs echoed once more. Songs that spoke of a child who would bridge the broken worlds, who would heal the ancient wounds between river and sea.

"The prophecies unfold," whispered an elder selkie, her silver-streaked hair floating in the currents of her underwater chamber. "The child of two worlds stands revealed."

"It is too soon," argued another, his face lined with centuries of caution. "The world is not ready. The old hatreds run too deep."

"When has the world ever been ready for change?" countered a younger voice. "The tide waits for no one's permission to turn."

Debates raged through the night, ending only when the High Queen of the Western Isles Selkie Court rose from her throne of pearl and coral.

"Send our emissary," she commanded. "We must know if this child is truly the one foretold—and if so, we must guide him before others can claim him."

In the deeper rivers, among the proud Kelpie clans who had once sworn fealty to Brannach, similar councils convened. But here, fear mingled with wonder.

"Brannach was a traitor to his kind," snarled a Kelpie lord, his green-black mane bristling. "He abandoned our ways for a selkie woman. His offspring carries tainted blood."

"Yet the waters answered his call," another pointed out. "The ancient guardians awoke for him. Can we ignore such signs?"

"Signs can be misinterpreted," said a third, her voice silky with danger. "Perhaps the child should be... tested. To ensure he is worthy of the legacy he claims."

As these deliberations continued, still more whispers traveled to places long forgotten by human memory—to the sunken temples of the Finfolk, to the mist-veiled domains of the Asrai, to the underground rivers where the Blue Men made their homes.

The boy himself felt these currents of change even in his healing sleep. Dreams came to him—vivid, powerful visions of faces he had never seen, voices speaking in languages he somehow understood.

On the fifth day, he awoke.

He sat up slowly, his body aching but whole. Through the small window of his chamber, he could see the loch, its waters touched gold by the setting sun.

"You had us worried," Maelis said, appearing at his side with a cup of herbal tea.

The boy accepted it, his hands steadier than she had expected. "How long?"

"Five days."

He nodded, sipping the bitter brew without complaint. "Things have changed. I can feel it."

Maelis settled beside him on the edge of the bed. "Yes. Your stand against Duncan did more than repel his forces. It announced your presence to all who have ears to hear such things."

The boy was silent for a long moment, watching the play of light on the loch's surface. Finally, he asked, "Do you think my parents knew? What would happen when they created the Heart?"

Maelis's weathered face softened. "They knew that love could create something powerful enough to change the world. The details... those they left to faith."

A small smile touched the boy's lips. "Faith. I felt them, Maelis. When I faced that wraith—when I thought I had nothing left to give—I felt them with me."

Maelis took his hand, her own eyes bright with unshed tears. "They have never left you. Not truly."

Later that evening, when his strength had returned enough to venture outside, the boy sat at the edge of the sacred pool. The waters were unnaturally still, reflecting the stars that had begun to appear in the twilight sky.

Maelis joined him, settling herself on a flat stone nearby. Neither spoke for some time, content to share the peace of the moment.

"They will come for me, won't they?" he finally asked, his voice steady despite the weight of the question.

Maelis sighed, her gaze fixed on the distant horizon. "Yes. Some will come to guide you. Others to test you. Some..." She hesitated. "Some will come to destroy you."

"And how will I know the difference? How will I know who to trust?"

She turned to him then, her eyes reflecting the wisdom of centuries. "You will know. In your blood, in your bones. The rivers and the seas will tell you."

As if in response to her words, a soft ripple disturbed the pool's perfect surface. From its depths rose a small, silver creature—neither fish nor bird, but something between. It hovered in the air for a moment, its translucent wings catching the starlight, before settling on the stone at the boy's feet.

The boy reached out slowly, drawn by an instinct he couldn't name. The creature pressed its delicate head against his palm, a gesture of such perfect trust that his throat tightened with emotion.

"What is it?" he whispered.

"A water sprite," Maelis answered, her voice hushed with wonder. "They are rarely seen, even by those of us who know the old ways. They appear only in times of great change."

The sprite's touch seemed to resonate with something deep within him—a chord struck that continued to vibrate long after the initial sound had faded.

"The heralds come," Maelis said softly. "The old magic stirs them."

The boy closed his eyes, feeling the creature's silent song merge with his own heartbeat. In that moment, he glimpsed fragments of what was to come—challenges, choices, sacrifices yet to be made.

"I am ready," he said, opening his eyes to meet Maelis's gaze.

She studied him—this child who had been born of love and sacrifice, who had grown in the shadow of prophecy, and who now stood at the threshold of a destiny larger than anyone could have imagined.

"Not ready for all that must come," she said gently. "But ready enough."

Beyond the protective mist, the first of the envoys were already crossing the ruined lands. Some carried banners of peace; others, blades hidden beneath cloaks of seeming friendship.

And high above the loch, unseen by mortal eyes, the ancient guardians circled, their silver forms cutting through cloud and darkness alike. Their songs, too high for human ears, threaded through the night sky like living constellations.

The world was changing. Ancient boundaries blurred, old certainties crumbled, new possibilities emerged from the shadows of what had always been.

And the tides of fate, once stirred, would not be stilled again.

Chapter 27: Envoys and Shadows

The first envoy arrived at dusk three days later, when the sky hung heavy with clouds the color of bruised plums. Sentries spotted the lone figure approaching from the east, moving with deliberate slowness along the shore of the loch.

"No weapons visible," reported Caelan, who had established a perimeter of river-warriors around the Heart. "Cloak of sea-green. Selkie markings on the staff."

Alasdair Fraser frowned, his hand never far from his sword hilt. "A peaceful approach means little these days. Duncan's spies came with smiles before they tried to slit our throats."

The boy had been standing silently on a rise overlooking the loch, the silver sprite perched on his shoulder like a living ornament. At Alasdair's words, he turned.

"This one comes in truth," he said, his voice carrying an certainty that none questioned. "I can feel it."

Maelis, who had been conferring with a circle of river-witches, approached the boy. "Even so, caution would be wise. Let us meet this envoy together."

They gathered at the outermost ring of standing stones—the boy, Maelis, Alasdair, Caelan, and Eira. A show of unity, but also of strength. The rest of their forces remained visible but distant, a silent reminder of the power that protected the Heart.

The figure in sea-green robes halted at the boundary, exactly as protocol demanded. With slow, deliberate movements, she bowed low, pressing one hand to the earth and the other to the sky—the ancient gesture that acknowledged the dual powers of water.

"I come in peace," the envoy said, her voice musical yet strong, carrying the subtle accent of the Western Isles. "I bring word from the Selkie elders."

Maelis tensed almost imperceptibly, her hand hovering near the pouch of protective charms at her belt. For all her outward calm, the boy could sense her anxiety—Maelis had left the Selkie courts long ago, under circumstances she rarely discussed.

But the boy stepped forward, the sprite still balanced on his shoulder. "Speak," he said, his voice carrying the quiet authority that had begun to emerge since his battle with Duncan's forces.

The envoy lifted her head, lowering her hood to reveal a face lined with wisdom and the subtle markers of great age. Her eyes, large and dark as deep pools, studied the boy with undisguised curiosity.

"I am Sorcha," she said, "Voice of the Western Court. The Selkie elders have long awaited the fulfillment of the Prophecy of Tides." Her gaze shifted to the pendant at his chest. "They send their blessing—and their warning. There are those among them who would see you raised to lead... and those who would see you drowned before your time."

The boy nodded gravely. "I expected no less."

Sorcha's expression softened slightly. "You are wise beyond your years, child of river and sea. The path ahead will be treacherous. Trust not in blood alone, nor in old alliances. Trust only in the waters, and in your own heart."

"Your court abandoned Nerina when she chose Brannach," Maelis said, her voice tight with old anger. "They turned their backs when Duncan's hatred first began to poison the rivers. Why come now, when the hardest battles have already been fought?"

Sorcha met Maelis's gaze steadily. "The courts move slowly, Maelis mac Finlay. Too slowly, perhaps. But they move nonetheless." She turned back to the boy. "What was done to your mother—the shunning, the denial of aid—it was wrong. Many now see this. But pride is a difficult current to swim against."

"I don't seek apologies," the boy said. "Only allies who will stand with us against the darkness that threatens all waters."

Sorcha smiled—a genuine expression that transformed her austere features. "Then perhaps there is hope for us yet."

She withdrew a small token from within her robes—a shard of abalone shell etched with ancient runes—and placed it carefully at the boundary stone.

"This will call us, should you have need. Three drops of water upon the shell, and a voice will answer."

With that, she bowed again and backed away several paces before turning to disappear into the gathering dusk, as silently as she had come.

Alasdair Fraser bent to examine the shell without touching it. "Genuine selkie craftwork," he confirmed. "The runes are old—protective sigils, mostly."

Maelis exhaled slowly, her shoulders relaxing slightly. "That was a true offer of alliance," she said. "The shell is a royal token—not given lightly."

"The first of many such approaches, I'd wager," Caelan said, his green-tinged skin darkening as night fell. "News travels fast through water."

The boy nodded, his expression thoughtful as he watched the spot where Sorcha had disappeared. "Others will come. Not all with honest intentions."

His words proved prophetic sooner than anyone expected.

Later that night, as the moon struggled to pierce thick clouds and most of the camp had settled into uneasy sleep, the boy woke with a sudden jolt. The sprite, which had taken to nesting near his pillow, was quivering with agitation, its silvery light pulsing in warning.

Something was wrong. The boy could feel it—a discordant note in the music of the waters, a presence that should not be there.

He slipped from his bed, moving silently to the door of his small chamber. Outside, the camp was quiet save for the murmur of the night sentries and the ever-present lapping of the loch against the shore.

Yet the wrongness persisted, a itch beneath his skin.

"What is it?" he whispered to the sprite. "What do you sense?"

The tiny creature flitted toward the western edge of the camp, its light dimming to a bare glimmer. The boy followed, staying to the shadows, one hand on the pendant at his chest.

Near the boundary stones, a shape moved—cloaked in rags and moving with unnatural swiftness. It didn't approach openly as Sorcha had done, but slipped from shadow to shadow, avoiding the sentries with disturbing ease.

The boy sensed the danger before he could fully process what he was seeing. The sprite hissed, its tiny body vibrating with alarm.

"Intruder!" Maelis shouted from somewhere to his left, having sensed the disturbance herself. "To arms!"

The ragged figure froze for just an instant—then lunged forward with inhuman speed, a blade gleaming wickedly in the faint moonlight.

The boy reacted instinctively. The pendant at his chest flared, casting a wall of protective light between him and the would-be assassin. The figure screamed—a sound of equal parts pain and fury—and recoiled as the light burned away the shadows that had cloaked it.

In that brief illumination, the boy caught a clear glimpse of his attacker's face—the greenish skin, the black eyes, the lips pulled back to reveal teeth too sharp for any human mouth.

A kelpie. But not like Caelan, whose form had been tempered by generations of adherence to the old covenants. This was a kelpie of the wild rivers, its features twisted by hatred and something more—a corruption that reminded the boy all too vividly of Duncan's wraith.

"Abomination!" the assassin hissed, its voice bubbling as if spoken through water. "The rivers reject your claim!"

Before anyone could respond, the creature retreated into the shadows, its form melting away with unnatural swiftness. The sentries gave chase, but the boy already knew they would find nothing.

Maelis reached him first, her face pale with fear and anger. "Are you hurt?"

The boy shook his head, the pendant's light already fading against his chest. "No. It never got close enough."

Alasdair Fraser arrived moments later, sword drawn, his expression thunderous. "How did it get past our wards?"

"The same way Duncan's spies did," Maelis said grimly. "It knew what to look for. What to avoid."

The boy stood for a long time at the boundary where the attacker had appeared, his thoughts racing. The sprite had returned to his shoulder, its light steadier now but still watchful.

"The waters grow restless," Maelis said, coming to stand beside him. "You have friends... and enemies now."

The boy nodded, his expression settling into lines of quiet resolve. "Let them come," he said, and there was a new hardness in his voice— not cruelty, but determination. "I will not hide from what must be faced."

Far across the misted lands, in stone halls where ancient blood still ran true, the Clan Fraser gathered in solemn council. They had kept the old oaths when others had forgotten—oaths to protect not just the land but the waters that gave it life, oaths that bound them to powers older than human memory.

"The signs are clear," said the clan's eldest, her white hair a crown in the firelight. "The child of two worlds has risen. The Heart awakens."

Young warriors shifted restlessly, hands never far from weapons. Elders nodded solemnly, recalling stories passed down through generations.

"Then we must honor our pledge," said the clan chief, rising to his feet. "Send the strongest of our warriors, those who still remember the old tongues. The Frasers stand with the Heart, as we have always done."

The ripples spread outward—river to sea, sea to shore, shore to glen, glen to mountain. The board was set, the pieces moving into position.

And at the center of it all, a boy who was becoming something more with each passing day stood watching the waters, waiting for the tides to bring what they would.

Chapter 28: Allies Awaken

The days following the boy's awakening were heavy with anticipation, each sunrise bringing with it the weight of prophecy. Though the mists clung stubbornly to the Heart of the Loch, beyond their boundaries, subtle changes rippled through the world like stones cast into still water.

Each morning, before the dew had lifted from the grass, the boy trained under Maelis' watchful eye. His muscles ached and his mind strained as he learned to command the gifts that ran through his veins like quicksilver.

"Again," Maelis urged, her voice stern but not unkind as she watched him struggle to maintain the column of mist he'd summoned. "Feel the water in the air. It is not separate from the water in your blood. They are one current, one tide."

The boy's brow furrowed with concentration. Sweat beaded on his temples as the mist wavered, thinned, then strengthened once more. "It fights me," he gasped.

"No," Maelis placed a weathered hand on his shoulder. "It tests you. There's a difference. The elements are not servants to be commanded, but allies to be respected."

"How will I ever be ready?" he asked, letting the mist dissipate as exhaustion claimed him. "The darkness is growing stronger every day."

Maelis' eyes crinkled at the corners. "Power without wisdom is a river without banks—destructive and directionless. Today you learn control. Tomorrow, purpose."

The boy nodded, drawing a deep breath. He was about to try again when the plaintive call of horns drifted through the morning air, low and resonant, carrying over the hills like the song of ancient earth.

Maelis froze, her hand tightening on the boy's shoulder. "Stay behind me," she whispered, then relaxed as she cocked her head, listening. "No... wait. That is no enemy's call."

They climbed to the ridge where the boundary stones stood like weathered sentinels. The mist parted before them, revealing a solemn procession winding its way up the eastern path. Men and women moved with measured steps, clad in cloaks of forest green and midnight blue, embroidered with symbols that spoke of river, stone, and sky. Though swords hung at their sides, their hands were empty—an offering of peace.

At their head rode a figure whose presence seemed to command the very air around him. Tall and broad-shouldered, with hair as dark as rain-soaked earth and eyes that held both steel and sorrow, he carried himself with the quiet dignity of one who has known both victory and loss.

"Clan Fraser," Maelis breathed, an uncharacteristic tremor in her voice.

The boy looked up at her, startled by the emotion he saw flicker across her normally composed features. "You know them?"

"I know of them," she replied. "The Frasers are guardians of the old pacts. They have kept faith when others forgot." Something passed across her face—relief, perhaps, or something more complex. "I had feared they too had fallen."

The leader of the Frasers dismounted with fluid grace when he reached the boundary stones. With deliberate movements, he removed his cloak and knelt, laying it upon the earth like an offering.

"I am Simon Fraser," he called, his voice deep and clear as mountain water. "Son of the Highlands, Brother to Alastair. Warden of Loch Ness, and Keeper of the Old Ways. We come in friendship, bound by oaths older than memory to serve the waters and the one who would heal them."

The silver creature on the boy's shoulder gave a soft, melodic trill that seemed to hover in the air like mist.

The boy felt a strange certainty settle over him. Without looking at Maelis for guidance, he stepped forward, the pendant warm against his chest.

"Why now?" he asked, his young voice steady despite the hammering of his heart. "Why come to me when the tide has already begun to turn against us?"

Simon's weathered face revealed a flicker of pain. "Dreams have haunted our sleep—visions of darkness seeping into the very heart of the waters. Then three nights past, the loch itself seemed to speak your awakening." His eyes, gray as storm clouds, studied the boy. "You have fought alongside my brother, and he has sent word of need."

"We have waited generations for this moment. I only pray we are not too late."

The boy considered the man before him, sensing no deceit in his words. Finally, he nodded. "Rise, Simon Fraser. There is much to be done, and I cannot—will not—stand alone."

Simon rose to his feet, and something fierce and proud blazed in his face. Behind him, as if responding to some unspoken command, the assembled Frasers knelt as one, heads bowed in silent oath to the child who stood before them—the child of waters, the child of prophecy.

"You honor us," Simon said softly.

"No," the boy replied, feeling the weight of their faith settle upon his shoulders. "You give me hope."

And for the first time since he had learned of his destiny, he truly believed that the seemingly impossible task before him might yet be accomplished.

Chapter 29: Gathering the Circle

The Heart of the Loch, once silent and secluded, now hummed with purpose. Each passing day brought new arrivals to its misty shores—those whose blood still remembered ancient pacts, those whose dreams had been haunted by visions of darkness and light.

"I never imagined so many would answer the call," the boy confessed to Maelis as they watched a group of Highland warriors establish camp along the eastern ridge. "How do they even know to come?"

Maelis smiled, the expression softening the weathered lines of her face. "The Heart speaks in many tongues—through dreams, through blood-memory, through the very currents of the earth. Those with ears to hear have heard."

Under her careful guidance, the boy began to form what would become his inner circle—those who would stand closest to him in the coming storm.

Alasdair Fraser proved himself indispensable, his knowledge of Highland paths and hidden ways was matched only by his quiet authority. The other humans deferred to him without question, and his brother Simon nodded acceptance to the bond Alasdair shared with the boy. Even the more elusive water-folk regarded Alasdair with cautious respect.

"My grandfather taught me the old stories," Alasdair explained one evening as they pored over crude maps drawn in earth and stone. "He made me memorize every word, though I understood little then. He said, 'A day will come when these tales are no longer just tales.' I thought him mad." He looked up, firelight catching in his eyes. "Now I understand he was preparing me."

The boy studied the weathered face across from him. "And what do your people think of serving a child they've never met?"

"They serve not a child, but a hope," Alasdair replied without hesitation. "Though I won't pretend there weren't doubts. Some called me a fool for following dreams and portents."

"And yet you came."

"And yet I came." Alasdair's expression softened. "Some truths can only be felt, not reasoned. When I stood at the shores of Loch Ness and felt its waters tremble... I knew."

And they all nodded, thinking back to their own arrivals, their own confirmation of hope in the boy…

From the Selkie courts had come Eira, arriving alone at dawn, her sealskin draped across her shoulders like a cloak of midnight. Her laughter spilled like sunlight on water, but her eyes held the ancient wisdom of the sea.

"Queen Mhairi sends her greetings," she had announced, bowing with liquid grace before the boy. "And her caution."

"Caution?" the boy asked.

Eira's smile dimmed slightly. "The sea-folk remember the last war all too well. Our songs still keen with grief for what was lost. The Queen will not commit her people lightly to another such conflict."

"Then why are you here?" Maelis asked, her tone sharp.

Eira turned, meeting the older woman's gaze steadily. "Because some songs cannot be left unfinished. Some wounds cannot be left to fester." She looked back to the boy, something fierce and tender in her expression. "I came to see for myself if you are truly the one spoken of in prophecy. If you are, then Queen Mhairi will honor the ancient pacts."

"And if I'm not?" the boy asked quietly.

Eira's smile turned sad. "Then I have given false hope to my people, and the darkness will claim us all."

The boy felt the weight of her assessment. "Fair enough."

And Caelan of the kelpies thought back to his arrival as twilight painted the waters in shades of amber and gold, his lone figure appeared at the edge of the mist. Tall and lean, with hair the color of river reeds and eyes like polished stone, he approached alone and unarmed.

The sentries had tensed, hands moving to weapons. Even Alasdair stepped forward, placing himself between the stranger and the boy.

"Hold," the boy commanded, feeling a strange resonance with the newcomer. "He means no harm."

"You can't know that," Alasdair warned.

"I can," the boy insisted. "He's kin to the waters, as I am."

The stranger stopped at a respectful distance, regarding them all with a gaze both wary and proud. "I am Caelan," he had strongly announced, his voice rough as though rarely used. "I come from the deep rivers."

"A Kelpie," Maelis breathed, her posture stiffening.

Murmurs rippled through the gathered folk. The Kelpies had long been feared, even among the water-folk—creatures of violent current and sudden depth, known for their fierce independence and unpredictable nature.

"Why are you here?" the boy had asked, stepping forward despite Alasdair's protective gesture.

Caelan's expression remained impassive, but something flickered in the depths of his strange, stone-colored eyes. "Because I have watched my kin turn to darkness one by one. Because I have felt the poison seeping into our waters, corrupting what was pure." His hands clenched at his sides. "Because I would rather die fighting for healing than live in slow corruption."

"You come alone?" Maelis pressed, suspicion clear in her tone.

"I come alone," Caelan confirmed, a trace of bitterness coloring his words. "My people are... divided. Many have already succumbed to the whispers of power that the darkness offers. Others wait, fearful and uncertain. I could convince none to join me."

The boy studied him for a long moment. "It takes courage to stand apart from your kin."

"Or foolishness," Caelan had replied, the corner of his mouth lifting in a humorless smile.

"Perhaps both," the boy acknowledged. "But I would rather have one courageous fool than a hundred cautious wise men."

And so the inner circle had been born, and now after many moons were as though brothers.

That evening, as the first stars pricked the darkening sky, the boy called his chosen few to the inner circle of ancient stones where the Heart pulsed most strongly. They gathered in silence—Alasdair of the Highlands, Eira of the Selkie courts, Caelan of the deep rivers, and Maelis, his first guardian and guide.

The boy stood at the center, no longer feeling like the child who had awakened to prophecy mere weeks before. The weight of their expectations should have crushed him, yet somehow it steadied him instead.

"We stand at the threshold of change," he began, his young voice carrying in the still evening air. "The old hatreds run deep. The darkness gathers strength. But together, we represent all that could be—river and sea, earth and humanity, united not by force but by choice."

The silver creature on his shoulder sang softly, its melody weaving through his words like silver thread through cloth.

"I cannot promise victory," the boy continued. "I cannot even promise survival. But I can promise purpose—a chance to heal what has been broken, to forge bonds stronger than the darkness that seeks to divide us."

Alasdair was the first to move. Kneeling, he pressed his hand to the earth. "By my blood and my breath, by the bones of my ancestors and the dreams of my children, I renew and swear loyalty to you and to the cause of healing."

Eira stepped forward next, her movements fluid as water. She knelt and placed her hand over her heart. "By the tides that bore me, by the songs of my people and the depths we call home, I lend you my strength and my sight."

Caelan hesitated before approaching. When he finally knelt, his movements were stiff, as though unaccustomed to such gestures. "By the rivers that shaped me," he said, his voice low and rough, "by the currents that run in my veins, I again vow to fight at your side until the waters run clear or I return to them in death."

Maelis was the last. She placed one hand on the boy's shoulder and the other on the ground beneath them. "By the old magic that binds all things," she murmured, "by the wisdom of ages and the hope of renewal, I guard your path and guide your steps."

The boy closed his eyes, feeling the weight of their vows settle around him—not as chains, but as a framework within which something new could be built.

The Heart of the Loch pulsed once, deeply, the sensation reverberating through stone and water and bone alike.

The Circle was solid as granite stone, formed in combat.

And in that moment, though none could have named how or why, the world shifted on its axis—a small change, imperceptible to most, but profound in its implications. The first tremor of a coming earthquake.

Chapter 30: First Steps into the Wider World

Dawn arrived with a sign that none could misinterpret. For as long as living memory stretched, the mists had enshrouded the Heart of the Loch, hiding its secrets from prying eyes. This morning, they parted like a curtain drawn back, revealing distant hills and forests that had remained hidden for generations.

"It's time," Maelis said quietly, finding the boy standing at the edge of the water, watching the mist retreat. "The Heart has awakened fully. It will not be contained any longer."

The boy nodded, feeling both terrified and strangely calm. "Neither will I."

By midday, preparations were complete. The Circle gathered at the great stone ring that marked the boundary between the Heart's domain and the wider world. Around them, warriors of river and mountain and sea waited in respectful silence, their faces solemn with the knowledge that once this threshold was crossed, there would be no returning to what had been before.

The boy stood atop the center stone—ancient granite, worn smooth by time and water, etched with symbols whose meanings had been forgotten by all but a few. The pendant that had been with him since birth—the Heart itself—pulsed gently against his chest, no longer a distant whisper but a constant companion.

"Are you certain of this path?" Maelis asked quietly, her eyes searching his face. "Once begun, it cannot be undone."

"I'm not certain of anything," the boy admitted. "Except that waiting will only give the darkness more time to spread."

Alasdair approached, his weathered face set in determined lines. "My scouts bring troubling news. The darkness has taken root in several of the western clans. They speak of their warlord Duncan who promises power over the waters to those who pledge themselves to him."

"Duncan," the boy repeated, the name tasting bitter on his tongue. "He serves the deeper darkness, whether he knows it or not."

"We cannot face him directly," Caelan warned, his voice sharp with tension. "Not yet. His forces outnumber ours, and many of my kin have been corrupted to his cause."

"We go first to gather strength," the boy agreed. "To Loch Ness, as planned." Strategically, Simon had already returned to Loch Ness to make ready for battle.

Eira stepped forward, her fingers absently stroking the sealskin draped over her shoulders. "The journey itself will be perilous. The old paths between the waters are treacherous, and not all who dwell along them remember the ancient pacts."

"Let them come," Caelan growled, a fierce light kindling in his stone-gray eyes. "Let them test our resolve."

The boy looked at each of them in turn—these four who had pledged themselves to him, who had placed their faith in a prophecy and a child. He saw their fear, their doubt, their determination. Most of all, he saw their hope, fragile but unquenchable.

"We won't seek conflict," he said firmly. "But neither will we hide from it. Our purpose is healing, not conquest."

He drew the Heart from beneath his cloak. Once a simple pendant of indeterminate metal, it now pulsed with its own light—not gold, not silver, but something deeper and more ancient, the glow of a memory older than human reckoning.

"The Heart is not a weapon," Maelis cautioned, her voice barely above a whisper. "It is a covenant. A bond between all waters, all lands, all peoples. If you call upon its full power, it will not fight for you—it will fight through you."

"And it will take from you as much as it gives," Caelan added, his expression grim. "That is the nature of such power. Balance must be maintained."

The boy nodded slowly. "I understand."

"Do you?" Maelis pressed, her eyes intent. "To bind the waters and the lands together is to bind yourself to them for all time. There will be no simple life for you afterward. No quiet hearth, no peaceful old age."

For a moment, doubt flickered in the boy's heart. He thought of Brannach and Nerina, of the promise they had made—a future carved not by violence but by choice. Was he betraying that promise by embracing this destiny?

As if sensing his thoughts, the silver creature on his shoulder trilled softly, the sound carrying notes of both sorrow and fierce joy.

"Some choices bind us," Alasdair said gently. "But they also free us to become what we were always meant to be."

The boy met his gaze, finding unexpected understanding there. He drew a deep breath and placed the Heart upon the center stone.

For several heartbeats, nothing happened.

Then the stones began to hum—a vibration so low it seemed to rise from the earth itself. The waters of the Loch shivered, rings spreading outward though no wind disturbed the surface.

The remaining mist thickened, coiling upward in spiraling tendrils that wrapped around the stones, the boy, the Circle. Symbols carved deep into the ancient rocks—forgotten by living memory—flared to life, threads of light racing outward from the Heart like veins of fire.

The boy placed both hands upon the stone, and pain lanced through him—not physical pain, but something deeper, as though his very soul were being stretched and reforged. Visions flooded his mind: ancient rivers carving their paths through newborn mountains; Selkies dancing beneath moonlight before human eyes had ever witnessed their grace; Highland warriors raising blades against a tide of shadow that threatened to devour all light.

The Heart showed him everything it had witnessed through ages uncounted. It showed him the price of the path he had chosen. And it offered him one last chance to turn back.

"I accept," he whispered, pressing his palms harder against the stone. "Whatever the cost, I accept."

Light exploded outward, a torrent of energy surging into the Loch, the rivers, the stones themselves. The ground trembled. Waters rose and fell. The assembled warriors cried out, shielding their eyes from the blinding radiance.

The boy felt himself unraveling, consciousness scattering like mist before a gale—and then, just as suddenly, he was whole again.

Changed.

When the light faded, the Heart hovered just above his chest, its glow steady, its pulse matching the rhythm of his own heart perfectly.

The boy looked to the hills where danger waited—where Duncan gathered his forces, where the deeper darkness festered unseen.

"We go now," he said, voice steady despite the power thrumming through him. "But not as conquerors. We go as healers, as bridge-builders, as keepers of a promise too long forgotten."

They departed as the sun began its westward descent, following ancient paths that wound through dense woodland and misty glens. Everywhere, the land seemed to whisper—sometimes welcoming, sometimes warning, but always alive with meaning that the boy was only beginning to understand.

As twilight gathered, they made camp beside a small spring whose waters sang a melody older than human speech. The boy sat apart from the others, watching the flames of their modest fire dance against the gathering darkness, feeling the currents of destiny tightening around him.

"Are you afraid?" Eira asked, settling beside him with the fluid grace of her kind.

"Yes," he admitted without shame. "But not of what lies ahead."

"What then?"

He considered her question carefully. "I'm afraid of becoming something I was never meant to be. Of losing myself in this power, this purpose."

Eira's gaze was steady. "That fear will keep you true," she said softly. "Hold to it. Let it guide you when the path grows dark."

Before he could respond, Alasdair approached, his expression grave. "Something stirs in the woods beyond our camp," he warned quietly. "Caelan has gone to scout, but I fear our journey will face its first test sooner than we had hoped."

The boy nodded, rising to his feet. The Heart pulsed against his chest, resonating with the unseen threat that approached through the gathering shadows.

The first true challenge of their journey was upon them—and with it, the first test of the Circle's strength and the boy's resolve.

Chapter 31: Shadows at the Crossroads

Morning broke heavy with mist, the air sharp with the distant bite of mountain snow. The boy woke before the others, watching his breath cloud in the pale light. The spring where they had camped now gurgled softly behind them, a whispered farewell as they prepared to continue their journey deeper into lands both ancient and perilous.

"Did you sleep?" Maelis asked, appearing silently beside him. Her weathered face showed concern as she studied his features.

The boy shook his head. "The Heart wouldn't let me. It... sings in my dreams. Shows me things."

"What things?" Maelis pressed gently, handing him a small wooden cup filled with a steaming herbal infusion.

The boy took a grateful sip before answering. "Memories that aren't mine. A war fought long ago. Rivers running black with hatred. And something else... something waiting." He looked up at her, his young face solemn. "Something I'm meant to face."

"The burden of prophecy," Maelis sighed, settling beside him. "It never comes with clear instructions."

"Would be easier if it did," the boy said with a wry smile that made him look suddenly older than his years.

By midday, their small company had reached a place where the path divided. Three ancient stones marked the junction, each taller than a man and worn smooth by countless seasons. Three paths stretched outward from this point: one winding through dense woodland shadows, another skirting the edge of a wide marsh where mist hung perpetually, and the third—steep and narrow—climbing toward the highland peaks.

Alasdair knelt by the central stone, his fingers tracing patterns in the lichen-covered surface. "This is Triad Crossing," he murmured. "A place older than clan memory. In better days, the peoples of river and hill would meet here under truce to settle disputes and renew alliances."

"And now?" the boy asked, sensing the unspoken warning in Alasdair's tone.

"Now it is as often a place of ambush as parley." Alasdair's expression darkened. "The old ways have been forgotten by many."

Eira moved silently to the edge of their group, her posture suddenly tense. "We are watched," she whispered, her eyes scanning the mist. "Many eyes. Not all friendly."

The boy felt it too—a prickling at the base of his neck, a subtle shift in the currents of the world around him. The Heart pulsed once against his chest, warm and warning.

"How many?" Caelan asked, his voice low as he loosened his blade in its sheath.

"Enough," Eira replied grimly. "They've been tracking us since dawn."

Caelan's expression hardened. "Better to meet them head-on than wait for a dagger in the dark," he growled, drawing his weapon with a soft hiss of steel against leather.

"Wait," the boy commanded, stepping forward. "We didn't come seeking battle."

"Battle has a way of finding those who carry destiny," Maelis murmured beside him, her fingers weaving subtle patterns in the air— protections and warnings, woven of magic more ancient than the stones themselves.

From the shadows of the woodland path, figures began to emerge. They wore the colors and tartans of Highland clans, but their faces were hard, their eyes wary and suspicious. Some carried longbows with arrows nocked but not yet drawn; others gripped swords or axes.

At their head rode a man whose presence commanded attention. His hair was the color of rusted iron, his beard cropped close to a face weathered by wind and war. A scar slashed down his right cheek, puckering the skin into a permanent sneer. His eyes, though—sharp and calculating—missed nothing.

Alasdair rose slowly, placing himself between the boy and the newcomers. His posture remained deliberately relaxed, but the boy noticed how his hand rested casually near his sword hilt.

"Name yourself," Alasdair called, his voice carrying easily across the clearing.

The leader reined in his horse, regarding them with open suspicion. He spat onto the ground between them—not quite an insult, but certainly not a greeting of respect.

"Duncan MacAuley," he replied, his voice rough as stone against stone. "And you tread dangerous ground, Fraser. These are troubled times to be crossing clan territories with such... unusual companions." His gaze flicked meaningfully toward Eira and Caelan before settling on the boy.

"We seek only passage to Loch Ness," Alasdair responded evenly. "Our business there concerns matters beyond clan disputes."

Duncan's mouth twisted into something that wasn't quite a smile. "Aye, so I've heard. Word travels fast in the Highlands, Fraser. Some say the old magic stirs again." His gaze sharpened on the boy. "Some say a child of river and sea walks the land, carrying powers that should have remained buried."

The boy stepped forward, feeling the Heart warm against his skin. The silver creature on his shoulder gave a soft, musical trill that seemed to make the very air vibrate.

"I am no child," he said quietly, but with a certainty that silenced the murmurs among Duncan's men. "And I walk where fate calls me."

Duncan leaned forward in his saddle, studying the boy with narrowed eyes. "Magic breeds trouble," he said flatly. "And we have enough trouble already. The clans are divided. Strange sicknesses poison the lakes. The very seasons seem turned against us."

"Perhaps that is why I am here," the boy replied.

An uncomfortable silence fell over the crossroads. The boy could sense the clash of forces—fear warring with curiosity, suspicion battling against ancient memory and half-forgotten prophecy.

One of Duncan's men, a burly warrior with elaborate knotwork tattoos covering his forearms, stepped forward. "The old stories speak of a time when the waters would rise against us," he said, voice tight with suspicion. "When creatures of river and sea would reclaim what was once theirs."

"Is that what you come for, boy?" Duncan asked. "To drown our lands and drive us from our homes?"

"No," the boy answered simply. "I come to heal what was broken. To bind what was sundered."

"Pretty words," Duncan scoffed. "But words are wind."

Alasdair stepped forward then, his voice resonating with quiet authority. "The Frasers remember the old oaths, Duncan MacAuley. We stand with him, as our ancestors swore to do. The waters and the land were never meant to war against each other." His eyes hardened. "Will you stand against us, against the ancient bonds, for fear of shadows and whispered threats?"

Duncan's men shifted uneasily, exchanging glances. The burly warrior with the tattoos muttered something that sounded like an old blessing—or perhaps a ward against evil.

Duncan himself seemed to wrestle with forces older than clan hatred or personal pride. His scarred face worked through conflicting emotions before settling into grim resignation.

"Pass, then," he finally said, throwing up a hand in reluctant permission. "But know this—others will not be so forgiving. The farther north you travel, the deeper the suspicions run." He leaned forward, lowering his voice. "And there are those who actively seek your destruction, boy. Those who whisper promises of power to any who will bring them your head."

"Do you speak of yourself, MacAuley?" Caelan challenged, his stance still combat-ready.

Duncan's gaze flickered to the Kelpie warrior. "If I sought your deaths, you would not have seen me coming." He straightened in his saddle. "No, I speak of others. Those who believe the old balance must be maintained—with blood if necessary."

The boy inclined his head. "Thank you for the warning," he said. "And for allowing us passage."

Duncan gave a curt nod. "We'll make camp here tonight. You'd best be continuing your march until morning." With that, he wheeled his horse around and barked orders to his men, who began establishing a perimeter around the crossroads.

As the boy and his companions gathered their belongings and chose the northern path that would lead them toward Loch Ness, Maelis fell into step beside him.

"Duncan MacAuley is a shrewd enemy," she murmured, "and he believes we do not know it was him hidden beneath that battle mask when last we met. This subterfuge bodes ill, he is luring us with tolerance when he means violence. Remember what I told you—trust not in blood alone, nor in old alliances. Trust only in the waters, and in your own heart."

The boy nodded, feeling the weight of her words. "We dealt him a painful defeat in our battle, one that cost him many men both in body and spirit. He is using time to rebuild the strength of his army."

The first steps have been taken," he said quietly. "But the true journey is only beginning."

Eira, walking ahead, looked back over her shoulder. "And the storm gathers with every step we take," she added, her eyes reflecting the gathering clouds above.

Chapter 33: Gathering Storms

The days grew harsher as they pressed northward. Bitter winds howled down from the mountains, carrying with them the scent of distant fires and the iron tang of blood. The mists thickened until even Alasdair, born to these highlands, found the familiar paths transformed into treacherous puzzles.

"The land itself resists us," he muttered one evening, nursing a hand cut open when a stone shifted unexpectedly beneath his grip. "It's as though the very hills have turned suspicious."

"Not the hills," Maelis corrected, applying a pungent salve to his wound. "Something deeper. Something that has poisoned the connection between water and earth."

The boy sat apart from them, watching the thin flames of their meager fire dance against the gathering darkness. In the days since leaving the crossroads, he had grown quieter, more focused. Though he rarely gave commands, his presence had become unmistakably that of a leader. The Heart pulsed continuously now, a steady rhythm that matched his own heartbeat so precisely he sometimes forgot it hadn't always been part of him.

"You've changed," Caelan observed, settling beside him with uncharacteristic gentleness. The Kelpie warrior usually kept to himself, maintaining a careful distance from the others.

The boy glanced up. "Have I?"

Caelan nodded. "You walk differently. Speak differently." His stone-gray eyes studied the boy. "Your river runs deeper now."

"Is that a good thing?" the boy asked, genuinely curious.

Caelan was silent for a long moment. "Power changes all it touches," he finally said. "Whether for good or ill depends on the vessel that contains it."

"And what do you see in me?" the boy pressed.

A rare half-smile crossed the Kelpie's face. "A surprisingly sturdy vessel. But even the strongest container can crack under enough pressure."

Before the boy could respond, Alasdair approached, his broad face tight with concern.

"We should move," he said quietly. "I don't like the signs I'm reading in the hills. Too many watchers, too many shadows moving against the wind. Duncan was at least honest that his men would camp the night."

"How far to Loch Ness?" the boy asked.

"Another day's journey if we push hard. But the path grows steeper, and the hidden ways I know are... changing." Frustration edged Alasdair's voice. "It's as though the land remembers paths I've forgotten, or never knew."

The boy stood, brushing earth from his clothes. "Then we'll follow where the Heart leads. It knows the way, even if we don't."

"A dangerous proposition," Maelis warned, joining their circle. "The Heart is ancient and powerful, but not always... precise in its guidance."

"We have little choice," the boy replied. "If the known paths are watched, we must find unknown ones."

Having put sufficient distance between them and the still weakened forces of Duncan MacAuley, they had bedded down for the night. Except one, for as the others slept, the boy stood watch, staring out into the impenetrable Highland mist. The silver creature perched on his shoulder, its melodic trills so soft they seemed to come from within his own mind.

"What are you trying to tell me?" he whispered to it.

In answer, the creature leapt from his shoulder, gliding a short distance before landing on a rocky outcrop. It turned back, waiting.

The boy followed, careful not to wake the others. The creature led him to a small hollow between two weathered boulders. There, protected from the wind, a tiny pool of water had gathered, its surface eerily still despite the gusting night air.

The creature trilled once more, then dipped one delicate silver foot into the water.

The pool's surface rippled, then stilled again. But now, reflected in its depths, the boy saw not stars but fires—dozens of them, dotting a dark landscape beside a vast body of water.

"Loch Ness," he breathed. "The clans are gathering."

The image shifted, showing faces illuminated by firelight—some familiar from his visions, others strange to him. Arguments, alliances, ancient feuds and fresh wounds—all played out in silent tableau within the tiny pool.

"They prepare for war," he realized, his heart sinking. "Not against some external threat, but against each other... and against those like me."

The silver creature withdrew its foot, and the vision faded, leaving only star reflections dancing on dark water.

"Thank you," the boy whispered, understanding the warning he had been given.

When morning came, he shared what he had seen with the others. Their faces grew grim, but no one questioned the vision's truth.

"Then we must hurry," Eira said, her usual lightness replaced by fierce determination. "Before blood is spilled that cannot be unshed."

They traveled hard that day, following paths that seemed to appear beneath their feet only as they stepped forward—ancient ways revealed by the Heart's guidance. Alasdair led them across swift streams where stepping stones had been laid generations ago, beneath arches of living trees that had grown together over centuries, and through narrow passes where the wind spoke in tongues forgotten by all but the oldest spirits.

It was nearing dusk when they crested a high ridge and caught their first glimpse of Loch Ness—a vast, dark mirror stretching between towering hills, its waters so deep and still they seemed to swallow the fading light rather than reflect it.

"The deepest loch in all the Highlands," Alasdair murmured with pride and reverence. "Some say it has no bottom. That it reaches down to the very heart of the world."

"They're not entirely wrong," Caelan said quietly. "There are passages beneath it that lead to places no human has ever seen."

Eira moved to the edge of the ridge, her keen eyes scanning the landscape below. "The clans have indeed gathered," she reported, pointing to a broad hollow near the loch's eastern shore.

Below, tents and makeshift shelters dotted the ground like a strange crop sprung suddenly from the earth. Campfires flickered like fallen stars, their smoke rising in thin columns to join the mist. Warriors moved through the gathering gloom, their clan tartans creating a patchwork of colors and loyalties. Some bore the Fraser stag, but many displayed crests and colors unfamiliar to the boy.

"Not all have come with peace in their hearts," Maelis observed, her eyes narrowing as she surveyed the scene. "I sense fear. Anger. Old grudges awakened."

"Then we shall show them what hearts bound by river and sea can do," Caelan said, his hand resting on his blade hilt.

"No," the boy said firmly. "We didn't come to fight. We came to unite."

Alasdair motioned for them to gather closer, his voice low. "We cannot simply march into their midst. Not yet. We must send a herald, declare our intent. Otherwise, we risk being met with drawn steel before a single word is spoken."

The boy considered this, then nodded. "I will go."

A chorus of protests rose from his companions.

"Absolutely not," Maelis said sharply. "You are the Heart-bearer. To risk you now—"

"Is necessary," the boy finished for her. "They must see me. Not just hear about me through legend or rumor. They must know who I am—and who stands with me."

He placed a hand over the pendant at his chest, drawing strength from its steady pulse. "If we are to change the world," he said quietly, "we must first show them we are unafraid to face it as it is."

Alasdair studied him for a long moment, then gave a grim nod. "Then we go together. As a Circle. As one."

"As it should be," Eira agreed, a fierce smile lighting her face.

As the sun sank behind the mountains, bleeding its last light into the dark waters of the loch, the boy and his Circle descended toward the gathering of clans. The Heart beat steadily against his chest, stronger with each step.

And above them, unseen save by the oldest of spirits, ancient powers circled, their songs weaving strength into every footfall, preparing the way for what must come next.

The tides of fate had indeed come to the Highlands. And they would leave nothing unchanged in their wake.

Chapter 34: The Voice of the Heart

The boy felt the weight of hundreds of eyes upon him as he and his Circle entered the hollow where the clans had gathered. Their approach had not gone unnoticed; a ripple of awareness spread through the encampment like wind across water. Conversations stilled mid-sentence. Heads turned. The haunting music of the Highland pipes faltered into uneasy silence.

"Keep walking," Alasdair murmured beside him. "Show no hesitation."

"Head high," Eira added softly. "You are not a supplicant here."

"And keep your hand away from the Heart," Maelis cautioned. "Some might take it as a threat."

Caelan said nothing, but his presence at the boy's left shoulder was reassurance enough—solid as stone, watchful as a predator.

At the center of the gathering stood a rough-hewn stone altar, ancient beyond reckoning. Its surface was worn smooth by countless seasons, marked with symbols whose meanings had been lost to all but a handful of living souls. Around it, the chieftains of the Highland clans had assembled—grizzled warriors whose scars told tales of countless battles, shrewd matriarchs whose eyes missed nothing, proud young lords eager to carve their names into legend.

The boy recognized fear in their expressions. Suspicion. Curiosity. And in some, a desperate, fragile hope they dared not acknowledge even to themselves.

When they reached the edge of the circle surrounding the altar, Alasdair stepped forward. His voice rang clear in the cold evening air, carrying to every corner of the hollow.

"Sons and daughters of the Highlands! Blood of the ancient covenant! I, Alasdair Fraser, stand before you to fulfill an oath sworn by my ancestors when the world was young. I bring before you one who bears the mark of the Heart, who carries the blood of river and sea in equal measure, who stands as bridge between worlds too long divided!"

Murmurs rose like the shifting of storm clouds. The boy heard snatches of conversation, fragments of argument and disbelief.

"—just a boy—" "—old prophecies best left forgotten—" "—Fraser always were dreamers—" "—but look at his companions—"

A tall chieftain with a streak of white in his dark beard rose from his place. The silver boar's head clasp on his shoulder marked him as head of Clan Campbell. "Fine words, Fraser," he called, his voice carrying the authority of one accustomed to command. "But what proof do you offer that this boy is anything more than a clever mascot for your ambitions?"

Before Alasdair could respond, a woman's voice cut through the gathering tension. "Are you blind, Dougal Campbell, or merely forgetful? Aye there is no good blood between the Campbells and the Frasers, but at least you know them to be honest men."

The crowd parted as an elderly woman made her way forward. Though stooped with age, she moved with purpose, leaning on a staff of polished blackthorn. Her face was a map of wrinkles, but her eyes—bright and keen as a hawk's—fixed on the boy with disconcerting intensity.

"I am Sarah MacLachlan," she announced, "keeper of the old stories, last of the true bards. And I have waited ninety winters to see this day."

She approached the boy without hesitation, studying his face. Then, with surprising swiftness, she reached out and placed her withered hand directly over the Heart.

A gasp went up from the gathered clans as a pulse of soft light bloomed beneath her palm.

"The mark is true," she said, her voice carrying strange harmonics that seemed to echo from stone and water alike. "The blood is true." She looked up into the boy's eyes. "But are you true, child of two worlds? Are you worthy of the burden you bear?"

The boy met her gaze steadily. "I don't know," he answered honestly. "But I am willing to try."

Sarah held his gaze for a long moment, then nodded once, satisfied. She turned to address the assembled clans.

"Our grandmothers' grandmothers spoke of this day," she said. "When the Heart would return to heal the rift between water and stone, between ancient enemies. When the blood of both would flow in a single vessel." Her voice hardened. "Will you turn your backs on prophecy now that it stands before you?"

"Prophecy is a dangerous thing to trust," another chieftain called out—a heavyset man wearing the MacAuley colors. "Especially in times like these, when strange sicknesses poison our waters and unknown threats gather at our borders."

"Aye," added a fierce-looking woman wearing the plaid of Clan Fraser, though her expression suggested no kinship with Alasdair. "How do we know this boy isn't the cause of our troubles rather than their solution? The timing is suspicious, at best."

The boy stepped forward then, feeling the moment balance on a knife's edge. He wore no armor, carried no sword. Only the pendant of the Heart shone at his chest, and the silver creature perched quietly on his shoulder, watching all with eyes that reflected the firelight like twin stars.

"I understand your fear," he said, his young voice somehow carrying to every ear. "Fear of change. Fear of the unknown. Fear that trusting the wrong person could bring destruction to all you hold dear."

He paused, looking around the circle of faces.

"I am not here to command," he continued. "Nor to conquer. I come because the old wounds still bleed. Because the rivers run sick, and the seas churn with sorrow. Because the hatred between our peoples has left the world broken."

A chieftain wearing a wolf's head brooch rose from his place by the fire. "Fine words, boy," he growled, "but words will not heal what has been torn for generations. My grandfather's grandfather died with Kelpie spears in his belly. My cousin's children sickened last spring after bathing in a river we'd trusted for centuries."

Others called out agreement, voices rising in a tide of centuries-old grievances and fresh suspicions.

The boy waited for the noise to subside, neither flinching nor attempting to speak over the outcry.

When relative quiet returned, he nodded. "You're right," he said. "Words alone will not heal such wounds. But neither will swords, nor hatred, nor hiding behind ancient walls while the world drowns in darkness."

He turned slowly, addressing them all.

"We are children of the same waters, whether born on land or in the depths. The time has come to remember that. To fight not each other, but the darkness that would consume us all."

"Pretty speech," muttered a young chieftain near the back. "But what exactly are you asking of us? To lay down our weapons? To trust creatures who have hunted our children for sport?"

Caelan stepped forward, his face tight with controlled anger. "And how many of my kin have died on human spears? How many Selkie skins have been stolen and burned? The blame flows both ways."

The hollow erupted again, accusations flying, old hatreds bubbling to the surface like poison from a festering wound.

"Enough!" The boy's voice cut through the cacophony, amplified not by volume but by something deeper—a resonance that seemed to vibrate in bone and blood alike.

Silence fell, abrupt and complete.

The boy placed his hand over his heart, and the pendant began to glow, casting a gentle light that illuminated his features from below.

"I am the legacy of sacrifice," he said quietly. "The child of river and sea. I offer my hand—not as a ruler, but as a bridge."

He took a deep breath.

"Tomorrow at noon, I will stand upon the Calling Stones at the heart of Loch Ness. Those who wish to see the truth of who I am—and what I offer—may meet me there. Those who prefer to cling to ancient hatreds may stay away. The choice is yours."

For a long moment, silence reigned.

Then Sarah, the old storyteller, stepped forward once more. From beneath her cloak, she pulled a faded banner—its colors dimmed by age but still recognizable as an ancient sigil of intertwined river and wave.

"The tides do not turn at a boy's command," she rasped, "but they do heed the pull of the moon. And the moon, as all know, governs both river and sea alike."

She raised the banner high.

"I remember the old songs," she declared. "The true songs, not the pale shadows we sing today. And I will stand with the Heart-bearer."

One by one, others began to move—some tentatively, others with growing conviction. A young woman from Clan MacLachlan approached and knelt briefly before the boy. "My brother drowned last spring," she said softly. "If you can prevent others from sharing his fate, I stand with you."

An old warrior with the Campbell colors limped forward. "I've lived long enough to know that the old ways are sometimes the truest," he said gruffly. "My sword is yours, if your cause is just."

Not all pledged allegiance. Some turned away, muttering darkly, retreating into the shadows that gathered at the edges of the firelight. Others watched with calculating eyes, withholding judgment until they could see what advantage might be gained—or what threat might be neutralized.

As the initial surge of declarations subsided, Alasdair stepped close to the boy's side. "You've made a beginning," he murmured. "But the hardest part lies ahead. The Calling Stones are sacred ground—and dangerous. The waters there run deep and swift."

"I know," the boy replied quietly. "The Heart has shown me."

Eira joined them, her expression both proud and concerned. "You speak of standing on the Calling Stones, but those stones haven't risen from the loch in living memory. They lie beneath the waters, hidden from human eyes."

The boy nodded. "They will rise for me."

Sarah, overhearing, gave a soft chuckle that turned into a wheezing cough. "Bold words," she said when she had recovered. "But if anyone can wake the stones, it would be you." She fixed him with her hawk-like gaze. "Just remember, child—ancient powers answer to their own rules, not ours. Be certain you're prepared for what you summon."

As the gathering gradually returned to its previous activities—though with a new current of tension and anticipation running beneath the surface—the boy and his Circle withdrew to a small clearing at the edge of the hollow. There, sheltered by ancient pines, they made their camp for the night.

"You risked much with that declaration," Maelis said as they sat around their small fire. "The Calling Stones are not merely a place—they are a threshold between worlds. A covenant written in stone and water."

"I know," the boy replied, staring into the flames. "But we need something more powerful than words to overcome generations of hatred and mistrust. We need a sign that cannot be dismissed."

"And if the stones do not rise?" Caelan asked bluntly. "If the powers that be deem you unworthy?"

The boy was silent for a long moment. "Then I am not what the prophecy promised," he finally said. "And we must find another way."

As the others drifted off to sleep, the boy remained awake, staring up at the stars that wheeled overhead. The Heart pulsed steadily against his chest, its rhythm matching the distant surge and retreat of the loch's dark waters.

Tomorrow would bring either a new beginning or a bitter end to their journey. He could only hope that the legacy he carried in his blood would prove strong enough for what lay ahead.

The Highlands would not change in a day. But tonight, by the shores of Loch Ness, the future had begun to stir. Whether it would rise like the Calling Stones or sink beneath the weight of ancient hatreds remained to be seen.

Chapter 35: Seeds of Rebellion

The dawn after the gathering rose chill and bright, a sharp wind clearing the mists from the loch. Sunlight spilled across the water in pale gold sheets, illuminating the ripples and eddies that marked the passage of unseen creatures beneath the surface. High above, an eagle circled—watchful, patient, borne aloft on currents only it could sense.

Where uncertainty had hovered the night before, now there was purpose—a fledgling alliance forged not by blood alone, but by choice. The encampment had transformed overnight, reorganizing itself around this new reality. Tents that had been rigorously separated by clan now intermingled. Banners that had once proclaimed ancient rivalries now flew side by side, the morning breeze tangling their colors together as if in foreshadowing.

The boy watched from the edge of the camp, the Heart warm against his skin. He could sense the currents of change, feel the subtle shift in loyalties and alliances. Some were drawn to him out of genuine belief, others from calculated self-interest, still others from simple curiosity. He accepted them all, knowing that unity began with small steps before it could become a tide.

Yet not all had accepted his offer. In the dark woods beyond the encampment, whispers brewed like storm clouds.

Among the muttering clans who had turned away, a hard core of dissidents formed—men and women who saw the boy not as a bridge between worlds, but as a threat to the old order. They had tasted power through division and would not easily surrender it to a vision of peace.

Their leader was Duncan MacAuley, the scarred chieftain who had once granted passage at the crossroads. His pride, wounded by the boy's calm strength, festered into something darker. There was history there that the boy did not yet understand—ancient grievances and personal losses that had shaped Duncan into the bitter opponent he had become.

In a clearing far from prying eyes, Duncan gathered his most trusted allies. The sunlight barely penetrated the dense canopy overhead, casting the meeting in perpetual twilight. Moss-covered stones formed a rough circle—an abandoned druid site, long forgotten by all but the most dedicated keepers of the old ways.

Gathered around a hidden fire, he spoke in low, urgent tones to the dozen chieftains and warriors who had answered his summons. Their faces were grim in the flickering light, marked by scars both visible and hidden.

"The boy carries magic not meant for mortal hands," Duncan hissed, his voice tight with controlled fury. "I have consulted the ancient texts—the forbidden ones, kept hidden from meddling eyes. The Heart he bears was not a gift but a theft—stolen from the depths by his ancestors in an act of war."

Murmurs circled the gathering, faces darkening with suspicion and fear.

"The old women speak of unity and healing," he continued, spitting into the fire. "But what they do not say is the price of such unity. The Heart demands sacrifice—blood sacrifice. Our blood. Our children's blood."

"How can you be certain?" asked a wary chieftain from Clan Ross, her hand instinctively moving to the hilt of her knife. "The boy speaks with conviction, and the MacLachlan woman is known for her wisdom."

"Wisdom?" Duncan scoffed. "Or madness? She is ancient beyond her years—who knows what bargains she has made to extend her life so unnaturally?

He rose, pacing the circle, his shadow thrown huge and distorted against the trees by the firelight. "He would upend the world we have bled to defend. If we do not act, the Highlands will be ruled by sorcery—and we will be ruled by him."

A young warrior from Clan MacPherson leaned forward, his face eager in the firelight. "What would you have us do, then? Strike now, while they are distracted with preparations?"

Duncan shook his head. "No. The boy is too well protected for a direct assault. And killing him outright would only make him a martyr to their cause." His smile was cold as winter frost. "We must discredit him first. Make the clans see him for what he truly is—a threat, not a savior."

"And how will we manage that?" asked an older woman whose plaid marked her as a member of Clan Fraser—one of the dissidents who had broken from Alasdair's leadership.

Duncan's smile widened, showing teeth. "The boy is calling for allies among the Highland clans. He believes they will rise for him—a miracle to validate his claims." He chuckled, a sound devoid of mirth. "But what if the miracle turns to tragedy? What if those who gather at his invitation find not salvation but terror?"

Understanding dawned on the faces around him. One by one, they nodded grimly.

Plans were laid. Oaths were sworn—not of loyalty, but of rebellion. Maps were drawn in the dirt and quickly erased. Weapons were examined and redistributed. Messengers were dispatched to sympathetic clans who had not attended the gathering.

As the meeting drew to a close, Duncan raised a cup filled with dark liquid that smelled of herbs and iron.

"To the true Highlands," he intoned. "Free of abomination. Free of compromise."

"The true Highlands," they echoed, drinking deep.

None noticed the small creature that clung to the shadows of a nearby tree—silver-scaled and silent, its luminous eyes taking in every detail of the secret council before slipping away to return to its master.

Meanwhile, at the heart of the loyal encampment, the boy and his Circle moved swiftly. The revelation of Duncan's treachery had not come as a complete surprise; they had suspected resistance would organize. But the scale and vehemence of the opposition was concerning.

Messengers were dispatched to distant lochs and glens, carrying invitations to those clans yet undecided. The boy had spent hours crafting these messages, each one personalized to address the specific concerns and histories of the recipient clan. Alasdair had taught him the importance of such details—how a remembered ancestor's name or an acknowledged deed could open doors that would otherwise remain firmly closed.

"Words are weapons and bridges both," the old warrior had told him, guiding his hand as he pressed the clan sigil into warm wax. "Choose them with the same care you would a blade or a foundation stone."

Smiths set to work forging new banners—ones bearing the sigil of river and sea united. The metalwork was intricate, requiring the combined skills of highland craftsmen and water-folk artisans. The boy watched as a burly smith with arms like tree trunks worked alongside a slender river-woman whose fingers moved with impossible delicacy, weaving strands of metal as though they were reeds. Neither would have spoken to the other a week earlier; now they exchanged techniques in hushed, reverent tones, each marveling at the other's skill.

"See how they learn from one another?" Maelis murmured, appearing silently at his side. "This is the first victory—small perhaps, but real. The sharing of knowledge long hoarded."

The boy nodded, hope flickering in his chest like the forge-fire before them. "Will it be enough?"

Maelis's expression turned grave. "Against what comes? I cannot say. But it is a beginning."

Eira trained scouts among the Selkies and Highlanders alike, teaching them the art of moving unseen, of listening to the whispers of the wind and water. Her methods were unorthodox by highland standards—focusing on patience and harmony with the environment rather than brute stealth.

"You do not conquer the land to move through it undetected," she explained to a skeptical group of young warriors. "You ask its permission. You become part of its song."

She demonstrated by seemingly vanishing before their eyes, though she had merely stepped behind a boulder. When she reappeared, the highlanders exchanged looks of grudging respect.

"The water-folk have survived among you for centuries," she continued. "Moving unseen when necessary. We can teach you these skills—if you are willing to set aside your pride and learn."

By midday, highland youths who had grown up on tales of Selkie treachery were practicing side by side with water-folk who had once feared human touch like poison. Their laughter mingled with the splash of the loch's waters—an unexpected harmony.

Caelan drilled the warriors who had pledged their swords, forging them into a force fierce and fluid, ready to defend not just the boy, but the fragile hope he represented. The massive highlander was a demanding teacher, accepting nothing less than absolute commitment.

"You think because water-folk are smaller, they are weaker?" he roared at a cocky young swordsman who had failed to take his water-born opponent seriously. "Size means nothing when your lungs are filled with water! Speed means nothing when the current turns against you! Learn to respect different strengths, or you'll die before you've drawn your second breath in battle!"

The warriors trained from dawn until dusk, muscles burning, weapons growing heavy in weary hands. But with each passing hour, their movements became more coordinated, their understanding of one another's strengths and weaknesses more nuanced. They were becoming something new—not quite highland warriors, not quite water-folk fighters, but something born of both traditions.

Alasdair moved among the clans, weaving a tapestry of alliances with quiet, stubborn grace. The Fraser chieftain had spent decades building relationships throughout the highlands; now he called in every favor, reminded allies of every oath, rekindled the embers of every old friendship. His white hair gleamed in the sunlight as he moved from fire to fire, sharing meals, exchanging stories, listening more than he spoke.

"My father fought alongside yours at the Battle of Glen Shiel," he would remind one chieftain. "We have been blood-allies for three generations." To another: "Did your clan not shelter mine during the Long Winter? The Frasers remember their debts." And to a third: "Your daughter's life was saved by river medicine when the fever took her. Would you now turn your back on the chance for lasting peace with those who helped you?"

Bit by bit, his patient diplomacy bore fruit. Clans that had been hesitant began to send representatives—first scouts, then warriors, then chieftains themselves. The camp grew, scattered fires coalescing into a single community.

Maelis watched over it all with wary eyes, sensing the undercurrents of betrayal gathering beyond the fires. The river-woman had lived longer than any human could guess, had seen alliances form and fracture like ice in spring thaw. She moved among the gathered forces like a shadow, listening, observing, occasionally whispering a warning in Alasdair's ear or redirecting a potential conflict before it could ignite.

One evening, as the boy stood gazing across the dark waters of Loch Ness, Maelis joined him. Twilight painted the surface of the water in shades of purple and gold, the distant mountains black silhouettes against a sky still flushed with the memory of sunset.

"The tides turn swiftly," she said, her voice barely above a whisper. A light mist rose from her skin, a sign of the deep water magic that ran in her veins. "I can feel them shifting beneath us all. But beware—it is not only the currents that shift."

The boy nodded. "I feel it."

He did—a tension in the air, a sense of forces gathering like storm clouds on the horizon. The Heart pulsed against his chest, its rhythm quickening as if in warning.

"Duncan's followers grow bolder," Maelis continued. "They move in the shadows, spreading whispers, sowing doubts. 'Why should we trust the water-folk after generations of conflict?' they ask. 'Why follow a boy who is neither fully of land nor of water?'"

"And what answer do they find?" the boy asked.

Maelis's eyes, reflecting the last light of day, seemed to darken. "Some resist their poison. Others drink it willingly. Fear is a powerful ally, and Duncan knows how to wield it."

She turned to face him fully, her expression grave beneath its usual serenity. "They will move against you soon. Perhaps not with open violence—not yet—but with something that may prove more dangerous."

"Doubt," the boy said. "They'll try to make the clans doubt me."

"Yes. And they will use the gathering at the Calling Stones as their opportunity."

The boy's hand moved to the Heart, feeling its steady pulse against his palm. "Then we must be ready."

"Then be ready," she said. "For soon you will face not the hatred of the past—but the fear of the present."

She reached out, briefly touching his shoulder—a gesture of rare physical affection from one who usually maintained careful distance. "Rest now. Tomorrow brings its own battles."

As she melted away into the gathering darkness, the boy remained at the water's edge, watching as the first stars appeared in the deepening sky. The silver creature emerged from hiding, climbing onto his shoulder and chirping softly in his ear.

"I know," he whispered to it. "I'm afraid too."

The creature nuzzled against his cheek, its touch cool and comforting.

The boy closed his eyes, feeling the pull of destiny like the tug of deep waters. Tomorrow they would journey to recruit more allies. Tomorrow he would either fulfill the prophecy or fail utterly. Tomorrow the future of the Highlands—of both peoples—would begin to take shape under his hands.

The seeds of rebellion had been sown. And soon, the storm would break.

Chapter 36: Breaking of the Storm

The pendant pulsed against the boy's chest, its uneven rhythm matching his restless heartbeat. Sleep had eluded him for hours, his mind too occupied with the weight of newfound responsibility. The fragile alliance formed just days ago felt both monumental and precarious.

"You should rest," Maelis had told him earlier, her weathered face softening with concern. "Leaders who do not sleep make poor decisions."

"And those who sleep too deeply miss the knife at their throat," he had replied, earning a rare smile from the old Selkie woman.

Now, alone in his tent, he traced the pendant's contours with his fingertips. The Heart of the Loch, they called it. A burden and a blessing both.

A sharp, acrid smell cut through his thoughts. Smoke—not the comforting scent of hearth fires, but the choking stench of destruction. He bolted upright just as the first screams tore through the night.

Maelis burst into the tent, her silver hair unbound and wild about her shoulders, her sealskin cloak trailing mist that seemed to cling to her like a second skin.

"They're here," she said, her voice unnaturally calm despite the chaos erupting outside. "Duncan MacAuley and his rebels."

The boy's fingers fumbled with the pendant chain. "How many?"

"Enough to make tonight memorable." Her eyes, black as deep water, held his. "Are you afraid?"

"Yes," he admitted, fastening the chain securely. "But fear doesn't matter now."

Outside, flames leapt skyward. The carefully crafted banners of unity—river and sea entwined—curled and blackened in the heat. Clansmen ran in all directions, some toward the fighting, others away from it, confusion ruling in those first terrible moments.

Alasdair Fraser's voice cut through the pandemonium. "Form ranks! To me, clansmen! To me!"

The aging warrior stood atop an overturned cart, his weathered face illuminated by the dancing flames, his claymore reflecting the firelight with deadly promise. His normally immaculate beard was singed on one side, but his eyes burned with clarity of purpose.

"The boy!" someone shouted. "Where is the boy?"

The boy stepped from his tent, and a hush fell over those nearest. Even in the chaos, his presence commanded attention—not from any imposing stature or battle scars, but from the calm certainty in his eyes.

Caelan materialized at his side, blood spattering his forearms and face. "They're coming for you," he said, his voice low and urgent. "Duncan himself leads them. He means to end this tonight."

"Does he?" The boy's voice remained steady even as his heart hammered against his ribs. "Where are Eira and the others?"

"Here," came a voice, and Eira slipped through the crowd, her hands glowing faintly blue with Selkie magic. Her normally braided hair hung in wild tangles, and a fresh cut marred her cheek. "The eastern flank is holding, but they're pressing hard from the north. Duncan brought more than we expected."

The boy nodded. "And how many of our own?"

"Not enough," Caelan answered grimly. "Not yet."

A harsh laugh cut through the air. "Not ever!"

Duncan MacAuley stood amid the flames, his scarred face twisted into a cruel mockery of a smile. A dozen men flanked him, their faces painted with woad and hatred.

"There he is," Duncan called, pointing a blood-stained dirk toward the boy. "The supposed savior! The one who would unite us all beneath his heel!"

The boy stepped forward, his Circle closing protectively around him. "I've never wished to rule, Duncan MacAuley. Only to heal what's been broken."

"Pretty words from a pretty mouth," Duncan spat. "But I've seen what your kind does with power. What your rivers did to my family when the floods came. What your Selkies did to our fishing grounds."

The boy's brow furrowed. "That was not my doing."

"No?" Duncan's eyes narrowed. "Then whose magic stirred the waters that drowned my sister? Whose tide pulled my brother's boat too far from shore?"

Murmurs rippled through the crowd. Even among the loyal, there were those who had lost loved ones to the unpredictable waters.

"I cannot change the past," the boy said, his voice carrying over the crackle of flames. "But I can offer a different future."

"The only future I want," Duncan growled, "is one where your kind knows its place!" He raised his sword high. "This ends tonight!"

He charged forward, and the battle erupted in earnest. Blades met with the screech of metal on metal. Selkie magic flashed blue and silver against the firelight. Clansmen fought clansmen, blood spilling onto the ancient earth that had seen too much of it already.

The boy stood at the center of the maelstrom, the pendant growing hot against his skin. He had never wanted this—never asked for blood to be shed in his name. But as Duncan's men pressed closer, he knew the time for regret had passed.

"Alasdair!" he called out, spotting the clan chief locked in combat with two of Duncan's men. "Hold them back!"

Alasdair roared and swung his claymore in a mighty arc, clearing space around him. "For how long, lad?"

The boy closed his eyes, feeling the pulse of the loch beyond the camp, the whisper of streams and rivers that fed it, the ancient magic that slumbered beneath the Highland soil.

"Just long enough," he answered, and thrust his hands toward the sky.

The pendant blazed with sudden, blinding light. The air grew heavy with moisture, and the ground beneath their feet trembled.

"What sorcery is this?" Duncan's voice cracked with fear as he stumbled backward.

Maelis watched the boy with ancient eyes. "Not sorcery," she murmured. "Birthright."

A wall of mist and water rose before them, towering twenty feet high. With a gesture from the boy, it crashed forward, sweeping rebels from their feet, dousing fires, creating chaos in the enemy ranks.

Duncan scrambled to his feet, wild-eyed. "Kill him!" he screamed at his followers. "Kill him now!"

But his men hesitated, terror plain on their faces as the boy called forth more water, more mist, drawing strength from depths even he had not known he possessed.

The boy's voice, when he spoke, seemed to come from everywhere and nowhere at once. "No more!"

The rebels faltered, weapons lowering. Several dropped to their knees, overwhelmed by the display of power.

Alasdair, seeing the turning tide, pressed forward with renewed vigor. "For the alliance!" he bellowed, and loyal clansmen echoed his cry.

Duncan, seeing his rebellion crumbling, let out a howl of rage and despair. He locked eyes with the boy across the battlefield—hatred meeting calm resolve—then turned and fled into the darkness, a handful of his most devoted followers trailing behind him.

Silence fell over the camp, broken only by the hiss of extinguished fires and the ragged breathing of the survivors.

The boy swayed on his feet, the pendant's light fading. Eira caught him before he could fall, her own strength nearly spent.

"It's over," she whispered.

"No," the boy said, looking toward the darkness where Duncan had vanished. "It's only beginning."

Chapter 36 (Continued): Aftermath

The battlefield lay silent under the pale light of dawn.

Where once the clash of steel and the roar of magic had filled the air, now there was only the whisper of the morning breeze through broken tent poles and charred banners. The boy moved slowly through the aftermath, his steps heavy with exhaustion and the burden of what had transpired.

Caelan fell into step beside him, his right arm bound tightly to his side with strips of linen already stained crimson.

"Twelve dead," he reported, his voice hollow. "Twenty-seven wounded. Five missing."

The boy nodded, absorbing the numbers, each one a weight upon his conscience. "And Duncan's men?"

"More casualties. Those who survived have scattered."

"He'll gather them again," the boy said, not a question but a certainty.

Caelan studied him with narrowed eyes. "You could have killed him, you know. When the waters rose. You had the power."

"And what would that have accomplished?" The boy stooped to retrieve a fallen banner—river and sea entwined—from the mud. "Another martyr for their cause? Another reason to hate and fear us?"

"Perhaps," Caelan admitted. "Or perhaps it would have ended this before it truly begins."

The boy shook his head. "This began long before I was born, Caelan. It won't end with a single death."

They continued in silence until they reached the shore of the loch, where Eira sat alone, her legs dangling over the edge of a stone outcropping. Her hands moved constantly, weaving river reeds into a complex pattern.

"What are you making?" the boy asked, settling beside her.

"A mourning wreath," she replied, her fingers never pausing. "For those who fell."

The boy watched her work, fascinated by the speed and precision of her movements. "I've never seen one like that before."

"It's how we honored our dead in the old days," she said. "Before the waters and the land grew so divided."

"My mother made something similar when my father died," Caelan said unexpectedly, lowering himself to sit on Eira's other side. "Though hers was rougher. She had no Selkie grace."

Eira's hands stilled momentarily. "I didn't know your father had passed."

"Three winters ago. He was a good man. Stubborn as Highland granite, but fair."

"Like his son," the boy observed.

Caelan's mouth twitched in what might have been the ghost of a smile. "Aye, perhaps. Though I've less of his patience."

Eira resumed her weaving. "Tell me about him."

And so Caelan did, speaking of his father's strength and kindness, his love of the mountains and his fearlessness in battle. As he spoke, others drifted to the shore—survivors seeking solace in the quiet aftermath—and they listened too, sometimes adding their own stories of those they had lost, not just in the night's battle but in the long years of strife that had preceded it.

The boy sat among them, listening, learning, feeling the bonds between them strengthen with each shared memory, each quiet tear, each solemn nod of understanding.

By midday, a considerable crowd had gathered. Alasdair Fraser joined them, his wounded jaw bandaged but his eyes alert. Maelis appeared with a cauldron of broth that steamed in the cool air.

"We must honor them properly," the boy said finally, rising to his feet. "All of them."

Together, they built a cairn at the water's edge—not grand or ornate, but solid and true. Each survivor came forward to place a token upon it: a lock of hair, a river stone, a bit of tartan, a weapon no longer needed.

When it was his turn, the boy knelt before the cairn and placed upon it the spiral-marked stone that Brannach had given him long ago. It had been a talisman of sorts, a reminder of the path he walked. Now it would be a marker of those who had walked it with him.

"I will not forget," he whispered, his words carried away by the breeze. "We will not forget."

Eira began to sing then—a low, keening melody that spoke of rivers lost and seas yet to be sailed. Others joined her, their voices weaving together across the water, a tapestry of grief and remembrance.

The boy stood back, watching as Highlanders and Selkies sang together, their differences momentarily forgotten in shared mourning. This was what he had hoped for—not unity forged in battle, but in understanding. In shared humanity.

"A fine tribute," Maelis said quietly, appearing at his side. "But they will need more than songs in the days to come."

"I know," the boy replied. "And I'll give them what they need."

Maelis studied him with those fathomless eyes. "You're changing," she observed. "The waters are rising within you."

"Is that good or ill?"

"That depends," she said enigmatically, "on whether you can navigate the currents."

The boy looked out over the loch, feeling the pull of its depths, the whisper of its secrets. "I'll find a way," he promised. "For all of them."

Chapter 37: Rebuilding the Circle

The work of rebuilding began before the songs of mourning had fully faded.

Tents were raised and repaired, fires rekindled, watches established. The camp, which had been a haphazard collection of clan groups, took on a more organized structure—a permanent settlement rather than a temporary gathering.

The boy moved through it all, directing, encouraging, his presence a steady anchor in the midst of change. The pendant at his chest no longer glowed with battle-fury, but it remained warm against his skin, a constant reminder of the power he had unleashed—and the responsibility that came with it.

"You're exhausted," Alasdair observed bluntly as the boy helped him reinforce a damaged palisade. "You've not slept since the battle."

"There's too much to do," the boy replied, driving a stake into the ground with more force than necessary.

Alasdair grunted. "Aye, and it'll still be there after you've rested. A leader who collapses is no use to anyone."

The boy straightened, wiping sweat from his brow. "Is that what I am now? A leader?"

"What would you call yourself?" Alasdair countered, his eyes shrewd beneath bushy brows.

The boy considered this. "A bridge," he said finally. "Between worlds that should never have been divided."

"A fine sentiment," Alasdair said, "but bridges bear weight, lad. And you've taken on more than your share."

Before the boy could respond, a shout went up from the eastern perimeter. Both turned sharply, hands going to weapons, but it was not an attack—merely the arrival of a new group. A small band of river-folk, led by a woman with silver-streaked hair and a determined set to her jaw.

"Moira," Alasdair breathed, surprise evident in his voice. "I didn't think she'd come."

"You know her?" the boy asked, watching as the newcomers were welcomed into the camp.

"Aye," Alasdair replied. "She's chieftain of the Aberdeenshire river clans. Refused my last three messengers." A wry smile crossed his face. "Also refused my hand in marriage, twenty years ago."

The boy glanced at him, startled. "You never mentioned—"

"Some wounds are better left undisturbed," Alasdair said gruffly. "Come, let's greet her properly."

They made their way through the camp, joined by Caelan and Eira, who had been training a mixed group of Highland and Selkie fighters in the art of synchronized combat.

Moira dismounted from her pony with the grace of a much younger woman, her eyes immediately finding Alasdair in the crowd.

"Fraser," she said, her voice carrying a musical lilt that marked her as river-born. "Still breathing, I see."

"Despite many who'd prefer otherwise," Alasdair replied, inclining his head. "Welcome to our camp, Moira of the Aberdeenshire."

"Is it welcome I'll be getting?" she asked, her gaze sweeping over the fortifications, the armed guards, the evidence of recent battle. "Or suspicion?"

"That depends," Caelan said, stepping forward, "on what brings you here."

Moira's eyes narrowed. "And who might you be, young hawk, to question my intentions?"

"Caelan," the boy interjected, moving to stand beside his friend. "One of my Circle. As are Eira and Maelis." He gestured to the others who had joined them. "And this is Alasdair Fraser, though it seems you're already acquainted."

"Aye," Moira said, her expression softening slightly. "We've crossed paths before." She turned her full attention to the boy. "So you're the one they speak of. The one who would unite water and stone."

The boy met her gaze steadily. "I seek to heal what's been broken, nothing more."

"Nothing more?" Moira arched an eyebrow. "I've heard tales of your battle two nights past. Of waters rising at your command. That sounds like something considerably more than healing."

"The waters answer to him," Eira said, a note of pride in her voice. "As they haven't answered to anyone in generations."

Moira studied the boy thoughtfully. "And what do you ask of them, these waters that obey you?"

"Only what is necessary," the boy replied. "I don't command them, Moira of the Aberdeenshire. I listen to them."

A smile flickered across Moira's face. "A wise answer. Perhaps there's hope for you yet." She turned to her companions. "We've ridden hard to reach you. My people are tired and hungry."

"Of course," the boy said. "Eira, would you show them to the eastern camp? There's room there, and fresh provisions."

As Eira led the newcomers away, Moira lingered, her eyes never leaving the boy's face. "There's something familiar about you," she said softly. "Something in the eyes."

The boy felt a jolt of surprise. "Did you know my mother?"

"Perhaps," Moira said enigmatically. "What was her name?"

The boy hesitated. His mother's name was a private thing, rarely spoken aloud, her kelpie name was not to be shared with landfolk, but her earthly name… something in Moira's gaze compelled him to answer. "Eilidh. Eilidh of the Western Isles."

Moira's sharp intake of breath was audible. "Eilidh," she repeated, her voice barely above a whisper. "So she survived."

The boy's heart quickened. "You knew her."

"Once," Moira said, her expression unreadable. "Long ago." She seemed about to say more, but then shook her head. "Another time, perhaps. For now, I need rest."

She followed after her people, leaving the boy standing with Alasdair and Caelan, questions swirling in his mind.

"What did she mean?" he asked Alasdair. "About my mother surviving?"

Alasdair's expression was grave. "I don't know, lad. But I suspect there's more to Moira's arrival than simple curiosity."

That evening, as the enlarged camp settled for the night, the boy sat with his Circle around the central fire. The flames cast flickering shadows across their faces—Alasdair's weathered countenance, Caelan's watchful eyes, Eira's thoughtful grace, Maelis's ancient wisdom.

"We need to expand our reach," the boy said, tracing patterns in the dirt with a stick. "The alliance is growing, but too slowly. Duncan will be gathering his forces again."

"And not just Highland rebels," Maelis added. "There are those among the Selkie courts who fear change as much as any land-dweller."

"What do you propose?" Alasdair asked.

The boy drew a circle in the dirt, then lines radiating outward. "A gathering. Not in secret, like before, but open. A declaration to all the clans—and to our enemies."

"A bold move," Caelan said, frowning. "And a dangerous one."

"Yes," the boy agreed. "But boldness is what's needed now. We must show strength, not just in battle but in our conviction."

"And if Duncan attacks again?" Eira asked.

The boy's expression hardened. "Then we'll be ready."

Maelis nodded slowly. "It could work. But you'll need more than flags and fires to draw them in. You'll need a name."

"A name?" the boy repeated.

"Not your birth name," she clarified. "Your true name. The one the waters whisper when you touch them."

The boy fell silent, considering her words. He had heard it, sometimes—a name carried on the current, a whisper in the depths. But he had never spoken it aloud, never claimed it as his own.

"I'm not ready," he said finally.

"You will be," Maelis replied with quiet certainty. "When the time comes."

Later, as the others sought their beds, the boy walked alone to the shores of Loch Ness. The water was calm tonight, reflecting the stars like scattered gems on black velvet.

He knelt at the edge, trailing his fingers through the cool water. "What am I becoming?" he whispered, not expecting an answer.

But a ripple spread from his fingertips, forming patterns too deliberate to be natural. The water rose slightly, curving toward him as if in greeting.

"Soon," came a whisper, like a mother's breath against a child's ear. "Soon you must take the name that is yours. Soon you must rise."

The boy drew back, startled yet strangely comforted. He looked up at the stars reflected in the dark water—countless, shimmering, steadfast.

The true war was coming.

And somehow, despite all that had happened, he knew he would be ready.

Chapter 38: The Call to the Highlands

The news spread like wildfire through the glens and valleys of the Highlands—a great gathering had been called, a moot not seen since the days when legends walked freely among men.

Flags of parley flew from the highest points around Loch Ness, visible for miles against the misty hills. Ancient watchtowers, long abandoned, now blazed with signal fires, their light a beacon to all with eyes to see and hearts to understand.

In the heart of the camp, which had grown into a small village in the weeks since the battle, the boy directed preparations with quiet authority. His Circle moved around him in constant motion—Alasdair organizing defenses, Caelan training warriors, Eira crafting symbols of unity, Maelis reading the signs in water and sky.

"Another three clans arrived during the night," Caelan reported, joining the boy at the central pavilion. "MacLeods from Skye, Camerons from the western valleys, and a small band of river-folk who call themselves the Bourne."

The boy nodded, marking their positions on a large map spread before him. "And Moira? Has she spoken further about my mother?"

Caelan's expression tightened. "Not to me. She keeps her own counsel, that one."

"She'll speak when she's ready," came Eira's voice as she entered the pavilion, her arms laden with bundles of woven talismans. "River-folk have their own sense of time."

The boy smiled faintly. "As do Selkies, it seems. Those were meant to be finished yesterday."

"Art cannot be rushed," Eira replied primly, but there was a teasing light in her eyes. She laid the talismans on the table—intricate weavings of rivergrass and driftwood, bound with threads of silver and blue. "Each one blessed with the old magics. They'll protect the wearer from minor harms."

"And what of major harms?" Caelan asked, fingering one of the talismans with unexpected gentleness.

Eira's smile faded. "For those, we'll need more than woven grass."

The boy studied the map, tracing the lines of clan territories with his finger. "We've heard nothing from the eastern shores?"

"Nothing," Caelan confirmed. "The MacAuleys hold sway there, and Duncan's influence runs deep."

The boy was silent for a moment, then looked up at his friends. "We need to send a delegation. A direct invitation."

"To Duncan?" Caelan's voice rose in disbelief. "After what he did? After our people he killed?"

"Not to Duncan," the boy clarified. "To his clan. To those who may not share his hatred."

"It's a risk," Eira said slowly. "But a calculated one."

"A necessary one," the boy insisted. "We cannot claim to seek unity while refusing to extend the hand of peace."

"And if they cut off that hand?" Caelan demanded.

The boy met his gaze steadily. "Then we'll know where they stand. And so will all the others who watch and wait."

Caelan muttered something under his breath but nodded reluctantly.

"I'll go," came a voice from the entrance. Moira stood there, her silver-streaked hair caught up in a complex braid, her eyes sharp with interest. "I have kin among the eastern clans. They'll hear me out, at least."

The boy inclined his head. "Thank you, Moira."

"Don't thank me yet, boy," she said. "I'm not doing it for you. I'm doing it for her." She did not need to specify who she meant.

That afternoon, Moira departed with a small escort—two of her own river-folk and a young Highland warrior who knew the eastern paths. The boy watched them go, a sense of unease settling in his chest.

"You're troubled," Maelis observed, joining him at the edge of the camp.

"I'm sending them into danger," he admitted.

Maelis nodded. "Yes. As leaders must sometimes do. But Moira is no fool, and she carries old magic of her own. Don't underestimate her."

"I don't," the boy said. "It's Duncan I worry about. There's something... broken in him. Something that goes beyond hatred."

"Fear," Maelis said simply. "The most dangerous emotion of all."

They stood in silence, watching as Moira's party disappeared into the mist that perpetually shrouded the eastern shores.

"She knew my mother," the boy said finally. "But she won't speak of it."

"Some memories are too painful to revisit," Maelis replied. "Give her time."

The boy nodded, but his thoughts were interrupted by a cry from one of the lookouts. He turned, alert, but it was not an alarm—it was a greeting. Far to the south, a new contingent approached, their banners unfamiliar even to his increasingly knowledgeable eye.

"Who are they?" he asked as Alasdair joined them, peering into the distance.

"By the saints," Alasdair breathed. "The Islesmen. I never thought they'd come."

The boy watched as the newcomers drew closer—tall, fierce-looking men and women clad in sealskins and woven cloth, their faces painted with blue spirals. They moved with the rolling gait of those who spend more time on water than land.

"Sea-Selkies," Maelis confirmed, a note of surprise in her voice. "From the Outer Isles. They rarely involve themselves in mainland affairs."

"Then why now?" the boy wondered aloud.

"Perhaps," Alasdair said, "your reputation grows."

As the Islesmen approached the camp, the boy moved forward to greet them. Their leader—a woman with storm-gray eyes and a face weathered by salt and wind—regarded him with open curiosity.

"You are the one they call the Bridge," she said, her voice carrying the rhythmic cadence of the waves. "The one who would unite river and sea, mountain and glen."

"I am," the boy replied, meeting her gaze steadily. "Though I have many names."

"As do we all," she agreed. "I am Sorcha of the Western Isles, Voice of the Tide Council. We have come to hear your words and judge their truth."

"You are welcome here," the boy said. "All who seek peace are welcome."

Sorcha smiled, a sharp, assessing expression. "Peace is a pretty word. But is it what you truly offer?"

"Peace through strength," the boy clarified. "Peace through understanding. Not surrender, not submission—but a new way forward."

"Bold claims," Sorcha observed. "We shall see if they hold water."

As the Islesmen were escorted into the camp, the boy found himself drawn to a small figure at the edge of their group—a child, perhaps ten years old, with sea-green eyes that seemed too old for her young face.

"Hello," he said, crouching down to her level. "What's your name?"

"Fionnuala," she replied, her voice surprisingly steady. "You're him, aren't you? The one the waters speak of?"

The boy blinked, startled by her directness. "What do they say about me?"

"That you understand their song," Fionnuala said. "That you can call them, and they answer." She tilted her head. "Can you really?"

Instead of replying, the boy held out his hand, palm up. A small pool of water gathered there, drawn from the moisture in the air itself. It swirled into a tiny whirlpool, then rose to form a delicate, crystalline flower.

Fionnuala's eyes widened. "Will you teach me?"

The boy closed his hand, the water soaking into his skin. "Perhaps," he said gently. "If that is your path."

He rose, feeling Sorcha's eyes on him. The Islewoman had seen the exchange, her expression unreadable.

"The child has the gift," she said quietly when he rejoined the adults. "As her mother did before her."

The boy turned, searching for the child in the crowd, but she had already disappeared among the tents.

"Does she know?" he asked, his voice barely above a whisper.

But a commotion at the northern edge of the camp drew their attention.

"Riders approaching!" came the call from the watchtower. "Flying the black thistle!"

The boy's heart sank. "Duncan."

Sorcha's expression hardened. "So the enemy shows himself at last."

"Not an enemy," the boy corrected automatically. "Not yet. Not if there's still hope for peace."

But as he moved toward the northern perimeter, the pendant at his chest grew warm with warning. Whatever Duncan MacAuley brought with him, it was not peace.

From atop the watchtower, the boy could see them clearly—a dozen riders, their cloaks black as night, their faces grim with purpose. Duncan rode at their head, his scarred visage unmistakable even at a distance.

But it was not Duncan who drew the boy's eye. It was the figure beside him—tall, hooded, with something unnaturally fluid about its movements. Something that made the waters within the boy recoil in instinctive recognition.

"What is it?" asked Alasdair, who had joined him on the tower. "What do you see?"

The boy's hand closed around the pendant, feeling its heat pulsing against his palm. "I don't know," he admitted. "But whatever it is, it doesn't belong in this world."

As Duncan's party drew closer, the boy descended from the tower, gathering his Circle around him. The time for preparation was over. The storm was breaking upon them once more.

And this time, it brought more than mere rebellion. It brought darkness from the depths—a darkness that whispered of ancient hatreds and forgotten fears.

The boy squared his shoulders, feeling the weight of responsibility settle upon him like a mantle. He had called the clans to unity. Now he would have to lead them through the darkness that sought to tear them apart.

"Are you ready?" Maelis asked quietly, her eyes knowing.

The boy nodded, the name the waters had whispered to him rising to his lips at last.

"I am," he said, and for the first time, he believed it.

Chapter 39: The Day of Reckoning

Dawn crept over the Highlands like a shy child, reluctant yet determined, painting the sky in pale blues and golds. The boy stood alone at the edge of the loch, watching as the morning light caught the ripples and transformed them into shimmering silver. Behind him, the encampment stirred to life—hundreds of fires rekindled, voices rising in anticipation of the day ahead.

"There you are," said Maelis, her approach as silent as always. In her arms, she carried a bundle wrapped in woven cloth. "I've been looking for you."

The boy turned, offering a tired smile. Dark circles shadowed his eyes—evidence of another sleepless night spent in preparation and prayer. "I needed to clear my head."

"And did you?" she asked, eyeing him shrewdly.

He glanced back at the loch. "The waters are restless today."

"As are you." Maelis unwrapped the bundle, revealing a cloak unlike any the boy had seen before. Woven from rivergrass and lined with the silvery down of Selkie seals, it caught the light in a way that seemed almost fluid, as if water had been spun into fabric. "This is for you."

The boy touched it hesitantly. "It's beautiful."

"It's more than that," Maelis said, draping it around his shoulders. "It's protection. A gift from both river and sea—a symbol of what you seek to unite."

The cloak settled against him with surprising weight, not heavy but substantial, like an embrace. The pendant at his chest—the Heart of the Loch—seemed to pulse in recognition, its light steady and sure.

"Do you think they'll listen?" he asked quietly.

Maelis adjusted the clasp of the cloak, her weathered hands gentle. "Some will. Some won't. That's the way of people, boy. Even in the face of truth, some choose blindness."

"Duncan is there."

"Yes." Maelis's expression darkened. "He and his shadow-ally both."

The boy frowned. "You know what it is—that thing that accompanies him?"

"I have suspicions," she replied carefully. "Old tales speak of creatures born from the hatred between water and land, nurtured in the darkness where neither sun nor moon can reach. Shapeless, ancient things that feed on division and fear."

"Can it be fought?"

"Everything can be fought," she assured him. "But first, you must win hearts. The battle with Duncan—and whatever stands behind him—will come soon enough."

They walked back to the camp together, where the rest of the Circle waited. Alasdair Fraser stood tall and proud, his clan tartan freshly pressed, his claymore gleaming at his hip. Beside him, Eira had braided river pearls into her hair, and her eyes shone with fierce determination. Caelan leaned against a tent pole, outwardly casual but with the coiled readiness of a warrior prepared for anything.

"Well," Alasdair said, eyeing the boy's new cloak with approval, "at least you'll look the part."

The boy smiled wryly. "The cloak doesn't make the leader, Alasdair."

"No," the older man agreed, "but it doesn't hurt to remind them that you stand between worlds."

Caelan pushed away from the tent pole. "The clans are gathering at the hollow. It's time."

As they moved through the encampment, the boy was acutely aware of the eyes that followed them—some reverent, some calculating, some merely curious. Clan chiefs straightened as they passed, common folk whispered behind their hands. A path cleared before them like water parting around a stone.

Some knelt in respect as they passed, pressing fists to hearts or touching foreheads to the earth in the old way. Others stood rigid, watchful, reserve etched in every line of their bodies.

"Not everyone is convinced," Eira murmured, noting the boy's attention to these details.

"They don't need to be convinced yet," he replied. "They just need to listen."

At the heart of the great hollow by the loch stood a platform built of ancient stones, draped in woven banners bearing the unified sigil—the river entwined with the wave. The stones were old—older than any clan's memory—placed there by hands that had understood the power of the loch long before the divisions of river and land began.

The boy climbed the steps slowly, feeling the weight of every gaze upon him. His Circle arranged themselves at the base of the platform—Alasdair and Caelan to his right, Eira and Maelis to his left, a living embodiment of the unity he sought to create.

Before him stretched a sea of faces—Highlanders in their clan tartans, river-folk in their woven garments of blue and green, Selkies with their silver-tinged hair and eyes that reflected the depths of the sea. Enemies who had put aside their feud for this one day, allies who had risked much to stand together, and those who wavered between, uncertain where their loyalties should lie.

Among them, the boy spotted Moira of the Aberdeenshire, her silver-streaked hair gleaming in the sunlight. Nearby stood Sorcha and the Islesmen, their faces painted with blue spirals. And farther back, half-hidden in shadow, was Duncan MacAuley, his scarred face twisted in what might have been contempt. Beside him, barely visible, lurked a cloaked figure whose presence seemed to bend the light around it.

The boy raised his hands, and a hush fell over the assembly, rippling outward until even the birds in the trees fell silent.

"Sons and daughters of the Highlands," he began, his voice carrying clear and strong despite his youth. "Children of river and sea, of hill and glen. I stand before you not to command, but to call."

A murmur rippled through the crowd.

"The darkness that has poisoned our rivers and sickened our seas does not come from one people, one clan, one race. It comes from the hatred that divides us. From the fear that blinds us."

He paused, letting his words settle. The pendant at his chest pulsed gently, lending strength to his voice.

"We have fought each other for too long," he continued. "We have forgotten that the river feeds the sea, and the sea gives rain to the river. We are bound, whether we will it or no."

From the crowd, a voice called out, gruff and skeptical. "Pretty words, boy! But what of the blood between us? What of the generations of strife?"

The boy recognized the speaker—a burly clan chief from the northern reaches, his beard braided with copper rings. "The blood calls for justice, not more bloodshed," he answered. "The strife has served none but those who would keep us weak and divided."

"And who would that be?" came another voice—sharper, more challenging. Duncan MacAuley had stepped forward, his face a mask of barely contained fury. "Who are these shadowy enemies you conjure to unite us against? Or is it just a clever tale to make us bow to you?"

The boy met Duncan's gaze steadily. "The enemy is not a clan or a people. It is the darkness that festers in the corners of the world—the corruption that seeks to turn brother against brother, clan against clan, river against sea. It is the poison that has seeped into our waters and our hearts alike."

"And what proof do you offer of this darkness?" Duncan demanded. "What proof beyond your own claims?"

The boy hesitated, aware that the moment had come sooner than he had expected. He had hoped to build more unity before facing this direct challenge. But Duncan had forced his hand.

He turned, sweeping his hand toward the great loch behind him, its waters gleaming like liquid silver in the morning light. "The Heart of the Loch has chosen," he said, his voice ringing with quiet certainty. "The old magic has awakened. It calls us to stand together—or to fall apart and be consumed."

As if in response to his words, the pendant at his chest flared to life, its light spilling outward like liquid moonlight. At the same moment, the surface of the loch rippled strangely, a pattern forming that could not be attributed to wind or current—concentric circles that spread outward from a central point, as if something vast moved in the depths below.

Many in the crowd gasped, some making signs of warding. Even Duncan took an involuntary step backward, though he recovered quickly.

"And what would you have us do, boy?" he sneered, though his voice lacked some of its earlier conviction. "Throw down our swords and sing songs to the waves?"

The boy stepped forward, the pendant flashing with each heartbeat. "I would have you fight," he said, his voice hardening. "But not against each other. Against the darkness that threatens all we hold dear. Against the forces that would reduce our lands to barren ash, our waters to poisoned mire."

He looked out over the assembled clans, meeting as many eyes as he could. "Join me, and we will heal what was broken. We will forge a new path—not forgetting the past, but building beyond it."

For a heartbeat, the world held still. Even the wind seemed to pause, waiting.

Then Alasdair Fraser stepped forward, unsheathing his claymore in one fluid motion and raising it high, the blade catching fire in the sunlight. "Clan Fraser stands with the Heart!" he declared, his voice a thunderous roar.

A great cry rose from the loyalists, a crashing wave of sound that rolled across the hollow. Others followed swiftly—Eira, lifting her hands to call a shimmer of Selkie magic that danced like aurora lights above the crowd; Moira of the Aberdeenshire, her face stern but resolved; Sorcha and the Islesmen, raising their spear-points to the sky.

Even some who had wavered now found their courage. A young clan chief whom the boy had never spoken to stepped forward, drawing his sword. "The MacKenzies stand with the Heart!" he declared, his voice cracking with emotion.

More followed, a cascade of pledges and raised weapons, voices joining in a chorus of unity that grew until it seemed to fill the very air with power. The boy stood at the center of it all, the pendant blazing now, the cloak streaming behind him though there was no wind.

But Duncan did not join the chorus. His face twisted with something beyond fury—something that might have been fear, or perhaps despair. Without a word, he turned and pushed his way back through the crowd, his shadowy companion slipping after him. His closest supporters followed, melting away into the mists that still clung to the edges of the hollow.

The boy watched him go, sadness mingling with the triumph in his heart. "He will return," he said softly, though only his Circle could hear him over the continuing clamor.

"Yes," Maelis agreed, her eyes tracking Duncan's retreat. "And not alone."

"Then we'll be ready," Caelan said grimly, his hand on his sword hilt.

The boy nodded, but his gaze lingered on the mists that had swallowed Duncan and his allies. Victory, he knew, was incomplete. The true battle—against the darkness that had tempted Duncan, and would tempt others—was still to come.

But today, here by the shores of Loch Ness, hope had taken root.

And from hope, a new world might yet rise.

Chapter 40: Murmurs from the Deep

Dusk settled over the loch like a heavy cloak, muting the sounds of celebration that still drifted from the encampment. Three days had passed since the gathering, and the glow of unity still burned bright among the clans. New alliances had been forged over shared meals and training grounds, old grudges set aside—if not forgotten—in the face of a greater purpose.

Eira sat alone on a flat rock at the water's edge, her bare feet dangling in the chill waters. Her fingers wove river reeds absently into intricate patterns as she watched the last light fade from the sky.

"You missed the evening meal," came Caelan's voice from behind her. "Alasdair was telling tales again. Something about how he single-handedly defeated a band of cattle raiders with nothing but a broken sword and his wits."

Eira smiled faintly but didn't turn. "I've heard that one before. The number of raiders grows with each telling."

Caelan settled beside her, his own feet remaining firmly on dry stone. For all their newfound alliance, some habits died hard—Highland warriors did not typically dangle their limbs in deep water.

"You're troubled," he observed after a moment of silence.

Eira sighed, her fingers stilling on the half-finished weaving. "I can feel it," she said, her voice low. "Something... wrong. In the water. It's like a taste at the back of my throat, a heaviness that wasn't there before."

Caelan frowned. "Duncan's doing?"

"No," she said, shaking her head. "This is older. Deeper." She glanced at him, moonlight silvering her features. "Have you ever stood at the edge of a storm and felt the air change? Felt the pressure building before the first lightning strikes?"

"Aye," he acknowledged. "We're standing at such an edge now, aren't we?"

Before Eira could answer, a figure emerged from the mist that had begun to gather along the shoreline—Maelis, her silver hair unbound, her expression troubled.

"You feel it too," she said to Eira, not a question but a confirmation.

Eira nodded, pulling her feet from the water and curling them beneath her. "When did it begin?"

"It's always been there," Maelis replied, settling on a nearby stone. "But it stirs now, awakened by the clash of fate and fear." She looked at Caelan. "Where is the boy?"

"With Alasdair, reviewing the training schedule for tomorrow," Caelan answered. "Why? What's happening?"

Instead of answering directly, Maelis knelt at the water's edge and withdrew a small leather pouch from within her robes. From it, she took seven smooth stones, each marked with a different spiral pattern.

"Divination?" Eira asked, leaning forward with interest. "I haven't seen the stone-casting in years."

"These times call for old ways," Maelis said simply, and cast the stones upon the surface of the loch.

For a moment, they skipped as ordinary stones might, creating ripples that expanded outward. But then, before they could sink, the ripples changed direction—flowing inward instead, converging toward a central point far out in the deeper waters of the loch. The stones themselves were pulled along, moving against all natural current until they disappeared beneath the surface.

Maelis drew in a sharp breath and stood quickly, backing away from the water.

"What does it mean?" Caelan asked, his hand instinctively moving to his sword hilt.

"It means we must speak with the boy," Maelis said, her voice tight with urgency. "Now."

They found him in the command tent, bent over maps with Alasdair Fraser, planning patrol routes for the expanded alliance territories. Both looked up as the three entered, Maelis in the lead with an expression that brought their discussion to an immediate halt.

"What's happened?" the boy asked, straightening.

"There is something old beneath these waters," Maelis said without preamble. "Older than Selkie or Kelpie, older even than the first clans. It stirs now, awakened by our actions here."

Alasdair frowned. "What manner of thing?"

"I cast the stones," Maelis explained. "They were drawn inward, to a central point deep beneath the loch. It's as if something there pulls at the very fabric of the world."

The boy's hand went to the pendant at his chest, which had grown noticeably cooler since the gathering. "I've felt... something," he admitted. "A presence at the edge of awareness. I thought it was just exhaustion."

"Is it an enemy?" Alasdair asked, ever practical. "Something Duncan has called up to use against us?"

Maelis shook her head. "It is neither ally nor enemy. It is what the world once was, before men or magic shaped it. It is hunger. It is tide. It does not care for our dreams or wars."

"But it's awakening now," Eira added, "when we've finally begun to unite the clans. That can't be coincidence."

"No," the boy agreed. "Not coincidence." He looked at each of them in turn. "I need to see for myself. To understand what we're facing."

Caelan straightened. "I'll come with you."

"No," the boy said gently. "This I must do alone."

Maelis looked as if she might object, but something in the boy's expression stopped her. Instead, she reached into her robes and withdrew a small vial filled with what appeared to be liquid moonlight. "Take this," she said, pressing it into his hand. "If what stirs beneath the loch is what I fear, this may offer some protection."

The boy accepted it with a nod of thanks.

"Be careful, lad," Alasdair said gruffly. "Some depths are not meant for the living to plumb."

"I'll return before midnight," the boy promised, and slipped out into the gathering darkness.

The night had deepened while they spoke, the mist thickening along the shoreline until it obscured all but the nearest trees. The boy moved through it confidently, guided less by sight than by the pull of the water, the pendant at his chest growing colder with each step toward the loch.

When he reached the shore, he found a secluded cove, hidden from the view of the camp by a stand of ancient pines. Here, the water lay black and still, reflecting nothing of the stars above—as if this small corner of the loch were somehow separate from the world above.

The boy knelt at the water's edge and uncorked Maelis's vial, letting three drops of the luminous liquid fall onto the surface. Where they touched, the water glowed briefly, then returned to darkness.

Taking a deep breath, he pressed his palm flat against the surface, not breaking it but making contact—a gesture of greeting, of questioning.

The effect was immediate and overwhelming. Visions surged through him with such force that he nearly fell forward into the loch— vast shapes twisting through primordial waters; storms that had howled before time began; a silence so profound it could unmake the world.

And beneath it all, a hunger beyond hunger, a cold intelligence that regarded humanity and its struggles with the same indifference a human might show to ants beneath their feet.

With a gasp, the boy tore his hand away, falling backward onto the shore. The pendant at his chest had grown so cold it burned against his skin, as if trying to shield him from what lay below.

He lay there for several minutes, his breath coming in ragged gasps, his mind struggling to process what he had touched. It wasn't evil—evil required intent, a desire to harm. This was beyond such concepts. It was primal, elemental, a force as fundamental to the world as gravity or time.

And it was waking.

When he finally returned to the command tent, his Circle was waiting, their faces tense with concern.

"You've been gone for hours," Eira said, rushing to his side. "We were about to search for you."

The boy looked surprised. "Hours? It felt like moments."

"The deep places have their own time," Maelis said softly. "What did you see?"

The boy sank onto a stool, his face pale in the lamplight. "The darkness we feared is not only in men," he said, his voice steady despite the tremor in his hands. "It is rising from the earth itself. From the oldest depths of the loch."

"What is it?" Alasdair asked, his voice hushed with uncharacteristic awe.

"I don't know what name to give it," the boy admitted. "But it's vast. Ancient. It slumbered for ages, but now..." He looked up at them, his eyes troubled. "Our conflict has disturbed it. The magic we've wielded, the passions we've roused—they've reached into the deep and touched something that should have remained untouched."

"Duncan," Caelan growled. "His hate and fear—could that have fed this thing?"

"Perhaps," the boy acknowledged. "Or perhaps it would have wakened anyway, in time. What matters is that it stirs now, and we must be ready."

Alasdair laid a steadying hand on his shoulder. "Then we will face it. As we have faced all things."

The boy looked around at the faces of those who had chosen him—Eira's quiet concern, Caelan's grim determination, Maelis's ancient wisdom, Alasdair's steady courage.

"We will need more than swords," he said. "We will need the oldest magics. We will need the courage of river and sea, of stone and spirit."

And in the deep places of the world, the ancient hunger uncoiled, sensing that soon, very soon, it would have cause to rise.

Chapter 41: Seeking the Forgotten Powers

Morning found the camp subdued, as if the same unease that troubled the Circle had seeped into the very air. The sky hung low and heavy, neither rain nor sun breaking through the uniform gray. The loch's surface seemed unnaturally still, reflecting the clouds above like a mirror of polished obsidian.

In the command tent, the Circle gathered around a table where ancient maps had been spread—some inked on vellum, others woven into cloth or carved into thin sheets of wood. Maelis traced her finger along a series of spiraling patterns that seemed to represent the network of lochs and rivers throughout the Highlands.

"The old powers are not entirely lost," she explained, her voice low as if the very walls might be listening. "They sleep in forgotten places, waiting to be called upon in times of great need."

"And this qualifies as great need?" Caelan asked, not challenging but seeking confirmation.

"What stirs beneath Loch Ness is beyond any power we currently possess," Maelis replied gravely. "Even united, the clans cannot stand against it with blade or common magic alone."

The boy studied the maps intently. "These patterns—they're more than just waterways, aren't they?"

"Yes," Maelis nodded approvingly. "The ancients understood that the rivers and lochs form a network of power—a web of energy that flows through the land itself. At certain points, that energy concentrates, creating wells of raw magic."

"And these wells could give us the power to face what's coming?" Alasdair asked, skepticism evident in his tone. The Highland chieftain had always been more comfortable with steel than sorcery.

"Not all of them," Maelis said. "Most have weakened over the centuries, as belief waned and the old ways were forgotten. But there is one..." She traced her finger to a point north of Loch Ness, where the patterns converged into a single, dense spiral. "The Well of the First Waters. It is the oldest and strongest of them all—the source from which all rivers in the Highlands originally sprang."

Eira leaned forward, her eyes widening. "I thought that was just a legend. A tale told to river children."

"Many legends have roots in truth," Maelis replied. "This one more than most."

"If it exists," Caelan said, "why has no one found it before?"

"Oh, many have found it," Maelis said, a shadow crossing her face. "Few have returned to speak of it. The Well guards itself fiercely. It tests those who seek its power—and most are found wanting."

All eyes turned to the boy, who had remained quiet during the exchange, his fingers absently tracing the contours of the pendant at his chest.

"You believe I can pass these tests," he said, not a question but a realization.

"I believe you must," Maelis answered simply. "For all our sakes."

The boy straightened, decision crystallizing in his eyes. "Then we'll seek this Well. How far is the journey?"

"In distance?" Maelis smiled grimly. "Perhaps three days' hard travel. But the path to the Well doesn't follow the rules of ordinary space. It might take us through places... elsewhere."

"You make it sound as if we're leaving the world entirely," Alasdair grumbled.

"In a way, we will be," Maelis confirmed. "The Well exists at the threshold between this world and others—places where the old magics still hold sway, where the veil between realities is thin."

Caelan crossed his arms. "And what happens when we find this Well? What exactly are we seeking there?"

"Power," the boy said quietly, his gaze distant as if seeing beyond the tent walls. "But not just any power. Understanding. A connection to the oldest magics of the land—the kind that might reach even the ancient thing beneath the loch."

"And if you gain this power," Eira asked carefully, "what then?"

The boy met her gaze steadily. "Then I use it to protect our people. All our people—Highland and river-born alike."

A silence fell over the group, heavy with the weight of what lay ahead.

Finally, Alasdair cleared his throat. "When do we leave?"

"Today," the boy decided. "As soon as we can make ready. The longer we wait, the stronger the awakening below grows."

"We can't all go," Caelan pointed out. "The camp needs protection, especially with Duncan still out there somewhere, gathering his forces."

"Agreed," the boy nodded. "A small party will travel north—myself, Maelis to guide us, and..." He looked around the circle thoughtfully. "Alasdair, Eira, and Caelan. The rest of the leadership will remain to oversee the clans and prepare them for what may come."

"Five," Maelis murmured. "A sacred number. Fitting."

Within the hour, preparations were complete. The party would travel light—carrying only what could be borne easily across difficult terrain. Word spread quickly through the camp that the boy and his inner circle were departing on a quest of great importance, and a crowd gathered to see them off.

Moira of the Aberdeenshire approached as they were making final checks of their gear. "So," she said, eyeing their provisions, "you seek the Well of the First Waters."

The boy looked up, surprised. "How did you know?"

"Little happens in this camp that I don't hear of," she replied with a thin smile. "Besides, what else would you seek, with what stirs below?"

She reached into a pouch at her belt and withdrew a small object wrapped in river-silk. "Take this," she said, pressing it into the boy's hand. "It belonged to your mother."

Unwrapping it carefully, the boy found a small carving of a seal, crafted from a single piece of driftwood so perfectly rendered that it seemed almost alive. "She carried this?"

"Always," Moira confirmed, a flicker of old sorrow crossing her face. "Until the day she gave herself back to the waters. She said it helped her remember who she was, when the land threatened to make her forget."

The boy closed his fingers around the carving, feeling its smooth contours, worn by years of his mother's touch. "Thank you," he said quietly.

Moira nodded, then stepped back. "May the currents guide you," she said formally, offering the traditional blessing of the river clans.

With a final word to the leaders who would remain behind, the boy and his companions set off, heading northward where the land grew wild and the boundaries between worlds grew thin.

The first day of travel was uneventful—a hard march through increasingly rugged terrain, the familiar landscapes of the central Highlands giving way to more desolate country. By nightfall, they had reached a high ridge overlooking a valley shrouded in mist.

"We camp here," Maelis announced. "Tomorrow, we begin the true journey."

As they ate a simple meal around a small fire, Alasdair surveyed the mist-filled valley below. "I've hunted these lands for forty years," he said, "but I don't recognize this place."

"The path to the Well reveals itself only to those who seek it," Maelis replied. "Already, we walk roads unmarked on mortal maps."

That night, as the others slept, the boy stayed awake, the seal carving clutched in one hand, the pendant cold against his chest. In the distance, he thought he could hear singing—voices neither human nor Selkie, weaving melodies that spoke of ancient waters and the birth of rivers.

When dawn broke, the world had changed. The familiar Highlands were gone, replaced by a landscape at once similar and profoundly different. The trees stood twisted into unnatural shapes, their bark spiraled like seashells. The very rocks seemed to hum with a subtle energy that vibrated through the soles of their boots.

"The borderlands," Maelis explained, seeing their confused expressions. "We stand now between the world of men and the older realms."

The day that followed tested them in ways none had anticipated. The land itself seemed alive and aware, sometimes helping, sometimes hindering their progress. Streams appeared where no water should flow, offering sweet refreshment when they grew thirsty. But later, stones shifted beneath their feet, nearly sending Caelan tumbling into a ravine that hadn't been there moments before.

By midday, they reached what Maelis called the Valley of Echoes— a desolate place filled with standing stones so ancient they seemed a part of the earth itself. They leaned at odd angles, some cracked, others worn to mere stumps by forces beyond ordinary weather.

"This is the first trial," Maelis whispered as they stood at the valley's edge. "In this place, the stones echo not sounds, but fears. They will show you what you most dread, and you must pass through it unchanged."

Alasdair's hand tightened on his sword hilt. "You might have mentioned this earlier."

"Would it have changed your decision to come?" Maelis asked, her eyes knowing.

The Highland chief grunted. "No. But I might have brought more whisky."

Despite the attempt at humor, tension hung heavy in the air as they entered the valley. Almost immediately, the mist thickened around them, isolating each member of the party despite their attempts to stay together.

The boy found himself walking alone through swirling gray, the sounds of his companions fading until all he could hear was the soft whisper of his own breathing. The mist before him thickened, coalescing into shapes—not enemies, but memories, fears, half-truths spun from the very fabric of his soul.

He saw his mother turning away from him, her eyes cold and unseeing. "You are not of the water," her shade whispered. "Nor are you of the land. You belong nowhere, to no one."

The boy's step faltered, an old pain twisting in his chest. He had sometimes wondered if his mother had left because of him—because he was neither fully Selkie nor fully human, a bridge between worlds but belonging to neither.

"That's not true," he said aloud, his voice steadier than he felt. "I belong to both worlds. And both belong to me."

The shade of his mother wavered, then dissolved into mist.

But the trial was not over. New shapes formed—the clans he sought to unite turned against each other, blood flowing into the waters of Loch Ness. And at the center of it all stood the boy himself, the pendant dark and lifeless at his chest, his efforts to unite them only driving them further apart.

"This is what awaits you," a voice whispered from the mist. "Failure. Destruction. The end of all you love."

The boy closed his eyes, focusing on the steady beat of his heart, on the cool weight of the pendant against his skin. "No," he said firmly. "This is what might be, not what must be. I choose a different path."

The vision wavered but did not fully disperse. It changed, showing him standing alone atop a barren hill, the last survivor of a war that had consumed both river and land. Solitude stretched before him like an endless, empty sea.

The loneliness was the worst of it. The feeling that all his efforts had been for nothing, that he was destined to watch everything he loved wither and die.

For one terrible moment, despair threatened to overwhelm him.

Then he remembered—the songs of the rivers, the loyalty in the eyes of his Circle, the warmth of communal fires and shared purpose. He remembered the trust placed in him by both Highlander and river-born, the hope that had begun to take root in the hearts of the clans.

And most of all, he remembered his mother's last words to him before she returned to the sea: "You carry both waters and earth within you. That is not weakness—it is your greatest strength."

The boy clenched his fists and shouted into the mist, "I will not be broken! I will not surrender to fear!"

The vision shattered like glass, the mist recoiling as if burned by his defiance.

Gradually, the boy became aware of sounds nearby—voices calling out in fear or anger, his companions fighting their own battles against the illusions of the valley.

He moved toward them, guided by instinct rather than sight. First, he found Alasdair, kneeling in the mist, his face a mask of shame and grief as he watched phantom members of his clan turn their backs on him, casting him out as a traitor for following a boy born of river and sea.

"Alasdair," the boy called, laying a hand on the chieftain's shoulder. "This is not real. Your clan stands with you—with us."

The older man looked up, recognition slowly dawning in his eyes. "Lad? Is that really you?"

"Yes," the boy assured him. "The stones show us what we fear, not what is true."

Together, they found Eira, who was trapped in a vision of the Selkie courts in ruins, her people scattered and forgotten, their songs lost to time. She too was freed of her fears when supported by the strength of the boy.

Shaken, still racked with fears and weakness, they set camp for the night.

Dawn broke reluctantly over the camp, its pale fingers of light hesitant to touch the expedition preparing at the edge of the Highland settlement. The boy stood silently watching the horizon as his companions made final preparations. The pendant at his chest pulsed with subtle warmth against his skin, almost like a second heartbeat.

Sixteen summers old now, the boy bore little resemblance to the uncertain child who had washed ashore from troubled waters years prior. His face had hardened, cheekbones more pronounced beneath eyes that shifted between stormy gray and the deep blue-green of the loch itself—his mother's eyes, or so Moira had once told him. His dark hair, perpetually damp as if still clinging to his aquatic heritage, was tied back with a leather cord adorned with small river stones.

"We should reach the borderlands by nightfall," Maelis said, approaching him with her staff in hand. The ancient oak, polished by decades of her touch, was wrapped with silver wire that caught the reluctant sunlight. At its crown sat a single stone—a droplet of polished obsidian said to have been formed when the First Waters touched the primal fires of the earth.

He nodded, studying the old woman's face. Maelis had been his first teacher, the one who recognized the dual nature of his being when others saw only a strange, half-drowned child. Her face was a map of the Highlands themselves—every crease and line a valley or ridgeline etched by years of weather and wisdom. But it was her eyes that betrayed her true nature—amber like autumn leaves, with flecks of gold that sometimes seemed to move independently, like motes of light dancing in deep waters.

"The others are afraid," he said quietly.

Maelis didn't deny it. "Fear is wisdom when walking into the in-between places. Only fools feel nothing when approaching the threshold of the otherworld."

From behind them came Alasdair's gruff voice: "Speaking of fools—are we certain this venture isn't pure madness?" The Highland chieftain approached, his considerable bulk somehow silent on the dewy grass. Despite his fifty-seven years, Alasdair Fraser moved with the fluid grace of a predator, his weathered face perpetually set in lines of stern concern beneath a mane of silver-streaked russet hair.

Alasdair's initial coldness for the boy had transformed first into grudging respect, then fierce loyalty after the boy had saved his youngest grandson from drowning in a flash flood the previous spring. The boy had moved through the raging waters as if they were calm seas, commanding currents that should have been beyond any mortal's control. Since that day, the Fraser clan had pledged their swords to the boy's cause, with Alasdair himself rarely straying from the boy's side.

"Madness? Perhaps." His voice carried a trace of his mother's lilting accent—a reminder of his Selkie heritage that emerged when emotion colored his words. "But what greater madness than standing idle while that ancient thing rises beneath the loch?"

He turned his gaze toward the distant waters of Loch Ness, where for weeks now the surface had been unnaturally still, despite winds that should have stirred it to waves. Something slumbered there, something drawn to the growing discord between the Highland clans and the river-born. Something that fed on their division.

Eira approached, her movements so fluid she seemed to pour across the landscape rather than walk upon it. Of all the Circle, she remained most deeply connected to her non-human ancestry. Her skin held the faintest silver sheen in certain lights, and her long dark hair, intricately braided with shells and river pearls, moved in currents invisible to others. As a full-blooded Selkie who had chosen to remain on land, she carried a melancholy that never fully left her eyes.

"The waters are restless this morning," she said, her voice like smooth stones rolling in a gentle current. "They know we're leaving. They fear what may happen in our absence."

He nodded, understanding her meaning. The river-born, particularly those with stronger ties to their aquatic ancestry, were growing increasingly anxious. The disturbance beneath Loch Ness affected them physically—many had complained of dreams in which they drowned on dry land, or where the waters turned viscous and black around them.

"Caelan will lead them in our absence," he said, his eyes seeking out the tall, silver-haired figure checking weapons at the camp's edge.

Unlike Eira, whose Selkie nature was evident in her every movement, Caelan's river-born heritage was less obvious. Only his unusual height and the webbing between his fingers betrayed his descent from the water spirits known as the Each Uisge. His mother had been one of them, though he never spoke of her. His father, a blacksmith from the lowlands, had raised him with calloused hands and quiet dignity until a Highland raid had left the boy orphaned at fourteen.

Now approaching thirty, Caelan had grown into a warrior of extraordinary skill, his halberd an extension of his own body, its blade catching what little sunlight penetrated the gloom. Despite the distrust many Highlanders held for the river-born, none questioned Caelan's prowess or loyalty. His voice, when he used it, carried the weight of oaths sworn and kept through the darkest of times.

"They're ready," he called across the clearing, his deep voice carrying easily despite its softness. Caelan never shouted—he'd once told the boy that his father had taught him that a man who must raise his voice to be heard has already lost half the battle.

The boy looked at the assembled party—five of them, as Maelis had noted with satisfaction the previous night. Five was a sacred number among the ancient peoples of the Highlands, representing the elements that composed the world: earth, air, fire, water, and the fifth element—spirit—that bound them all together.

"We travel light," he reminded them. "Only what can be carried easily across difficult terrain."

Each member of the Circle had prepared accordingly. Maelis carried only her staff and a small pouch of herbs and ritual implements. Alasdair bore his clan sword, passed down through sixteen generations of Fraser chieftains, its handle worn smooth by the hands of his ancestors. A dirk rested at his hip, and a small pack containing provisions was slung across his broad shoulders.

Eira carried almost nothing—a small silver knife, a pouch of water from her birth-loch, and a seal-skin cloak that rippled with unnatural life when the wind touched it. The Selkie woman needed little to survive in even the harshest conditions; her kind had evolved to thrive in the cruel northern waters where other creatures perished.

Caelan's gear was meticulously arranged—his halberd, a short sword, a hunting knife, and a pack containing practical essentials. No wasted space, no unnecessary weight. Everything with purpose, like the man himself.

The boy carried only the pendant—the Heart of the Loch, as some called it—and now, tucked safely in an inner pocket of his leather vest, the small wooden seal carving Moira had given him. His mother's talisman. Its smooth contours, worn by years of her touch, gave him comfort in a way few material possessions ever had.

As the party prepared to depart, a crowd gathered from a ragtag mixed encampment of Highlanders and river-born. Once bitter enemies, the two peoples had formed an uneasy alliance—bound together by the threat lurking beneath the loch and the prophecies that surrounded the boy born of both worlds.

An old river-woman stepped forward, her body bent like a willow by the weight of years. In gnarled hands, she offered a small bundle wrapped in river-silk. "Water-bread," she explained, her voice rippling like the surface of a disturbed pool. "Made with the first flow of spring. It will sustain you where other food fails."

He accepted the gift with a formal bow that recognized her status among the river-born. Her answering smile revealed teeth filed to points in the old way of her people—a tradition largely abandoned by the younger generation.

A Highland warrior, his face marked with the blue woad patterns of the ancient Picts, approached next and offered him a small flask. "Whisky," he said gruffly. "Not for drinking, mind—though Alasdair will ignore that instruction, no doubt." He cast a knowing look at the chieftain, who responded with a noncommittal grunt. "Pour it on wounds that won't close, or into water you don't trust. It burns away impurities of both flesh and spirit."

More gifts followed—small tokens of protection, respect, and hope from both peoples. A river-stone carved with protective runes. A sprig of rowan, bound with red thread against evil. A small vial of water from the sacred spring at the heart of Fraser lands. He accepted each with growing solemnity, understanding the weight of trust being placed upon his shoulders.

Finally, Duncan's wife approached. Her husband—once Alasdair's trusted friend —had betrayed them all, fleeing with a contingent of Highland warriors who refused to ally with the river-born. Now he gathered forces in the north, calling the boy a deceiver and the river-born an abomination to be purged from the Highlands.

The woman's face was a careful mask, her grief and shame hidden beneath layers of Highland pride. "My husband follows a darkened path," she said quietly. "But not all in our family share his hatred." From around her neck, she removed a small amulet—a simple stone wrapped in copper wire. "This was my grandmother's. She was an outsider too, brought to the Highlands as a bride from distant shores. It protected her. Perhaps it will protect you as well."

The exchange silenced the gathered crowd. For her to publicly support the boy was to declare against her own husband—a declaration that could not be undone.

He took the amulet with gentle hands. "When I return, I hope to bring wisdom that will heal the divisions between us all—including Duncan, if he will listen."

The woman's smile was sad but genuine. "May the old gods walk with you, water-son."

With the morning light strengthening, the party set off northward, away from the temporary safety of the encampment and into lands increasingly touched by powers older than human memory. The path led them through ancient pine forests where the trees stood like sentinels, their needled branches sighing in winds that smelled of snow and secrets.

By midday, they had reached the high moors—vast expanses of heather and gorse stretching toward distant mountains wreathed in mist. Here, the land seemed to breathe beneath their feet, the very earth rising and falling in slow, measured rhythm like the chest of a slumbering giant.

The boy led the way, drawn forward by some inner compass that none of the others could perceive. The pendant at his chest grew warmer with each step northward, occasionally pulsing with soft blue light when they reached crossroads or places where the path grew indistinct.

"The Heart knows the way," Maelis observed, watching the boy navigate an unmarked trail through a field of standing stones that seemed randomly placed to casual observation but formed perfect alignments when viewed from the correct angle. "It remembers the old roads."

Alasdair scowled at the stones as they passed. "My grandfather warned me about circles like these. Said they were doorways, left ajar by those who walked before us."

"He wasn't wrong," Eira replied softly. "The ancients understood that certain configurations of stone and earth could thin the boundaries between worlds. Not all who step through such doorways return unchanged—if they return at all."

The chieftain's hand tightened on his sword hilt. "Comforting."

As afternoon waned into evening, the landscape began to alter in subtle ways. The colors seemed too vivid—the purple of the heather almost painful to behold, the green of the scattered pines so deep it appeared black in shadows. The sky above took on a peculiar quality, as if the very air had thickened, damping sound while magnifying light.

"We've reached the borderlands," Maelis announced, her voice hushed as if afraid to disturb the unnatural stillness. "From here, the rules of the mortal world grow thin."

They made camp that night on a high ridge overlooking a valley shrouded in mist. Though exhausted from the day's hard travel, none slept easily. Strange lights danced at the corners of their vision, and the stars above seemed to arrange themselves in unfamiliar constellations that shifted when directly observed.

The boy sat apart from the others, the small seal carving cradled in his palms. In the faint moonlight, the wood seemed almost alive, the grain flowing like water across the surface of the miniature creature. He thought of his mother—Nerina, of the Western Shores Selkie Court—who had given up her sealskin to walk upon the land with his father, Brannach, King of the Kelpie nation.

Their union had been unprecedented—a Highland warrior and a daughter of the sea. Their love had defied ancient prejudices, crossing boundaries that had separated their peoples for generations. They had lived in fragile happiness at the edge of the loch, until the growing hostility between river and land had forced a choice no parent should face.

Nerina had returned to the waters, believing her absence would protect her child from those who saw his mixed heritage as an abomination. Brannach had fallen defending the boy against his own kin, who feared the power that might come from such a union. Orphaned at birth, the boy had been found half-drowned at the loch's edge by Maelis, who recognized in him the fulfillment of prophecies older than the clans themselves.

"You should rest," Caelan's quiet voice interrupted the boy's thoughts. The warrior settled beside him, his movements fluid despite his size. "Tomorrow will test us all."

He nodded, tucking the carving away. "Do you ever wonder if we're doing the right thing? Seeking more power when power is what divided our peoples in the first place?"

Caelan was silent for a long moment, his silver eyes reflecting the strange stars above. "Power itself is neither good nor evil," he finally said. "It is like water—it takes the shape of the vessel that contains it. Some vessels are corrupt and twist it to destruction. Others channel it toward healing." He looked directly at the boy. "You are a worthy vessel."

The simple statement, coming from the usually taciturn warrior, carried more weight than flowery reassurances might have. He felt some of the tension ease from his shoulders.

"Thank you, brother," he said quietly.

Caelan's mouth twitched in what might have been the ghost of a smile. "Sleep now. I'll take first watch."

As he settled into his bedroll, the sounds of the night enveloped him—the soft murmur of Eira's prayers, the occasional crackle of their small fire as Alasdair fed it broken twigs, the rhythmic tapping of Maelis's staff against stone as she warded their campsite with ancient symbols. Familiar sounds, comforting despite the strangeness of their surroundings.

Just before sleep claimed him, he thought he heard singing—voices neither human nor Selkie, weaving melodies that spoke of ancient waters and the birth of rivers. Whether dream or reality, the song followed him into slumber, wrapping around his consciousness like gentle currents drawing him deeper into mysteries yet to be revealed.

When dawn broke, the world had changed.

The familiar Highlands were gone, replaced by a landscape at once similar and profoundly different. The trees stood twisted into unnatural shapes, their bark spiraled like seashells. The very rocks seemed to hum with a subtle energy that vibrated through the soles of their boots.

"The borderlands have accepted us," Maelis explained, seeing their confused expressions. "We stand now between the world of men and the older realms."

The boy studied the transformed landscape with a mixture of wonder and apprehension. The distant mountains now curved like waves frozen in mid-break, their peaks crystalline and shimmering with colors that had no names in human tongue. Streams flowed in impossible directions—some moving uphill, others splitting to form perfect geometric patterns before rejoining in choreographed precision.

"How is this possible?" Alasdair whispered, his usual gruffness replaced by childlike awe.

"The rules of earth and stone are younger than you think," Maelis replied, her amber eyes reflecting knowledge accumulated through decades of communion with powers most Highlanders preferred to forget. "Before men hammered the world into rigid laws of nature, the elements danced to older rhythms."

They walked in silence after that, each lost in private wonder or fear as the landscape continued its gradual transformation around them. Though the sun still rose overhead, its light fell differently here—casting shadows that sometimes moved independently of their owners or stretching in directions that contradicted its position in the sky.

Near midday, they encountered their first direct challenge from the borderlands. A ravine appeared before them—too wide to jump, too deep to descend safely. Unlike natural formations, this chasm seemed newly formed, the earth at its edges still crumbling as if torn open moments before their arrival.

Eira approached the edge cautiously, her Selkie senses more attuned to the patterns of this half-world. "The land tests us," she murmured. "It asks if we are worthy to proceed."

"And how do we prove our worth to a hole in the ground?" Alasdair demanded, though his voice lacked its usual edge.

The boy stepped forward, drawn by an intuition he couldn't explain. The pendant at his chest pulsed more strongly now, its rhythm syncing with his heartbeat until he could no longer distinguish between the two sensations. He knelt at the ravine's edge and pressed his palm against the exposed earth.

"We mean no harm," he said, his voice dropping into a lower register that seemed to resonate with the stones themselves. "We seek the Well of the First Waters to protect both worlds—your world and ours."

For a moment, nothing happened. Then, with a sound like a great indrawn breath, the ravine began to close—slowly at first, then with increasing speed until the earth knit itself back together, leaving only a faint seam to mark where the chasm had been.

Alasdair crossed himself—a gesture from the new religion that had begun to displace the old ways among some Highland clans. "Mother of God," he whispered.

"Not here," Maelis corrected gently. "The new god has no dominion in these lands."

They continued onward, the landscape growing stranger with each passing hour. Trees whispered warnings in languages none could understand yet all somehow comprehended. Stones shifted beneath their feet, sometimes helping, sometimes hindering, their progress. Streams appeared where no water should flow, offering sweet refreshment when they grew thirsty, only to vanish when they tried to refill their water skins.

At the far end of the valley, they found a narrow path descending into darkness. Upon a stone marker at the path's mouth, worn nearly smooth by countless centuries of wind and rain, was a single symbol—a spiral descending into a point.

"The Well lies beyond," Maelis said, her voice hushed with reverence and trepidation.

The boy placed his hand on the stone, feeling the pull of the old magic. It recognized him—not as Highland or river-born, but as something new, something that bridged ancient divides. The stone warmed beneath his touch, the spiral briefly glowing with the same blue light as his pendant before fading once more into weathered obscurity.

"This is what we came for," he said quietly. "The power to face what rises beneath the loch."

Without another word, they stepped into the deepening gloom, the path winding downward, ever downward, toward the forgotten heart of the world.

Chapter 43: The Descent to the First Waters

Darkness enveloped them like a living entity, pressing against their skin with almost tactile weight. The air grew cold and dense, heavy with mineral scents that spoke of depths where sunlight had never reached. Their breathing echoed strangely, sometimes seeming to precede the actual intake of air, as if time itself flowed inconsistently in this place between worlds.

The boy led the way, the pendant at his chest now glowing with steady blue radiance, pushing back the shadows that threatened to consume them. The light revealed a tunnel that could not have been fashioned by human hands—its walls too perfectly smooth in some places, too organically twisted in others, as if the very earth had been persuaded rather than carved to form this passage to the deep.

"How far down does this go?" Alasdair whispered, his naturally booming voice muted by some quality of the tunnel that seemed to absorb sound.

"Distance has little meaning here," Maelis replied, her staff tapping rhythmically against the stone floor, each contact producing tiny sparks that momentarily illuminated ancient symbols etched into the rock. "We descend not just through earth, but through layers of memory and time."

The path narrowed as they proceeded, forcing them to walk single-file. Eira moved directly behind him, her Selkie senses providing additional guidance where the path grew treacherous. Behind her came Maelis, then Alasdair, with Caelan—as always—guarding their rear. The warrior's eyes, with their unusual silver quality, penetrated the gloom more effectively than human sight, allowing him to spot potential dangers before they materialized.

He felt the weight of responsibility pressing down on him with each step deeper into the earth. Leading his companions into this place of ancient power and unknown dangers—was it hubris or necessity? The question haunted him as they descended further from the world they knew.

As if sensing his thoughts, Eira spoke softly from behind him. "Second thoughts, water-son?"

He didn't turn, keeping his eyes fixed on the path ahead. "Not about our purpose. Only about my right to bring others into danger for my sake."

"For your sake?" Her laugh was gentle, like water flowing over smooth stones. "We do not follow you for your sake, but for the sake of both our peoples. For the future that might exist if water and land can finally live as one."

Her words steadied him, reminding him that this journey was larger than his own doubts or fears. It was about preserving a fragile peace that had begun to take root between peoples divided by centuries of mistrust and violence.

The tunnel continued its winding descent, occasionally opening into small chambers where luminous fungi clung to the walls, casting eerie blue-green light across wet stone. In one such chamber, they paused to rest, the endless downward journey having taken its toll even on Eira's Selkie endurance.

Alasdair sank onto a relatively dry boulder, massaging his knee where an old battle wound troubled him in the damp cold. "If this Well is so blessed important," he grumbled, though without real rancor, "why bury it so deep that only the half-dead can reach it?"

"To protect it," Maelis said, settling cross-legged on the chamber floor, her staff laid across her knees. "And to test those who seek it."

"Test our patience, more like," the chieftain muttered.

Caelan, who had been examining the chamber's far wall with intense concentration, suddenly spoke. "There are carvings here. Old ones." He beckoned the others closer.

Indeed, beneath the luminous fungi and centuries of mineral deposits, intricate patterns had been etched into the stone—spirals interlocked with straight lines, forming complex geometries that seemed to shift when viewed from different angles.

Maelis approached, her amber eyes widening. "The language of the First Ones," she breathed, tracing the patterns with reverent fingers. "I've seen fragments in the oldest stone circles, but never so complete a text."

"Can you read it?" the boy asked, fascinated by the way the carvings seemed to pulse with subtle life beneath Maelis's touch.

"Not read, exactly," the old woman replied. "These are not words as we understand them, but... impressions. Memories captured in stone." She closed her eyes, her fingers continuing to trace the patterns. "This tells of the creation of the Well—how the First Waters were gathered from the tears of the sky and the blood of the earth, mixed with the breath of the first living creatures."

Eira moved closer, her own fingers joining Maelis's on the ancient carvings. As a Selkie, her connection to primal forces ran deeper than most humans could comprehend.

"There's more," she said softly. "A warning." Her face grew troubled as she deciphered the patterns. "The Well gives according to the vessel that approaches it. Like calls to like. If darkness seeks the Waters, darkness will be granted. If light approaches, light is bestowed."

A heavy silence fell over the group as they contemplated this revelation.

"What happens," Alasdair asked carefully, "if the vessel contains both light and dark? As all humans do?"

Maelis and Eira exchanged glances, a wordless communication passing between them.

"Then the Waters will reveal that duality," Maelis finally answered. "And force a choice upon the seeker."

All eyes turned to the boy, whose mixed heritage represented a different kind of duality—not of moral character, but of fundamental nature. What would the Waters reveal in him? What choice might he be forced to make?

He met their gazes steadily, despite the cold knot of apprehension forming in his stomach. "Whatever the Well shows me, my purpose remains clear. I seek power to protect, not to destroy."

"Intentions are slippery things," Maelis cautioned. "Many who began with protection in mind have ended with domination. The line between them is thinner than you might believe."

Before he could respond, a low rumble vibrated through the chamber, dislodging small fragments of stone from the ceiling.

"We should move on," Caelan said, already positioning himself near the exit tunnel. His silver eyes tracked the falling debris with practiced wariness. "This place grows restless with our presence."

They gathered their belongings quickly, the ominous trembling of the earth adding urgency to their movements. As they filed into the continuing passage, he noticed that the pendant at his chest pulsed more rapidly now, its rhythm almost anxious.

The tunnel beyond the chamber descended more steeply, the walls closing in until their shoulders occasionally brushed against cold stone. The air grew increasingly dense and moist, each breath a conscious effort as they pushed deeper into the earth's embrace.

"We're approaching a threshold," Maelis warned, her voice barely audible above the soft percussion of water droplets falling from unseen heights. "The boundary between physical realm and spirit realm thins ahead."

As if to confirm her words, the passage before them began to shimmer with a faint aurora-like quality, colors that had no business existing so far from sunlight dancing across the stone surfaces. He felt a strange doubling of his senses—simultaneously perceiving the solid tunnel around them and something else, something that existed in the same space but followed different rules of form and substance.

"What am I seeing?" he whispered, half to himself.

"The memory of water," Eira answered from behind him. "All water remembers where it has been, every vessel that has held it, every creature that has drunk of it. The First Waters remember everything since the world's beginning."

The shimmering intensified as they continued downward, the tunnel walls now appearing almost translucent, revealing glimpses of other spaces, other times—ancient forests where trees towered like mountains; vast shallow seas teeming with creatures long extinct; ice fields stretching to the horizon, carving the young landscape into the form the Highlands would one day assume.

Alasdair muttered prayers under his breath, his hand never straying far from his sword hilt despite the obvious futility of steel against whatever powers dwelled in this place. Caelan maintained his stoic silence, but his knuckles were white around his halberd shaft, betraying his tension.

After what seemed like hours—though time had become increasingly difficult to judge—the tunnel widened abruptly, opening into a vast cavern that defied the logic of their descent. By all rights, they should have been deep beneath the earth, yet the space above them seemed limitless, stretching upward beyond the reach of the pendant's light. The air was no longer close and stifling but fresh and charged with energy that raised the hairs on their arms and made their skin tingle with something between pleasure and pain.

At the cavern's center lay the Well.

It was not what he had expected. Not a simple pool or spring, but a swirling vortex of light and shadow, its surface shifting between mirror-bright reflection and bottomless darkness. Around it stood six great stones, each etched with runes older than any language spoken in the world above. The stones seemed to hum with contained power, vibrating at a frequency just beyond human hearing but felt in the marrow of their bones.

"Six stones," he noted quietly. "Not five."

"The sixth is for the one who is absent," Maelis explained, her voice hushed with reverence. "The one who came before and the one who will come after. Time itself stands guardian here."

As they drew closer to the Well, the mist that swirled around its edges began to coalesce into forms—not solid, but substantial enough to perceive. Guardians of the First Waters, beings neither alive nor dead, shaped from memory and magic as ancient as the earth itself.

One stepped forward, a tall figure robed in flowing silver. Its features were fluid, sometimes appearing feminine, sometimes masculine, sometimes neither, shifting like reflections in disturbed water.

"Who seeks the blessing of the First Waters?" the guardian intoned, its voice like the rushing of hidden streams beneath winter ice.

The boy felt his companions' eyes upon him, their combined gaze a weight of expectation and trust that straightened his spine and steadied his voice.

"I do," he said, stepping forward. "Born of river and sea, child of sacrifice and hope, guardian of the covenant between land and water."

The silver figure studied him with eyes like deep pools—eyes that seemed to look not at him but through him, examining the very essence of his being.

"Many come seeking power," the guardian said. "Few understand its price."

"What is the price?" he asked, though something in him already knew the answer.

"Balance," the figure replied. "All power demands balance. What will you give in exchange for what you seek?"

He did not hesitate. The answer formed in his heart before his mind could question it.

"My strength. My will. My life, if need be."

Behind him, he heard Eira's soft intake of breath, felt Alasdair's tension and Caelan's focused attention. Only Maelis seemed unsurprised, her ancient eyes watching the exchange with the calm acceptance of one who had always known how this moment would unfold.

A long silence followed the boy's declaration, the cavern holding its breath around them. The guardian's form rippled like a stone-disturbed pool, its silver robe flowing upward as if gravity had temporarily relinquished its hold.

Then, slowly, it nodded.

"Then step forward, child of two worlds. And be tested."

The mist thickened around them, the ground trembling beneath their feet. The Well of the First Waters flared with blinding light, its swirling surface rising into a column that stretched toward the unseen ceiling of the cavern. Within that column, the boy thought he could perceive shapes—faces, landscapes, creatures both familiar and utterly alien—all composed of liquid light that flowed and merged and separated in endless permutation.

Without fear—or rather, with fear acknowledged but not yielded to—he stepped toward the column of light.

"Wait," Alasdair called, a note of desperate protectiveness in his gruff voice. "Lad, you don't know what's in there."

The boy turned back briefly, taking in the faces of his Circle. Alasdair's weathered features creased with concern; Eira's otherworldly beauty rendered ethereal in the Well's light; Caelan's steadfast presence, a pillar of quiet strength; and Maelis, whose amber eyes now glowed with an inner fire that matched the Well's radiance.

"I know what awaits me," He said softly. "The truth. My truth. Whatever it may be."

With those words, he turned and walked into the heart of the light.

CHAPTER 44: The Well and the Test

The boy fell.

There was no up or down, no sense of direction in the void that engulfed him. Only falling, endlessly, weightlessly, into the heart of the Well. Colors blurred past him—silver like moonlight on water, deep green like forest pools, the fierce blue of a storm-tossed sea. Sounds pulsed in his ears: children's laughter, women's screams, the mournful cry of gulls, the gentle whisper of rivers against ancient stones.

And then—stillness.

He stood upon a shore that was no shore, a twilight world suspended between memory and dream. The sand beneath his feet shifted with each step, sometimes solid, sometimes flowing like water. Before him, a vast expanse stretched endlessly, a mirror to depths within himself he had not known existed.

"Where am I?" he whispered, though he had not meant to speak aloud.

Where you need to be, came the answer, though no voice had spoken.

From the mist that shrouded the water's edge, three figures emerged.

The first was a woman cloaked in the flowing silver of the Selkies, her features shifting between human beauty and something wilder, older. Her eyes held the memory of deep currents and hidden grottos, of secrets kept beneath the waves for millennia.

"Who are you, child?" she asked, her voice both gentle and unyielding. "Will you be river—ever changing, ever restless—rushing forward without thought for what lies behind? Never rooted, never sure, always seeking the next bend, the next fall?"

The boy opened his mouth to answer, to proclaim himself the son of Brannach and Nerina, bearer of the Heart—but found he could not speak. No words would come, no certainty to anchor him against the weight of her gaze.

The second figure stepped forth—a man, proud and wild, his form shifting like the kelp-laced waters of the Kelpies. Sometimes he appeared noble, sometimes bestial, but always fierce, always untamed.

"Who are you, child?" he asked, and his voice was the crash of waves against ancient cliffs. "Will you be sea—deep and vast, but cold, forever hungry, swallowing all who draw too close? Will you drown the lands in your pursuit of power?"

Again, the boy struggled to answer, to defend himself against the accusation in those storm-dark eyes. But again, he faltered, doubt creeping like cold water into his bones.

The third figure approached—an old woman, her face lined with river-worn wisdom, her eyes pools of bottomless knowing. She wore simple garments of undyed wool, and around her neck hung a pendant that matched his own, though hers was weathered by countless years.

"Who are you, child?" she asked, and her voice was that of every grandmother who had ever told tales by firelight, every elder who had passed down wisdom from generation to generation. "Will you be both— or neither? Will you forge a new course, or drown beneath the weight of what was?"

The questions hammered at him like waves against a shore, each one eroding his certainty a little more. He fell to his knees before the waters, his hands clutching at the shifting sand-that-was-not-sand.

Who am I?

He was the child of Brannach the Riverman and Nerina of the Selkie folk, born of river and sea, of sacrifice and sorrow. He carried their blood, their legacy, their hopes.

But he was not only their son, he realized with sudden clarity. He was not only their legacy.

He was his own.

Slowly, deliberately, he rose to his feet, feeling a new strength flow through him—not the borrowed strength of ancestry or prophecy, but something that welled up from within.

"I will be river," he said, his voice gathering power with each word. "I will be sea. I will be storm and stillness, light and darkness." He touched the pendant at his chest, feeling it warm beneath his fingers. "I will not choose one path or the other—I will weave them together, as they have always been meant to be."

The three figures exchanged glances—and then, as one, they smiled.

"Well answered, child of two worlds," the Selkie woman said.

"Well answered, bearer of the Heart," the wild man echoed.

"Well answered, hope of what is to come," the old woman concluded.

And then, as swiftly as they had appeared, they dissolved into mist, leaving only their voices echoing across the waters.

Remember who you are.

The Well surged upward, engulfing him once more in light so intense it burned away all thought, all fear, all doubt. For a moment that might have been an eternity, he was one with the Waters, one with the ancient magic that flowed through land and sea alike.

When the boy opened his eyes, he was back in the cavern, kneeling at the Well's edge. But something had changed. The air felt different—clearer, somehow, as though a storm had passed. And he himself felt changed, reforged, as though something essential within him had been both broken and remade.

The guardians stood in a silent ring around him, their heads bowed in acknowledgment.

The tall figure in silver stepped forward and placed a spectral hand upon his brow.

"You have been weighed," it said, its voice resonating through the chamber like the toll of a great bell. "And found true."

The Well's light flowed from the waters into the boy's pendant, filling it with a new brilliance—the ancient strength of the First Waters, renewed for a new age.

Around him, his Circle watched with expressions ranging from awe to fierce pride. Maelis's eyes shone with unshed tears; Alasdair stood straighter, as though the boy's triumph was his own; Eira nodded in quiet satisfaction; and Caelan—gruff, skeptical Caelan—offered a rare, genuine smile.

"Welcome back," Maelis said softly. "We knew you would return to us."

The boy—no, the young man now, for something of childhood had been left behind in the Waters—rose to his feet. The pendant at his chest glowed with steady purpose, its light no longer simply illuminating the darkness but pushing it back, transforming it.

He was ready.

And the world above, trembling on the brink of darkness, would soon know it.

The climb from the depths of the Well was both swift and solemn. The passages that had once seemed labyrinthine now appeared straightforward, the misted paths that had once resisted them now yielding before the young man who carried the blessing of the First Waters. It was as though the very earth recognized the change in him and bent to his purpose.

"The tunnels are different," Alasdair observed, his hand tracing the wall as they ascended. "The symbols... they're changing."

He was right. The cryptic markings that had adorned the stone now rippled and flowed like living script, rearranging themselves as the group passed. What had once been warnings now seemed to be proclamations, heralding their passage.

"Not different," Eira corrected, her wise eyes following the shifting patterns. "Awakened. As he is awakened." She nodded toward the young man who led them upward.

Maelis walked beside him, matching his steady pace. Though they did not speak, a new understanding flowed between them—the shared knowledge of what had been risked, and what had been gained.

"What did you see?" she asked finally, her voice hushed. "In the Waters?"

The young man was silent for a long moment, remembering the shifting figures, the questions that had pierced to his very core.

"Myself," he said at last. "All that I was, all that I am, all that I might become."

Maelis studied his profile, noting the subtle changes—the new steadiness in his gaze, the quiet certainty in his bearing.

"And was it terrible?" she asked softly.

A ghost of a smile touched his lips. "Yes," he admitted. "And wonderful."

Behind them, Alasdair and Caelan kept close watch at the flanks. The warrior's hand remained near his blade, his eyes scanning the shadows with ingrained wariness.

"Still expecting trouble?" Alasdair asked, a hint of amusement in his tone.

Caelan shrugged broad shoulders. "Always," he replied, but there was less tension in his posture than before. "Though I'll admit, we've done well. Better than I expected."

"High praise, coming from you," Alasdair observed dryly.

"Don't let it go to your head," Caelan growled, but there was no real heat in his words. "We've still got a long road ahead."

Eira moved ahead, her staff tapping rhythmically against the stone, her senses keen to any shift in the currents of magic that flowed around them.

"The veil grows thin," she murmured, more to herself than to the others. "The old ways stir."

As they neared the surface, a strange stillness settled over them—a breath held by the world itself, waiting. The quality of the air changed, becoming fresher, carrying with it the scent of peat and heather and the distant tang of the loch.

Their journey back to the camp went almost in silence, though it spanned three days travel. Each of the five lost in personal thought of the time spent in the well.

When they finally neared the loch, blinking into the gray Highland daylight, they found the camp around Loch Ness transformed.

More banners had joined those already raised—the crimson and black of Clan Fraser, the green and gold of the McKinnons, the blue and silver of the McTavishes. More warriors, more clans, had come—drawn by the whispers of awakening magic, by the ancient call that now pulsed through the very stones and rivers of the Highlands.

Where there had been dozens, now there were hundreds, perhaps thousands—a gathering not seen since the days of Robert the Bruce. Campfires dotted the shores of the loch, and the air rang with the sound of steel being sharpened, horses being readied, preparations being made.

The young man's return was met not with fanfare, but with a reverent silence that spread outward like ripples on still water. One by one, those gathered lowered their weapons, their heads, their doubts.

"Is that him?" The whisper came from a young Fraser warrior, his face still soft with youth. "The one from the prophecy?"

"Aye," his companion replied, awe threading through his voice. "The Child of Two Worlds."

The young man walked through the parting crowd without speaking, the light of the Heart shining steadily at his breast, a beacon to all who saw. His Circle followed close behind, their faces set with purpose.

At the great stone altar—ancient even before the first clans had settled these lands—he turned to face them. The gathered hosts fell silent, waiting.

"For generations," he began, his voice carrying with the weight of storm and tide, "we have been divided. River folk and sea folk, Highland clans and Lowland lords. We have fought each other while a greater darkness gathered."

His hand rose to touch the pendant at his chest, and its light flared brighter.

"I have been to the First Waters," he continued. "I have walked the paths of those who came before. And I tell you now—the time of hiding is over. The time of waiting is past."

A murmur passed through the crowd, a current of both hope and unease.

"The darkness that gathers does not care for our ancient feuds, our petty grievances. It will devour river and sea alike if we stand divided."

He paused, his gaze sweeping across the assembled warriors, meeting the eyes of chieftains and common soldiers alike.

"But united—" His voice rose, carrying to the farthest edges of the gathering. "United, we are stronger than any shadow. United, we can forge a future worthy of our children, and our children's children."

He raised his hand, and the pendant flared with blinding brilliance, its light reflecting off the waters of the loch, off the blades of a thousand swords raised in answer.

"Now we rise together—river and sea, land and sky. We rise for the future yet to be born."

A great cry went up, echoing off the hills, rolling across the loch like thunder. Clan banners waved, weapons clashed against shields, and for the first time in centuries, the divided peoples of the Highlands stood as one.

Yet beyond the shouts of hope, a darker sound stirred.

Across the water, from the farthest, mist-wreathed shores of the loch, a second cry answered—low, ancient, and filled with hunger. A sound that spoke of corruption and hatred, of ancient grudges nursed in darkness.

Caelan was the first to hear it, his hand flying to his sword. "We have company," he growled, nodding toward the far shore.

The boy's trial had ended.

The true war was about to begin.

Chapter 46: The Gathering Storm

The mist over Loch Ness thickened with unnatural speed, swirling into dark shapes that writhed and twisted above the water. Every soul gathered at the shores felt the change—a shift not only in the air, but in the very bones of the earth. A wrongness that set teeth on edge and caused horses to stamp nervously, their eyes rolling with fear.

"Form ranks!" Alasdair Fraser's voice cut through the growing tension, steady and commanding. "Archers to the high ground, pikemen to the fore!"

The clans moved with practiced efficiency, ancient rivalries forgotten in the face of the common threat. Claymores gleamed dully in the fading light, bowstrings were checked and rechecked, prayer-stones clutched in callused hands.

The young man's Circle gathered around him atop the stone altar. Maelis's fingers worked quickly, weaving protective sigils in the air, her lips moving in silent incantation.

"What are we facing?" Caelan demanded, his weathered face grim as he scanned the far shore. "MacAuley and his lot, yes, but there's something else out there. Something that stinks of old death."

"The corruption has spread further than we feared," Eira said, her voice tight with strain. She leaned heavily on her staff, her other hand pressed to her temple. "It's in the water, in the air... It's feeding on the fear and hatred that MacAuley has nurtured."

The young man stood silent, watching the darkening mist with eyes that had seen beyond the veil of the mortal world. The Heart at his chest pulsed with steady light, pushing back the encroaching gloom.

"Scouts to the western ridge," he said at last, his voice quiet but firm. "Signal fires prepared atop the three peaks. If we're overwhelmed, the northern clans must be warned."

Alasdair nodded sharply and moved to relay the orders, his confident stride belying the gravity of the situation.

Maelis stepped closer, her dark eyes searching the young man's face.

"It is no longer only men we must face," she said, pitching her voice low so only he could hear. "The Shadows have found vessels in those whose hearts were already dark."

He nodded, unsurprised. "I have felt it. The hunger that stirs. It's not just MacAuley's ambition now—it's something older, something that has waited centuries for this moment of weakness."

"Can we stand against it?" she asked, and though her voice was steady, he heard the tremor of doubt beneath.

His hand found hers, squeezing gently. "We must," he said simply.

Far across the loch, shapes began to emerge from the mist—a dark procession winding down to the water's edge. At first they seemed like warriors—clansmen clad in tattered plaids, bearing twisted weapons. But as they drew nearer, pushing boats into the water, it became clear they were something else entirely.

"Gods preserve us," whispered an old McKinnon warrior, making the sign of protection. "What manner of men are those?"

They were not men—not anymore. Creatures born of corrupted waters, their forms part flesh, part shadow. Where eyes should have been, sickly green light glowed. Mouths gaped with silent screams. They moved with jerking, unnatural motions, like puppets in the hands of an unskilled master.

Among them strode Duncan MacAuley, changed from when they had last seen him. His body was still that of a man, but his face was hollow, his skin etched with dark veins like rivulets of poison. The proud chieftain who had once fought for his clan's honor was gone, replaced by something that wore his form like an ill-fitting garment.

"Hold steady!" Alasdair called as murmurs of fear rippled through the ranks. "They're trying to frighten us. Don't let them into your heads!"

The boats reached the midpoint of the loch, and Duncan MacAuley rose to his feet, balancing with inhuman stillness despite the rocking vessel.

"You see what unity has brought!" he roared across the water, his voice warped and layered, as though many throats spoke through his. "You gather behind a half-blood child, trusting in water-magic and old wives' tales!"

The clans stirred, uncertainty flashing through their ranks.

"You would chain us to weakness, to compromise!" Duncan continued, gesturing with arms that seemed too long, fingers that bent at unnatural angles. "I offer freedom! I offer power! The old ways—the true ways—before river and sea diluted our strength!"

The young man stepped forward, the Heart of the Loch pulsing bright against his chest. Its light struck the water, creating a path of radiance across the dark surface.

"You offer death," he said, his clear voice carrying across the water. "And we choose life."

Duncan's face contorted with rage, the veins beneath his skin pulsing with sickly green light. "Then come and claim it, little half-breed! Show these fools what their hope is worth!"

With a howl that no human throat could produce, Duncan raised a blackened sword high. The blade seemed to drink in the fading light, and where it cut the air, reality itself seemed to tear.

"Now!" he screamed, and the corrupted army surged forward, their boats cutting through the water with impossible speed.

Alasdair Fraser gave a cry, rallyingthe Highlanders. "For river and sea! For the Heart! HOLD FAST!"

Archers nocked arrows, their hands steady despite the horror approaching. Pikemen braced their weapons, forming a bristling wall of steel.

"Maelis," the young man said quietly, "the water wards. Now."

She nodded, her face pale but determined. From a pouch at her waist, she drew a handful of small stones, each inscribed with ancient sigils. One by one, she cast them into the loch, whispering words of binding with each throw.

For a moment, nothing happened.

Then, with a sound like the indrawn breath of a giant, the waters of the loch rose—not in a wave, but in a wall, shimmering with the same blue light that emanated from the Heart.

The first of the corrupted boats crashed into this liquid barrier and... stopped. Not broken, not overturned, but held fast as though embedded in amber. The creatures within thrashed and howled, their unnatural limbs clawing at the water that would not yield.

A cheer went up from the Highland forces.

But Duncan MacAuley only smiled—a terrible rictus that split his face like a wound.

"Did you think it would be so easy?" he called, and then he plunged his blackened blade into the heart of his own vessel.

The sword pierced wood and water alike, and where it struck, corruption spread—dark veins racing through the barrier, turning the clear blue light to sickly green.

"The wards won't hold for long," Maelis gasped, sweat beading on her forehead from the effort of maintaining the spell. "There's something... something in that blade. Something that devours magic."

The young man placed his hand on her shoulder, lending her his strength. "They don't need to hold forever," he said. "Just long enough."

With a sound like shattering glass, the water barrier began to crack. Corrupted warriors spilled through the gaps, their bodies twisting in impossible ways as they swam toward the shore.

"MAKE READY!" Alasdair bellowed.

The clans tightened their formations, banners snapping like whips in the rising wind. Prayers mingled with battle cries as the distance between the armies dwindled.

"Caelan," the young man said, "guard Maelis. Eira, the elders and children in the rear camp—get them to higher ground."

"And you?" Caelan asked, his knuckles white around his sword hilt.

The young man's eyes never left the approaching horde. "I'm going to meet Duncan MacAuley."

"That's not Duncan anymore," Eira warned, her ancient eyes filled with sorrow. "Whatever has taken him, it's old. Older than the clans, perhaps older than the First Waters themselves."

"I know," the young man said simply. "But it must be faced. It must be named."

As the last of the water barrier collapsed, the corrupted army surged forward, spilling onto the shores with inhuman shrieks. The clans met the charge with a thunderous roar, the ground trembling under the collision.

Steel clashed against shadowed flesh. Magic flared against corruption. Blood mingled with water and earth as the battle was joined in earnest.

Above it all, the young man moved like a force of nature, the light of the First Waters driving back the dark with every step. Where he passed, the corrupted creatures recoiled, their sickly green light dimming before the pure radiance of the Heart.

And across the battlefield, Duncan MacAuley—or the thing that had once been Duncan MacAuley—watched with ancient, hungry eyes, and waited.

The battle had begun.

And the fate of the Highlands—of river, sea, and sky—hung in the balance.

Chapter 47: Clash at the Loch

The clash on the shores of Loch Ness was unlike anything the Highlands had ever witnessed in all their blood-soaked history. Dawn had given way to a strange twilight that seemed to hang between day and night, as though time itself hesitated to move forward in the face of such momentous conflict.

The corrupted forces poured forth from the mist like a nightmare made flesh, their twisted forms shrieking with a sound that made the stones weep and the rivers writhe. Some bore the remnants of clan colors, tattered plaids hanging from emaciated frames. Others had shed all semblance of humanity, their bodies reshaped by the ancient darkness that rode them.

"Hold the line!" Alasdair Fraser's voice carried across the battlefield, steady as stone. "For your homes! For your children!"

Against the corrupted horde stood the united clans—Highlanders with claymores and dirks flashing in the dim light, Selkies weaving waves of water magic that crashed through enemy ranks, Kelpies charging on phantom steeds conjured from mist and memory, their hooves striking sparks against stone and corrupted flesh alike.

"They come in waves," Caelan growled, his blade already dark with ichor as he fought shoulder-to-shoulder with a Fraser warrior. "Like the sea at storm tide. No end to them."

"There's always an end," the Fraser man replied, his young face grim with determination. "Even the sea retreats eventually."

A corrupted creature—once perhaps a McKinnon by the tattered remains of his plaid—lunged at them, its fingers elongated into claws that glistened with venom. Caelan ducked beneath the strike and drove his blade upward, through what remained of the creature's heart.

"Retreat faster, would you?" he muttered to the thing as it dissolved into foul-smelling mist.

The young man fought at the center of it all, the Heart's light blazing from his chest like a second sun. Wherever he moved, the corrupted creatures faltered, their shadowed forms recoiling from the purity of his power. The pendant pulsed in time with his heartbeat, each surge of light driving back the darkness a little further.

"They fear it," Maelis said, appearing at his side like a shadow, her hands flickering with complex sigils of binding. A corrupted warrior that had been lunging for the young man's back suddenly froze mid-stride, its limbs locked by her magic. "The Heart remembers what they once were, before the corruption. It reminds them of their betrayal."

The young man nodded, dispatching the bound creature with a swift stroke. "Not just the Heart," he said, his voice carrying an authority that belied his years. "They fear what it represents. Unity. The joining of what they would keep divided."

Across the battlefield, Alasdair Fraser led the Highlanders with ferocity and precision, his sword carving a path through the enemy ranks. His voice rose in the ancient battle cries of Clan Fraser, each shout lending strength to those who fought alongside him.

"For river and sea!" he bellowed, his blade claiming another corrupted form. "For the Heart and the Highlands!"

The cry was taken up by a hundred throats, then a thousand—a tide of sound that pushed back against the unnatural shrieks of the enemy.

Near the altar stones, Eira stood with the oldest of the clan mothers and the youngest of the river-born children. Her silver hair streamed in the wind as she sang ancient battle songs, her voice weaving protective enchantments that shielded the warriors from the worst of the darkness.

"Coinnich an t-saighead, till an trùpan, dìon an cridhe," she chanted, her gnarled hands tracing patterns in the air. "Meet the arrow, turn the blade, guard the heart."

Around her, a dome of faintly shimmering light formed, growing stronger with each repetition of the chant. The children joined their high, clear voices to hers, their innate magic—untrained but potent—strengthening the barrier.

Caelan, grim and relentless, waded into the thickest fighting, his blade flashing with the cold certainty of one who had sworn an unbreakable oath. Blood matted his beard and stained his leathers, some of it his own, but he showed no sign of slowing.

"You fight well," called a Kelpie warrior who rode beside him, the creature's horse-form shifting between solid and mist with each stride. "For a landborn."

Caelan grunted, cleaving through another corrupted form. "You talk too much," he replied. "For a horse."

The Kelpie's laughter rang out, wild and free, as it charged into another knot of enemies.

Maelis moved through the battlefield like a shadow, striking where needed, whispering words of binding that unraveled the magic animating the darkest foes. Her sealskin cloak billowed around her like living water, deflecting blows and ensnaring enemies who drew too close.

"The source," she called to the young man as they fought back-to-back. "We must find the source. Duncan channels something ancient, something that predates even the First Waters."

The young man nodded, his gaze scanning the battlefield. The tide of battle swelled and ebbed around them, each side surging forward only to be driven back. For each corrupted creature that fell, another seemed to rise from the mists. For each defender who faltered, another stepped into the breach.

And then he saw him.

At the heart of the enemy host, Duncan MacAuley stood, a monstrous figure now barely resembling the man he had once been. His body had grown, stretching to inhuman proportions. His skin had darkened to the color of deep-water silt, crisscrossed with veins that pulsed with sickly green light. Dark magic poured from him in visible waves, twisting the earth, souring the air, feeding the corruption that animated his forces.

"There," the young man said, his voice steady despite the horror before him. "Duncan is the conduit. The darkness feeds through him."

Maelis followed his gaze and paled. "He's no longer human," she whispered. "Whatever bargain he struck, whatever power he invited in—it's consumed him completely."

The young man saw the truth of it—and knew the battle could not be won while Duncan still stood. So long as that channel to ancient darkness remained open, their forces would eventually be overwhelmed.

He turned to Maelis, his decision made. "Rally the others," he said. "Hold the line here. I'm going for Duncan."

Alarm flashed across her face. "Alone? That's madness! Whatever's wearing Duncan's skin now has power we can barely comprehend."

"And I have this," he replied, touching the Heart at his chest. "It was made for exactly this purpose—to stand against the darkness when it rises."

She held his gaze for a long moment, searching for doubt and finding none. With a swift, fierce movement, she leaned forward and pressed her forehead to his—an ancient gesture of blessing among the Selkie folk.

"Then go," she said softly. "But remember—you carry all our hopes with you."

With a nod, he turned away. With a shout that carried above the din of battle, he charged toward the center of the enemy host, the Heart's light blazing before him like a living shield. Corrupted creatures scattered from his path, shrieking in pain where the light touched them.

Duncan turned at his approach, a sneer twisting his ruined face.

"The half-breed whelp," he growled, his voice layered with unnatural harmonics that grated against the ear. "Come to play the hero?"

"I've come to end this," the young man replied, raising his blade. "To send back whatever darkness you've invited into our lands."

Duncan threw back his head and laughed—a sound like stones grinding against each other in the depths of the earth. "You cannot stop what has already begun!" he roared, striking with a blade blackened by corruption. "The old powers rise! The true masters return!"

Steel met steel with a crash that sent sparks of conflicting magic scattering across the battlefield. Light met shadow, ancient power against ancient power. Their clash sent shockwaves rippling across the battlefield, warriors on both sides staggering under the force.

"You never understood, boy," Duncan snarled as they broke apart, circling each other. "This land was never meant for peace. It was forged in blood and darkness, and to blood and darkness it must return!"

"You're wrong," the young man countered, the Heart's light surging brighter with his conviction. "The Highlands were born from the marriage of river and sea, of earth and sky. Unity, not division, is their true nature."

With a howl of rage, Duncan attacked again, his corrupted blade moving with impossible speed. The young man parried, feeling the impact shudder through his arms, but he held firm. Every strike was met, every thrust turned aside. The Heart's power surged through him, lending him strength beyond his years, skill beyond his training.

He pressed forward, the Heart's light pushing Duncan back step by step. For the first time, uncertainty flickered across the corrupted chieftain's face.

"Impossible," Duncan hissed. "You are nothing! A mongrel child playing at prophecy!"

"I am exactly what I need to be," the young man replied, his voice steady despite the strain of combat. "What the land needs me to be. As were you, once, before fear poisoned your heart."

For the briefest moment, something flickered in Duncan's eyes—a ghost of the man he had been, the leader who had sought only to protect his people from a changing world. Then the darkness surged back, stronger than before.

"Enough!" Duncan roared. "If I cannot defeat you alone, then I shall call upon older powers!"

He raised his corrupted blade high and plunged it into the earth at his feet. The ground split with a terrible crack, and black water welled up from the fissure, spreading outward in a widening circle.

"From the depths!" Duncan cried, his voice no longer his own. "From the oldest dark! I call you forth!"

The waters of Loch Ness churned in answer. A massive shape rose from beneath the surface, sending waves crashing against both shores. First one spined ridge broke the surface, then another, and another—until a creature of nightmare proportions revealed itself.

Its scales were like shattered stone, ancient and crusted with the sediment of centuries. Its eyes burned like twin coals, holding malice older than human memory. Its maw opened in a roar that shook the very heavens, revealing rows of teeth that could crush stone.

"Behold the true master of these waters!" Duncan cried in triumph. "The Devourer of Light, the Ender of Ages!"

The battle around them faltered as both sides turned to witness the horror rising from the loch. Fear gripped even the bravest hearts. Some of the Highlanders fell to their knees, weapons forgotten. Even the Kelpies drew back, their ancient memory recognizing a power that predated their own.

The young man alone stood firm, though his heart hammered in his chest. The creature before him was beyond his imagining—a being from the oldest stories, whispered around fires on the darkest nights. Yet he knew with bone-deep certainty that this was the moment for which he had been prepared, the darkness against which the Heart had been forged.

The final battle had truly begun.

And the outcome would shape the fate of river, sea, and sky for all time.

Chapter 48: Heart Against Darkness

The creature rising from Loch Ness was vast beyond comprehension, a nightmare leviathan that seemed to swallow the light itself. Water cascaded from its ancient scales as it rose higher, its spine ridges breaking the surface one after another in a seemingly endless procession. Its head alone dwarfed the altar stones; its body stretched half the length of the loch.

"The Great Wurm," Eira whispered, her aged voice tight with horror and recognition. "The Oldest Shadow. It should not be possible..."

The warriors on the battlefield faltered at the sight, fear gripping even the bravest hearts. The mist thickened around them, laced now with the creature's malice, choking the air with the stench of stagnant water and ancient decay. Brave men who had faced death countless times found themselves unable to move, paralyzed by a primal terror their ancestors had carried in their blood.

Only the young man stood firm before the rising horror, though he felt its ancient malevolence pressing against his mind like a physical weight.

The Heart of the Loch at his chest blazed anew in answer to the darkness, casting a brilliant beam of light across the waters. Where that light touched the creature's scales, steam rose with a hissing scream, momentarily pushing the darkness back.

Duncan MacAuley laughed—a terrible, broken sound—as he watched the young man face the ancient evil. "Do you see now?" he called, spreading his corrupted arms wide. "This is the true power of the lochs! Not your pitiful unity, not your halfbreed magic! THIS is what sleeps beneath our lands!"

"You fool," the young man answered, his voice carrying despite the creature's continued roar. "You've unleashed something you cannot control. Something that will devour your people as readily as ours."

"I am its voice!" Duncan shrieked, his body contorting as the corruption spread visibly through him, blackening his skin, elongating his limbs. "Its chosen vessel! I will rule when all else is consumed!"

With another inhuman cry, Duncan hurled himself at the young man with renewed fury, his corrupted blade now wreathed in the same malevolent energy that poured from the Great Wurm. Their weapons met again, the clash sparking currents of raw magic that scorched the earth where they fell.

"You are nothing!" Duncan roared, pressing his attack with supernatural strength, his blade moving faster than mortal eyes could follow. "A dream that will drown like all the others!"

The young man matched him blow for blow, the Heart's light flowing through him, guiding his movements. Yet he could feel the tide turning against him. The Great Wurm's presence strengthened Duncan, feeding him power drawn from the darkest depths, while its aura of fear weakened the allied forces with each passing moment.

This was not a battle that could be won by strength of arms alone.

The young man parried another vicious strike, then leapt back, putting space between himself and Duncan. As his opponent prepared to charge again, the young man did something unexpected.

He closed his eyes.

The battlefield, the creature, Duncan—all faded from his awareness as he turned his focus inward, to the Heart that beat in time with his own. He recalled the vision in the Well of the First Waters, the three figures who had asked him who he truly was.

I will be river, he had answered then. I will be sea. I will be storm and stillness, light and darkness. I will not choose one path—I will weave them together.

Now, with darkness rising around him, he reached deeper into that truth.

The Heart at his chest began to pulse with a new rhythm, its light shifting from brilliant white to a deeper, richer blue—the color of the deepest waters, where light and darkness meet and mingle.

When the young man opened his eyes again, they too shone with that same blue light. Power radiated from him in waves, not the harsh, driving force of Duncan's corruption, but something deeper, steadier— the patient strength of water that can wear away mountains given time.

The young man answered Duncan's rage not with words but with will.

"What is this?" Duncan faltered, uncertainty creeping into his voice as he sensed the change.

"The truth you've forgotten," the young man replied, his voice resonating with power that seemed to come from the land itself. "That darkness and light are not enemies, but parts of the same whole. That river and sea are not separate, but one continuous flow."

Drawing on the strength of the rivers, the patience of the lochs, and the fierce freedom of the sea, he drove forward. Each step was purposeful, each strike of his blade guided by something beyond mere skill. Duncan found himself retreating, step by step, toward the churning waters where the Great Wurm waited.

"Stay back!" Duncan screamed, his attacks growing wild, desperate. "You cannot defeat what has always been! What will always be!"

"I don't seek to defeat the darkness," the young man answered calmly, deflecting another strike and countering with a blow that sent Duncan staggering. "Only to restore the balance you have broken."

Behind him, the clans began to rally as the Heart's changed light pushed back against the creature's aura of fear. Alasdair Fraser, his face bloodied but his spirit unbroken, led a countercharge, Highlanders locking shields and pressing forward with grim determination. The clans moved as one, each warrior finding strength in the unity they had forged.

"FOR THE HEART!" The cry went up, hundreds of voices joining as one. "FOR THE HIGHLANDS!"

Eira wove barriers of water and air from atop the altar stones, her ancient voice rising in songs not heard in the Highlands for generations. The spells shielded the clans' flanks, turning aside the worst of the corrupted attacks.

"The ancient ways remember," she called to the frightened children who huddled around her. "Join your voices with mine. Let the waters hear their children call!"

Caelan struck down any creature that dared to breach their line, his blade a blur of constant motion. Though exhaustion pulled at his limbs, he fought on, drawing strength from the oath he had sworn to protect the boy who now stood as a man against the darkness.

"Come on, you shadows!" he bellowed, his voice rough with exertion. "Is this all you bring? I've fought midges with more bite!"

Maelis, standing atop the stone altar alongside Eira, called upon the ancient guardians, her voice rising in a chant so old it shook the stones beneath her feet. The air around her shimmered as she drew upon the deep magic of her Selkie heritage, summoning the memory of times when the waters were pure, before corruption had tainted their depths.

"Hear me, Waters of the Beginning," she intoned, her eyes gleaming with the same blue light that emanated from the Heart. "Remember your first flowing, your first song. Remember what you were meant to be!"

The Great Wurm roared again in answer to her call, a sound of ancient rage and hunger. It lunged forward, massive jaws snapping at the air, sending waves crashing onto the battlefield. Warriors were swept off their feet, the corrupted creatures riding the wave to press their attack.

In that moment of chaos, the young man pressed his advantage against Duncan.

With a desperate, rage-filled cry, Duncan swung his corrupted blade in a wild arc—but the young man was ready. He caught the blade with his own, the metals shrieking against each other, and with a sudden twist born of river-water fluidity, he broke Duncan's weapon with a crack that echoed across the hills.

The corrupted blade shattered, its fragments dissolving into foul-smelling mist. Duncan staggered backward, his face contorted with shock and fear as the magic that had sustained him began to unravel.

"No," he gasped, clutching at his chest where the corruption had taken root. "No, this cannot be!"

The young man stepped forward and placed his hand upon Duncan's chest, over the place where a heart once beat.

"You chose fear," he said softly, his voice pitched for Duncan alone despite the chaos around them. "I choose hope."

Duncan's eyes widened, and for a moment—just a moment—the man he had once been looked out from them, confused and sorrowful.

"I only wanted to protect them," he whispered, his voice briefly his own again. "To keep them safe from change..."

"I know," the young man replied gently. "But there is no safety in stagnation, only slow death. Life is change, Duncan. River becoming sea, sea feeding sky, sky nourishing earth."

The Heart's light surged forth at his words, flowing through his hand and into Duncan's corrupted form. Blue radiance filled the chieftain from within, illuminating his veins, his eyes, the very marrow of his bones. For a heartbeat, Duncan MacAuley stood transformed, cleansed of the darkness that had consumed him—and then he dissolved into mist, carried away on the currents that flowed between worlds.

The Great Wurm shrieked in rage, its connection to Duncan severed. Without its chosen vessel, its hold on the mortal world weakened. It thrashed wildly in the waters of the loch, its massive body sending waves crashing against both shores, its roar now tinged with something almost like fear.

The young man turned to face it, feeling both the terrible weight of what must be done and the strength to do it. He raised his blade—now shining with the same blue light that emanated from the Heart—and called out to the gathered clans, his voice rising above the creature's rage.

"Now! Together! As one people, one land, one water!"

The warriors—Selkies, Kelpies, Highlanders, riverborn and sea-born alike—lifted their voices in a single, thunderous cry. It was not a battle cry, but something older, deeper—a song of belonging, of coming home, of waters running clear and free.

Magic flared across the battlefield as each fighter contributed what strength they had left. Arrows tipped with Selkie spellcraft flew in gleaming arcs. Blades blessed by generations of Highland warriors flashed in the strange half-light. Kelpies called to the waters of the loch, reminding them of their true nature.

The Heart of the Loch pulsed one final time, and at the young man's command, a great torrent of pure water—bright as the first dawn—rose from the loch. Not forced or compelled, but freely given, the waters answered the call of their champion.

The torrent struck the Great Wurm with the force of centuries of restrained power. The creature reared back, its ancient scales unable to withstand the purity of the waters it had once corrupted. With a deafening roar that shook the mountains, the ancient darkness shattered, its essence dissolving, its pieces sinking back into the depths from which they had been summoned.

As suddenly as it had begun, it was over.

Silence fell over the battlefield, broken only by the soft lapping of waves against the shore.

The mist that had shrouded the loch for days parted like a curtain, revealing a sky where the first stars were beginning to appear.

Warriors stood frozen, weapons half-raised, scarcely daring to believe what they had witnessed. The corrupted creatures, without the dark will that had animated them, collapsed into piles of mud and stone that rapidly dissolved back into the earth.

And on the shores of Loch Ness, beneath the watching stars, the young man lowered his blade, the Heart at his chest now pulsing with a gentle, steady light.

A new world had been born.

Chapter 49: A World Remade

Dawn broke over Loch Ness with a brilliance unseen for generations. The first light touched the waters, scattering the last remnants of mist and shadow. The loch shimmered like polished silver, reflecting a sky washed clean of all taint. The land, battered but unbowed, drank in the newborn peace like a parched traveler discovering a clear spring.

The young man stood at the water's edge, watching the gentle ripples carry away the echoes of the battle. His body ached from wounds both seen and unseen, but his spirit felt strangely light, as though a burden carried all his life had finally been set down. The Heart of the Loch, now a steady glow against his chest, pulsed with quiet, enduring life.

"It's beautiful," Maelis said softly, coming to stand beside him. Her face was drawn with exhaustion, a fresh cut marking her cheek, but her eyes were clear and peaceful. "I had almost forgotten what the loch looked like in true sunlight."

"As had I," the young man admitted, turning to study the transformed landscape. "Though I was born beside these waters, I think this is the first time I've truly seen them."

Behind them, the survivors gathered in small groups across the battlefield. Warriors of river and sea, land and loch—bloodied, weary, but standing. They tended to their wounded, counted their dead, and shared what supplies remained. Their faces bore the exhaustion of hard-won victory, and the dawning realization that the world they had fought to save had, indeed, been remade.

"What happens now?" Maelis asked, her voice barely audible above the gentle lapping of the water. "The prophecy spoke only of the battle, not what comes after."

The young man smiled faintly. "Perhaps because what comes after is not fated, but chosen. By all of us, together."

Alasdair Fraser approached them, his movements stiff with fresh bandages visible beneath his torn clothing. His sword rested across his back, his expression a complex mixture of grief for those lost and pride in what had been accomplished.

"Three hundred and seventeen," he said without preamble.

The young man turned to him, questioning.

"Our dead," Alasdair clarified, his voice rough but steady. "Three hundred and seventeen brave souls who will never see the world they helped to save." He gazed out across the loch, his weathered face solemn. "We have seen the darkness fall, but the price was high."

"Too high," the young man agreed quietly.

"No," Alasdair corrected him, his hand coming to rest on the young man's shoulder. "Not too high. Exactly what was needed, freely given. They knew what they fought for." His grip tightened briefly. "Now we must build something brighter in its place. Something worthy of their sacrifice."

Eira came next, moving slowly through the gathered survivors. Despite her age, she had worked through the night, weaving healing waters through the wounded, singing songs that wove hope into broken bodies and weary hearts. Her silver hair hung loose around her shoulders, and deep exhaustion lined her face, yet still she moved from warrior to warrior, offering what comfort she could.

"The waters remember now," she said as she joined them, her voice thin but determined. "I can feel it. The corruption is gone, not just from the surface, but from the depths."

"Will it last?" Maelis asked.

Eira's eyes, ancient and knowing, met the young man's. "That depends on him. And on all of us. Balance is never static—it must be maintained, nurtured."

Caelan, ever vigilant, stood a few paces away, his stance alert despite the bandages wrapped around his arm and torso. His sword was cleaned and sheathed, but his hand never strayed far from its hilt. Some habits, forged in decades of wariness, would take time to fade.

"The southern clans are asking to speak with you," he said gruffly to the young man. "The ones who came late to the fight. They're not sure where they stand now."

"Where we all stand," the young man replied. "Together, or not at all."

Maelis, her sealskin cloak heavy with morning mist, studied him with thoughtful eyes. "It is not over," she said softly, voicing what all of them felt but hesitated to name. "It is only begun. The darkness may be banished for now, but there will be other challenges. Other battles, though perhaps not of steel and spell."

"Building is always harder than destroying," Alasdair agreed. "And what we must build now is a new way of living. Not river against sea, not clan against clan, but something... different."

The young man absorbed their words, feeling their truth settle in his bones. The Heart at his chest hummed in quiet agreement. This victory, hard-won and precious, was not an ending but a beginning—the first uncertain step into an uncharted future.

He turned to face the gathered clans. The sun had risen higher now, its light casting long shadows across the battlefield. He saw in their eyes not only loyalty born of shared struggle, but expectation—the unspoken question of what came next, now that the ancient enemy had been defeated.

He stepped forward, feeling hundreds of eyes track his movement. The pendant at his chest caught the morning sun, sending fractals of blue light dancing across the gathering.

"Last night," he began, his voice carrying across the hushed assembly, "we fought as one people. Not as river folk or sea folk, not as Highland clans or Lowland lords, but as defenders of a shared home." His gaze swept across their faces—some familiar, many not, all united by what they had endured together. "We fought for more than mere survival. We fought for a world where river and sea, land and sky, are bound not by fear, but by trust."

A murmur of agreement rippled through the crowd. Heads nodded, weapons were raised in salute.

"This victory," he continued, "is not the end of our journey. It is the first stone of a bridge that will take generations to build." His voice grew stronger with conviction. "But we have laid its foundation—together. And together, we will continue the work our ancestors began: creating a Highlands where all waters flow free, where all people stand equal, where the old magics and the new ways strengthen rather than oppose each other."

He paused, seeing doubt flicker across some faces. Change, even necessary change, was never easy to embrace.

"I do not ask you to forget the old ways," he said, addressing that unspoken fear. "Our traditions, our histories—they are the bedrock upon which we stand. But I do ask you to look forward as well as back. To see not just what was, but what might be."

He lifted his hand, and from the Heart of the Loch a soft wave of magic flowed outward, touching each warrior, each survivor. Not a binding or a compulsion, but an invitation—a glimpse of the world that could be, if they chose to build it together.

"The waters are cleansed," he said. "The land begins to heal. Now we must do the same—healing the divisions between our peoples, the ancient grievances that have kept us apart. It will not be easy. There will be disagreements, setbacks, moments when the old fears resurface. But if we remember this day—remember what we accomplished when we stood as one—there is nothing we cannot overcome."

For a long moment, silence held the gathering in its grip. Then, from the back of the crowd, a single voice called out:

"For the Heart of the Highlands!"

Others took up the cry, weapons clashing against shields, voices rising in a chorus of renewed purpose:

"For the Heart! For the Highlands!"

The young man felt something stir within him—not the fierce battle-joy of the previous night, but something deeper, more enduring. A sense of rightness, of purpose discovered and embraced.

As the cheers faded, the clans began to disperse, moving with new energy despite their exhaustion. There were wounded to tend to, fallen comrades to honor, plans to be made for the days ahead. But beneath the practicalities ran a current of hope stronger than any the young man had ever felt.

Alasdair approached, offering his arm in the traditional warrior's clasp. "Well said," he murmured as they gripped forearms. "They needed to hear that—especially from you."

"Will it be enough?" the young man asked quietly.

"Words never are," Alasdair replied with a slight smile. "But they're a start. The rest will come with time, and work, and patience." He glanced toward the loch, where the waters glittered in the morning sun. "And perhaps a bit of magic, now and then."

For the remainder of that day, and many days after, they stood together at the shores of Loch Ness—the young man and his Circle, the leaders of clans once divided, the children of river and sea. They talked and planned, argued and compromised, laying the foundations of a new order that honored both past and future.

And far beneath the loch, where once the ancient darkness had slept, only stillness remained—a stillness that promised the world, for now, had been set right.

The tides of fate had turned.

And the future, at last, belonged to them.

Epilogue: The Watcher in the Mists

Years passed.

The Highlands flourished in ways no song had ever foretold. Rivers ran clear again, and the seas sparkled with new life. The clans, once divided by blood and bitterness, now stood bound by a tapestry of old magic and hard-earned trust.

The young man—no longer a boy, but a leader whose name was spoken with reverence—guided the alliance with wisdom far beyond his years. His Circle remained close: Alasdair Fraser, steadfast and loyal; Eira, the song-weaver whose voice healed more than wounds; Caelan, whose silent strength steadied them all; and Maelis, guardian of the old ways.

The Heart of the Loch, worn always against his chest, had grown quiet—not dead, but sleeping, its great task completed for now.

But peace, like the tides, is never still forever.

Far across the seas, beyond the edges of the maps, a new shadow stirred. Not the crude, festering darkness that had once poisoned the lochs, but something colder, older—a hunger born from the spaces between stars, from the places where light had never shone.

On quiet nights, when the mists curled low across the hills, Maelis would sometimes pause and lift her gaze to the north, her brow furrowing.

"Not yet," she would whisper to herself. "But soon."

And in a hidden glen known only to the oldest of the riverborn, sealed within stone and guarded by the songs of the deep, a name slept.

Not the name given by Brannach and Nerina.

Not the name the world now called him.

A truer name.

A name of binding and power, of promise and peril.

Waiting.

Waiting for the day it must be spoken aloud—and claimed.

In the great hall by Loch Ness, the young man would sit by the fire, his fingers tracing the worn spiral etched into the Heart's surface. He would feel the faintest tremor—a warning ripple, a pulse of distant storm.

And he would smile, not in fear, but in readiness.

For he knew that the tides of fate, once turned, would forever call to those brave enough to shape them. And this time, the tides of fate would carry him far beyond the shores he had once called home.